Scribe Publications
BUCKLEY'S HOPE

Craig Robertson was born in Melbourne in 1944, studied at Melbourne High School, and completed a mathematics-science degree at the University of Melbourne. He has travelled widely and, after having worked at a variety of jobs, established a career as a technical writer.

He began writing seriously while living in the bush in Gippsland in the early 1970s. *Buckley's Hope* was originally published by Scribe in 1980. *Song of Gondwana*, a science fantasy adventure set in Victoria's Otway Ranges, was published by Penguin in 1989. He lives with his wife in Melbourne.

William Buckley's Victoria
Map drawn by Patrick De Largy Healy

Buckley's Hope

A Novel

CRAIG ROBERTSON

SCRIBE

Melbourne • London

Scribe Publications Pty Ltd
18–20 Edward St, Brunswick, Victoria 3056, Australia
50A Kingsway Place, Sans Walk, London, EC1R 0LU, United Kingdom

Copyright © Craig Robertson 1980, 1997
First published by Scribe 1980
Second edition 1997
Reprinted 2002
This edition published 2014

Printed and bound in England by CPI Group (UK) Ltd, Croydon, CR0 4YY

Cover image: *Buckley's Escape* by Tommy McRae, c. 1890's

National Library of Australia
Cataloguing-in-Publication data

Robertson, Craig, 1944 –.

Buckley's hope: a novel.

New ed.

9781922247223 (UK paperback)

A 823.3

scribepublications.com.au
scribepublications.co.uk

Contents

Acknowledgements

This book owes most to the one it is based on: *The Life and Adventures of William Buckley*, by John Morgan, (1st edition printed and published by Archibald MacDougal, Hobart, 1852; 2nd Edition edited with an introduction and notes by C. E. Sayers, Heinemann, Melbourne 1967).

Special mention should be made of the following books for the original versions of the myths. For the cloud myth: *Aboriginal Myths* by Streten Bozic in conjunction with Alan Marshall (Gold Star Publications, Melbourne 1972); for the Bullum-Boukan myth: *Bunjil's Cave: Myths, Legends and Superstitions of the Aborigines of South-East Australia* by Aldo Massola (Lansdowne, Melbourne, 1968); the magpie myth: *The Dawn of Time* by C. P. Mountford with Ainslie Roberts (Rigby, 1969); the platypus myth: *Myths and Legends of Australia* by A. W. Reed (A. H. & A. W. Reed, 1965); the dog and cat myth: *Aboriginal Fables and Legendary Tales* by A. W. Reed (A. H. & A. W. Reed, Sydney 1965).

I would like to thank all the friends whose help made it possible to complete this book; in particular Keith and Sue Betties, Carlo and Caroline Canteri, Don Carless, Patrick and Alma De Largy Healy, Cheryl Grant, Chris and Ann Koller, Julie Kotlin, Mark Lazarus, and Sue Robertson. My thanks also to the staff of the Latrobe Library for their assistance, and to Stephanie Grey, Margot Blackburne, Maureen Mills and Betty Snowball for their typing.

Foreword

The tale of William Buckley puts me in mind of a spirit caught between the Dreamtime and the earth; a spirit in limbo, always trying to do the right thing, both spiritually and in the way he treated his fellow man. But the greed and lust for the land of his more detached colleagues was far more powerful. It overwhelmed and claimed him, just as it had claimed the original inhabitants of this land.

William Buckley wanted to be free, and to be a free spirit. It is hard to imagine how he felt about his own culture, so imprisoned was he by his own past and his own kind; so much so that he took extreme risks to be free to start a new life in a strange new land.

He knew nothing about this land. He was frightened by it. And he was frightened by the original people of the land. There were many Aboriginal tribes. Nevertheless, Buckley took the risk to be free. He became a man on the run, faced with hunger, scarcity of water, and sheer exhaustion.

But his life was about to change. He did not know that the spear, which symbolised the spirit of possession of the dead black man, would not only save his life, but also empower him in another life. Buckley had deserted his own culture and found another. The spirit of the dead had returned to its people. Buckley soon came to understand that he had become the spirit of the dreaming. He treasured and valued this right, and equally protected his new friends the best way he knew how.

He did not realise that, by doing just this, he would be torn between two cultures. And abused by both. The Aboriginal way of living became his way of life. The other culture, however, did not understand so easily, nor did it want to understand. Those who tried were not rewarded.

Buckley was excited by his new way of life. And also, often frustrated as he tried to learn how to hunt, to fish, to survive, and not be seen as wasteful in the eyes of his new friends. He seems to have understood and respected many of the customs, the ceremonies and rituals of his Aboriginal friends. It seems also that he knew he was fortunate to have become a witness of these ancient ways. All this took place just 140 years ago. William Buckley had the rare privilege to be inducted into an age of timelessness.

Buckley found it very difficult, at times, to come to terms with the bloodshed caused by infighting between tribes. But Buckley was still able to memorise and respect the Aboriginal customs and way of life.

Buckley was a true witness of the occupation and so-called civilisation of this country. He lived within two worlds, one of which he deserted and the other in which he became lost and confused. He came to know the Aborigine, but he no longer knew the white man.

He tried to bring the two together, in harmony, but he underestimated the power of the occupier. How could two completely different cultures live together in harmony, with different languages, different practices, different customs? What place was there in the new order for the indigenous people, and for a William Buckley?

So Buckley ended life as a lonely man. And perhaps only then, with his death, did his spirit become truly free.

The Aborigines battled the invasion. And they managed, despite it all, to beat the attempt to wipe out their race.

The Aborigines have survived. Still, today, there is a continuing battle taking place, as Aborigines seek to challenge the laws that have denied them for so long. In fact, what they are asking for is understanding, respect, and acknowledgement; in other words, they are asking that the system return the favour they bestowed upon Buckley, when they allowed him to share in their way of life.

The spider web will always spin, as will the Dreamtime. And as the sun shines through, the vision of the free spirit may be seen once again.

When I read *Buckley's Hope* I felt that time had slipped by so quickly. Yet while the haunting story of William Buckley continues to be reinvented and brought back to life, it has proved much more difficult to develop people's sensitivity to differences between cultures and respect for the natural environment.

When I look around our beautiful country today, I am constantly reminded of the absolute devastation and destruction, and the dredging of our natural resources, and I can only dream of the old ways.

However, there appears to be a positive move to build relationships between the peoples of Australia. Too many hearts have been broken, and too many hearts are aching. Let the healing begin. Perhaps 'Buckley's Hope and none' may become a phrase that will be put to rest.

Joy Murphy,
Wurundjeri elder

Preface

It is a rare privilege to be able to write a second preface to a book after seventeen years. I am deeply grateful to my publishers, Henry and Margot Rosenbloom, and to all the readers who have supported the book over this time. Since I first set out to write the story of William Buckley, many novelists, dramatists, poets, painters and film-makers have now dealt with either his story in particular or its paradigm situation. One can now ask, what is the source of this phenomenon? What is it in our culture that has made it possible to re-publish this book after a long period?

A full answer cannot be given here. But a glimpse might by provided by tackling the question I myself have been asked most frequently over the years. The question is: 'Is that the Buckley who had the cave down the coast?' My reply is at first affirmative, but then I always feel compelled to make it clear that I do not believe Buckley ever spent more than a night or two in a cave, anywhere — that he did not 'live in a cave'. This is a kind of myth about Buckley, and a powerful one, too. But myths are a central concern of this book; so what is the problem?

The young William Buckley trained as a builder. He built huts and lived in them. So did the Aborigines. The very earliest accounts make it clear that the people living around the Port Phillip area — for example, on the shores of Corio Bay and other parts of Victoria — had substantial groups of permanent dwellings. They were destroyed very quickly. In some cases, at least, they had been used on a seasonal basis as their owners moved about the territory they occupied in a regular cycle of food gathering. This was the society that Buckley joined and where he spent most of a long exile from his culture of origin. The problem is, why is this not so well known? Why has it not become the kind of myth with the power of the man in a cave?

The cave has become a powerful imaginative archetype in Western culture, even before we think of Buckley's story. One thinks of the 'primitive caveman' idea engrained by post-Darwinian archaeology; this is another kind of myth, re-enforced by the popular culture of the Flintstones, the fascination of an Altamira, Lascaux or Koonalda, perhaps even by the pervasive intellect of Plato.

Also there is the notion of man-alone-in-the-wilderness. One thinks not only of Defoe's character, but of a long Romantic and romanticised history: Rousseau, Wordsworth, the landscape painters, Beethoven's *Pastoral Symphony*, Thoreau, Tarzan, even *Star Trek*. The list goes on. It remains a powerful influence, for example, in the value placed on nature and our desired place in it that permeates modern environmentalism. It certainly influenced me. Robinson Crusoe, and living in a cave — the appeal is irresistible.

I return to the first Preface. Regardless of what was said in it, I do not believe Buckley should ever be seen as a Robinson Crusoe. The myth of a man alone, away from society, in a wilderness, in a cave — whatever its appeal belies the historical reality. To my mind, the important thing about Buckley's survival is that he was 'a man cast out by one society and welcomed by another', one that occupied the land in a structured and culturally developed manner. Its environment was not a wilderness. The land and the culture — including its mythology and gastronomy — were all integrated. Where the Europeans saw wilderness, often there was none. To the original inhabitants it was the settlers who created one by axe and title deed.

But there is also a great irony late in the story (see Chapter 25), when the ageing Buckley — the man who crossed the lines in his youth — wanted to spear the young Aborigine, Derrimut, for inadvertently betraying a plot to drive out the settlers — for crossing the lines, too. We don't really know why Derrimut was attracted to the household of the settler Fawkner. Perhaps it was simple friendship. All societies have internal conflicts that may drive people under pressure to seek refuge within another society, even when it is a declared enemy. For the fact is, when common humanity prevails we do relate to each other as individuals and families — which is as it should be — not as 'tribes' nor, worse still, as nations and races.

The importance of William Buckley, especially today, is that he was a man who, for a brief, fleeting moment in our history, stood for reconciliation between two societies by their simply living together. Then, as now, he demonstrated that there was something to be found in the idea of 'the best of both worlds'.

Finally, while I wish to restate the fictional nature of this account of Buckley's life, the factual element is important. Please note that I took poetic licence in two instances:

- With the name 'Murrangurk' having the connotation of 'soul': this was based on one flimsy etymological record;

- With the last of Buckley's tattoos: Todd recorded it as a monkey, but it looked more like a bird, albeit a bizarre one, with arms.

I should also like to correct one error: the shepherd killed with Franks (see Chapter 26) was named Fisher, not James Smith (see *the Historical Records of Victoria* Vol. 2A, 'The Aborigines of Port Phillip 1835–1839', Chapter 2).

Craig Robertson
Melbourne, 1997

Preface to First Edition

This is a story about William Buckley, a convict who ran away from a settlement on the shores of Port Phillip in southeast Australia, in 1803. For nearly thirty-two years he lived among the tribes of the district. He learnt the ways of the nomad, forgot his English language, lost his sense of time, and enjoyed a better diet and better health than his countrymen. He survived to greet the founders of the city of Melbourne and to suffer savage disillusionment over his 'deliverance'.

His adventurous life seems unique, even bizarre. From the time of his return to white society Buckley presented an enigma. He had transcended the racial conflict that is still with us, yet became an early victim of it. He was referred to as everything from a 'man of thought and shrewdness' to a 'mindless lump of matter'. He achieved what few others in Australia ever have, and yet has been despised by most of the few historians who have given him more than a footnote.

Buckley was a true Robinson Crusoe, a random being thrust into a challenge to his individual survival. But the enigma arose because he was also more than that. He was a man cast out by one society and welcomed by another – the two apparently so different, so antithetical, that they have yet hardly met without conflict. How was it that he could survive and thrive on his passage from European civilisation where others failed and perished? And why is it that a failure like Burke is revered, while Buckley is half-forgotten? How do we choose our heroes, the subjects of our statues and our monuments?

The answers to these questions strike at the foundations of white society in Australia. Buckley had to be heaped with abuse and consigned to obscurity in order to preserve our society's assumptions and values. For Buckley's story is also a story about the land, about how and why it became property. His life was entwined with this vexed question from beginning to end.

At the time of Buckley's birth the new steam-powered factories were already burgeoning a few miles away in the next county. But modern industry would not have a direct impact on his life, or most of his countryman's for decades. His boyhood was spent in the countryside, close to nature. That way of life was, however, in its death throes. His father was among one of the last generations of English peasants. Soon they would all be gone, replaced by a far smaller number of modern farmers.

Then, in his final years, Buckley witnessed the situation described in 1840 by Assistant Protector Edward Stone Parker, of the Loddon District, the north–west quarter of the Port Phillip Protectorate. In his first report to Chief Protector Robinson, just four years after the founding of the settlement on the Yarra Yarra, and with Batman's treaties swept aside, he depicted the situation thus:

> Several important facts materially affecting the condition and prospects of the aboriginal population, as well as the security of persons and property of the colonists ...
>
> The first is the rapid occupation of the entire country by settlers, and the consequent attempts made to deprive the aborigines of the natural products of the country and even to exclude them from their native soil. The entire country of the Waverong and Witourong tribes with scarcely any exception, is now sold or occupied by squatters ...

It is a common opinion among the settlers that the possession of a squatting licence entitles them to the exclusion of the aborigines from their runs.

Lately, Mr Munro, having pushed his stations on both sides of the 'Colaband' and up the tributary creeks to Mount Alexander (Leanganook) complained in a public journal that 'the blacks are still lurking about the creeks — that they seemed determined to act as lords of the soil' etc. etc. The plain fact is that this is their ordinary place of resort, as furnishing them with the most abundant supplies of food.

Precisely similar is the relative situation of the native and colonial population in other parts of the district — both parties mutually regarding each other as intruders.

There was a single social factor at work in both situations, common to both Buckley's youth and old age. It was the relentless expansion of the wool market. The most efficient way to grow wool is simply to graze sheep on pasture under the control of fences. For this reason the English peasantry was deprived of the common lands it had used for a thousand years, and was hence destroyed as a class. Over one-fifth of England was fenced by hedgerow and ditch, and turned into private property after 1760. In the years of Buckley's exile the Irish were subjected to the same process, and the Scottish clan chiefs threw thousands of their clansmen out of the highlands. The Australian blacks and other subject peoples of the growing empire were simply the next to lose their lands.

Buckley was unique to colonialism only in that he lived the common experience of British peasant and Australian nomad. He came to a crossroads and, by a combination of factors of personality and circumstances, took the opposite direction to everyone else. By the time he returned to civilisation the mass of his countrymen had been adapted to the values of secular, urban industrialism.

Except in favourable circumstances, such as in islands of the South Pacific, tales such as his became rare. But, before Buckley's time, his experience was not even unusual. In every colonial situation there have been people who preferred the society of the subject race. Whether they were renegades or outcasts, they found in the adopted culture something which enhanced the quality of their lives; something denied them in their culture of origin.

Buckley became a strange kind of Australian who was unacceptable to a society hell-bent on the unending accumulation and investment of capital. His reserved attitude to the merchants and graziers was regarded — had to be regarded — as evidence of stupidity, laziness, torpor and moral backwardness. If he had gone further, and supported the aboriginal resistance by involving himself in raiding the graziers, his detractors would have added 'treachery' to his sins.

And so Buckley became the victim of both class and racial prejudice. As an uneducated working man who did not go to church every Sunday he was looked down upon, anyway. He was also subjected to the stigma of being an ex-convict; he had to be careful not to give away the identity of his old shipmates because of its intensity. But he had broken a far stronger taboo by 'going native', by having 'sunk' or 'fallen' to the level of the brutish savage — which was the only way his preference for life with the tribes could be explained comfortably. So, instead of being recognised for his efforts to achieve peace and harmony between the races, he was accused of the same 'faults' as the blacks, and criticised for not having tried to 'raise them up'. He acquired such a bad reputation that he was thought best forgotten.

Hopefully, this book will help give Buckley his rightful place in our history. Nearly all of the available material relating to his life has been used; it has been judged critically, but not by the standards of the historian or the biographer. This is essentially a work of fiction. The values of the novelist have prevailed in the task of interpreting the records and filling in the gaps they leave. For those who wish to read further, or who want to check where the boundaries of fact and fiction have been crossed, a bibliography has been provided.

Part One

I

In the undulating green countryside of the English county of Cheshire there is a small village called Marton. Only a few dozen families lived there when William Buckley was born in 1780. They knew little of far away London where, not long before, an *Act of Enclosure* had been passed through Parliament on the petition of a few local gentlemen, giving them the right to fence in the commons — exactly where the villagers, as far back as anyone could remember, had run their pigs, sheep, cows and geese, gathered wood, and hunted and fished. Now only sheep occupied the area, and a lad was called a poacher if he were caught there while hunting rabbit for the family stew.

But the villagers of Marton had been luckier than others. Instead of all of them being forced out of the village, many of the men had been granted a few acres each. It was, however, not like the old times, when they had shared different strips of land so that each got a fair share of the good soils; now, they each occupied one small holding and, in some cases, only on a yearly lease basis.

Each day Buckley's father went out to his plot and worked in the tiny fields. Like his neighbours, he grew oats and corn, milked a couple of cows and made cheese, and planted potatoes in the lighter soils. Whenever possible his wife and two sons and two daughters worked with him. Most of what they produced they ate themselves; any surplus was sold at market, but the prices they received gave the family a paltry income.

They always found it difficult to buy seed or livestock, implements, or even clothes. They all knew well enough that their life on the land would not last, and that they would have to do what everyone did in the end — sell out to a bigger neighbour. The village itself offered nothing but poverty and idleness, as landless men and women sat waiting for some seasonal work with the farmers, or the planting of hedges and digging of ditches for new enclosures.

Hoping to find a better future for their son, young William's parents sent him to live with his maternal grandparents in Macclesfield — the nearest large town, five miles to the north east. The old people treated him kindly, indulgently by some standards of the time. They even sent him to an evening school where he was taught to read, but not to write. The purpose of his education was to make sure that he could read the scriptures, so that he would be able to judge matters affecting his liberty for himself and not be left at the mercy of any priest.

But by the time Buckley was in his teens the scriptures were not able to help him understand the great events that were affecting the life of his country. There had been a revolution in France, with whom England was at war, and great turmoil at home. By 1795 people were starving to death in the streets of London; radical leaders were haranguing vast crowds across the country; and even the King was mobbed by a crowd of 200,000 on his way to open Parliament. The Government reacted to these events savagely, passing laws that made it treasonable to oppose the King, Constitution and Government, and giving magistrates the power to use the death penalty to suppress public meetings. For the time being, the country was under control again.

Buckley was now fifteen and his foster-parents were able to apprentice him to a bricklayer, Robert Wyatt, with the intention of seeing him learn the house-building trade. Macclesfield is a market town set in a deep gorge on both banks of the Bolton River and surrounded by the bleak upland folds on the western edge of the Pennine mountains. In the 1790s the silk and cotton trades came to the town, encouraged by the humid atmosphere of the valley. It smelt of far-off places and exciting changes as new worlds were opening up, and the possibility of travel was in any aware youngster's mind. Buckley had spent years playing on the banks of the river, roaming the town on market days, encountering all kinds of people he would never have known in his father's village.

These influences and the easy discipline of his grandparents encouraged what he himself felt to be an unsettled nature. He believed in God but, beyond that, the subject failed to hold his attention. He longed for adventure, and chafed under the arduous tutelage of Mr Wyatt.

This artisan, to be fair, genuinely tried to instruct his apprentice in a manner which would ensure that he became an independent small master of the trade in his own right. They worked together nearly four years. During that time Buckley worked hard. By the thousand he carted bricks and sandstone blocks — excellent building stones quarried from several ridges which ran north-west of Macclesfield up toward the new industrial heartland of Lancashire. He learned to work, to do it all week, and to apply himself with imagination to the many odd jobs and minor skills that such a trade demanded. Naturally, his labours made him fit and strong, and this contributed to a certain dare-devil fearlessness.

So did something else. If there is one thing to be known about Buckley, it is that he was a big man. He passed the six-feet mark in his mid-teens and stopped at six feet six inches not long before leaving Mr Wyatt. His hazel eyes twinkled in a round face topped by a shock of dark brown hair. Sinewy but well built, he always walked erectly; and this at a time when the average height of his countrymen was only about five feet three inches. It was a mixed blessing; the other lads didn't dare look for trouble, but it made things difficult with the girls of Macclesfield, and in his own mind his stature marked him off from others. This intensified his restlessness and growing desire to find what life had to offer in other places.

In these years England did nothing but encourage such feelings. The war with France continued, new colonies were founded, and civil disturbances continued to flare around the country. There was mutiny in the navy, and then a civil war in Ireland that renewed fears of a French invasion.

Not long after he had turned nineteen, Buckley took the call to arms. His discontent with work, his yearning for adventure and the mood of patriotism made the decision to leave his apprenticeship easy. But he needed money so, rather than join the Volunteers, he chose the Militia — a standing army whose units were based in their own counties, and which paid a fat bounty of ten pounds. Thus he joined the Cheshire Militia, determined to win glorious laurels on the battlefield and become a colonel or a corporal. He didn't really know the difference between the two, any more than he knew the disasters he would encounter.

In fact, Buckley became a pivot man in his unit. Companies were sized by placing the tallest men on the flanks and the shortest in the centre. By height alone Buckley was a natural choice, but because of the drilling and combat procedures a pivot man was also required to display steadiness and correctness of movements as a guide to others. Buckley certainly mastered this position, as failure would have seen him run out of the army. At first, his life of adventure was anti-climactic. He spent about a year at the barracks, doing nothing in particular except taking part in some rather farcical training sessions. However, it was better than carting brick and stone, at least until his money ran out. Feeling more secure on the home front by the summer of 1799, the prime minister, William Pitt, planned another attack on the French in Holland. In July he passed an Act to reduce the numbers in the Militia in order to make men available for the expeditionary army, and named a number of regiments of the regular army which they could choose to join for a bounty of ten pounds.

This new venture in Holland was to be another disaster from beginning to end. Forming an army in July for an invasion in August was based on the wishful thinking that it would arrive in time to assist a supposedly imminent Dutch counter-revolution.

Amsterdam lies near the base of a neck of land running north about fifty miles to a tip called Den Helder, beyond which stretches a chain of islands sweeping around the north of Holland towards Germany. The North Sea coast on the neck is lined with large sand dunes forming a natural dyke. The plan was to land and invade through a certain gap in the dunes a few miles from Den Helder. The Duke of York had been given command mainly so he would outrank anyone coming with the Russian contingent, which was to join the British. The navy was ill-prepared and the army little more than a collection of men in red coats so poorly equipped that some of them were almost naked. There were practically no supplies throughout the campaign.

They sailed in mid-August and ran straight into a series of unusually violent gales. After being forced to beat about for days before invading the mainland, the landing was finally made in rough surf at 5 a.m., so that many men were drowned. The French, calmly watching and bringing up reinforcements, opened up a withering fire of grapeshot and the heavy casualties commenced. The landing was secured, but the Dutch did not defect.

Meanwhile, throughout August the ten pound bounty men from the Militia were rolling into Barham Downs in the south-east of England where the invasion force was being organised, and Buckley was with them. They were drunk and riotous and the locals were locking up their daughters. Pitt came for an inspection tour not long before the force was to sail and join its beleaguered comrades at Den Helder. The officers had to raid the taverns and brothels in the nearby town of Canterbury in order to round up the men. Not more than one in twenty was sober and the troops were dismissed after a summary review, the commanding officers not wanting to risk a march past.

Buckley had enlisted in the Fourth, or King's Own Regiment of Foot after leaving the Militia under Pitt's *July Act*. For the first time he travelled down through England by coach to join them where they lay at Horsham Barracks, about thirty-five miles south of London. The regimental commander was Lieutenant Colonel Dixon, who impressed him as a competent officer. A couple of weeks later they moved to Barham Downs and prepared to sail.

The second wave of the invasion, about thirty-three thousand men, landed in Holland in mid-September, where they were joined by the Russian contingent. Before long, thousands of them were sick in hospital, mostly with dysentery; but the battle continued. The thrust south was made by four columns so spread across the country that they were not strong enough in any one sector. Buckley's regiment was put in a brigade under the Earl of Chatham, a man of notorious indolence and incapacity. They were in the fourth column, on the left flank, which marched on Hoorn, a small port town about twenty miles from Amsterdam. The column was under General Abercrombie, who seemed to be one of the few commanders who knew what he was doing. With about twenty miles of bad winding road to cover they marched in the afternoon and arrived at two o'clock the following morning. The commandant and his garrison were all asleep and easily taken.

The other columns met with disaster, especially the Russians who were crushed. Exhausted from their march, Abercrombie let his 10,000 men rest a day. When he finally found out what was happening they were forced to retreat through torrential rain and a river of mud. Buckley and his friends were quite sober by now and far from impressed with this. Stragglers began to fall by the wayside all around them.

Another attack was mounted at the end of September, but a south-westerly gale drove the sand so hard into the faces of the troops that they were forced to give in. Chatham's brigade was now in a column on the right flank in the sand-dunes. The next fine morning was 2 October, and they attacked again towards the town of Bergen. The dunes were up to a hundred and fifty feet high, covered in heather and coppices of stunted trees. It was easy to get lost in them, and various battalions soon lost sight of each other and began to lose formation. The big militiamen like Buckley were outfought by the nimble and experienced little French light infantrymen. They played a retiring, game, keeping clear as the militiamen exhausted themselves running up and down the dunes with their heavy muskets and backpacks. Suffering heavy casualties, the British managed to fight their way past Bergen and on towards Haarlem over the following few days.

On 5 October another major skirmish took place several miles from Haarlem. It was chaotic, no one commander having any idea what was happening or where everyone was. Chatham showed his true form by running his exhausted men through more sand dunes infested with French infantry, and his brigade suffered the worst casualties. Buckley was lucky to receive only a bad wound to his right hand from a musket shot.

By the evening of 6 October, York's armies had fought five major actions without gaining anything more significant than enough casualties to seriously weaken them. The militiamen had proved good fighters despite their lack of training. Although they were totally exhausted, wet weather had made encampment impossible. There was mutual dislike between the English and Russians, whose commander made a point of disobeying York and fighting his own campaign. The Dutch were unfriendly if not hostile, and were simply content to see who won before declaring their allegiance. So, on 7 October, York gave up in disgust and ordered the retreat. On the 20th an evacuation fleet arrived at Den Helder and the campaign was over.

No-one was more glad to retreat than Buckley. He could hardly hold his musket, let alone use it. His regiment was eventually marched to Chatham on the Thames, about thirty miles from London, where he was to spend over two years.

2

The turn of the century came, but few could rejoice. Napoleon had blockaded continental Europe, cutting off Britain's trade. Industries stagnated, unemployment grew; manufacturers were petitioning for peace; and a fresh round of food riots spread across the country. The pressure for peace finally resulted in a brief truce — the Peace of Amiens — from April 1802 to May 1803.

Buckley, whose wound had now healed, and his comrades-in-arms watched pensively the day the London crowd drew Napoleon's emissary in triumph through the streets. Having fought a losing battle and seen men die in a not altogether popular war, they could not entirely share the feelings of the crowd about this obviously popular settlement. Yet, after only one abortive campaign and nearly four years in the army, most of it spent in wasting time and always tied to the barracks, Buckley felt there had to be more to life, and that perhaps the new peace would bring new developments. England had been at war since he was thirteen and it was hard to imagine the alternatives.

Events were to move quickly in determining his future over the period of peace. Shortly after the settlement he received another bounty. This was a reward for his length of service and for being a good soldier. He had impressed his officers with his attention to duty and generally sober conduct, and his build and manner of bearing himself also left a favourable impression on the military mind.

But now it was peace time and the army was less and less interesting as a future. He had some money in his pocket, and in the town the tavern life of girls and ale had many attractions. Sometimes he and his friends would go up to London and do the round of East End pubs. Many people were flocking over to Paris to see the new republic, and the general populace was caught in election fever. Extraordinary campaigns were being held across the country and a number of reformist candidates were elected.

The people with whom Buckley drank and caroused around the taverns were swept up into renewed agitations and hopes for better times, and he was more and more cynical about being a good soldier for Old Corruption.

Shortly after the elections he was given a six-week furlough and, in the summer of 1802, he set out to see his family and friends in Cheshire for what was to be the last time.

Life in Macclesfield seemed at once dull after London, but also strange. The spirit of the new century walked the streets. There were more factories with more machines thumping away in the humid gorge, but the people looked morose. Many went to revival meetings looking for a way to relieve their feelings, which were deliberately aroused during the preaching, often to the point of hysteria. Some people used opium whenever they could, and its haphazard availability often resulted in great tensions building up. Malnutrition aggravated these problems. All kinds of prophets arose, playing on this emotional imbalance which could swing people from sober resignation to revolutionary enthusiasm. The orthodox clergy were outraged, much to Buckley's amusement.

A local ranter-type group, the Independent Methodists', attracted a following to their emotional and noisy meetings where the leaders railed against the Whore of Babylon (the corrupt Establishment), the corrupt clergy, robbing gentry and merchants, and against 'the Beast', Napoleon. In the Delamere Forest several miles west of Marton, there were stories of a cult calling itself the 'Magic Methodists' whose members practised falling into trances or seeing visions.

Such developments added some relief to the ascendant gloominess, but Buckley couldn't help seeing how his friends were affected by it. Some had become serious, dedicated to their jobs, and were even going to church regularly. There they listened in silence to sermons against friends who were still going out of town together on weekends for sinful 'revels'. These revels, while not what they were in the old days, still afforded some fun. The practices of eating, drinking, whoring, cursing and wasting money were carried on in the face of continued attack from the clergy, who also could not abide card playing, colourful clothes, personal ornaments, theatre, singing and dancing or anything else that might encourage happiness.

Buckley's parents had finally given up their land to a local gentleman and moved into Macclesfield. Only an uncle now lived in the village. They were much as he remembered them. They were older of course, and perhaps lonelier, as only one of his sisters still lived with them and she was soon to be wed. His brother had gone to Middlewitch to work at one of the salt-works that provided industry for a number of small towns in the south of the county. He had not been able to get land of his own, nor had most of the other lads that Buckley dimly remembered running with through the maize fields all those years ago.

Coming back to this situation after some years made Buckley realise that it was not land that he wanted. He wanted his independence, his liberty, however vaguely he could imagine what this meant. He thought in terms of adventure and excitement, and to have them he would have to cast this life behind him and never look back. His grandparents had died not long after he had been in

Holland and, although he assumed he might see his family again one day, he left Macclesfield for London gladly, and with some ease of mind. At least he knew now that, whatever life had to offer, it was not to be had in his native Cheshire. The young Buckley considered himself the equal of any other man and was determined to make the world his oyster.

Soon after his return to the barracks Buckley met his destiny. One day at the end of July he was crossing the barracks yard when a woman he had not seen before approached him. She asked him to take a bolt of cloth to a woman in the garrison who would make it up into clothes. England's law was harsh, and it was also inefficient, indeed random in its effectiveness. But Buckley was apprehended, accused of receiving stolen goods and convicted at the Sussex Assizes on 2 August.

As a soldier his 'trial' was a mockery, the judge effectively handing him to the military police. He was never told exactly what the charges were nor the extent or nature of his sentence. Considering the burgeoning number of hangable offences he was lucky to be alive. Within a matter of a few days he had been reduced from being a relatively free man to being in a state of slavery. He was put to work in a prison gang building the new fortifications at Woolwich, on the banks of the Thames a few miles from central London.

His life was now more miserable than he had ever thought possible. Not only was he again carting brick, stone and mortar through a long working day of fourteen hours; the food was rotten, there was no pay, no days off, nights and Sundays were spent in confinement along with scores of other unhappy souls, and his whole life was spent under the threat of the lash. He hated authority with all his heart, and swore every waking hour that the next time he found himself free he would kill, murder, die, before he would submit to such agonies again.

Month after month of this misery passed, broken by only one significant piece of news. In November word spread that a Colonel Despard and his associates had been arrested for treason.

Allegations were made at the trial that Despard had planned a coup d'état in which the Tower and the Bank of England were to be stormed and the King assassinated, signalling the London crowd to rise. It was also alleged that sympathetic guardsmen at the Chatham and London barracks had recruited many of the soldiers and the civilian working men from the surrounding districts into a large paramilitary organisation. But none of this could ever be proved.

Buckley knew nothing of a national underground organisation or any imminent seizure of power, but he knew well enough that the conspiracy was real. In his own barracks at Chatham there had been many soldiers and guardsmen including some close friends who were quietly sympathetic to Colonel Despard's ideas. The Colonel had been known well enough around East End taverns such as the Flying Horse, the Two Bells, the Brown Bear and the Bleeding Heart. It seemed obvious now that some of his own friends had been involved.

The bitter thought came to Buckley one day, as word spread about the trial, that perhaps he never knew why he had been arrested because the watchful officers had had orders to round up anyone whose loyalty was suspect. In those final months, especially after the visit to Cheshire, Buckley had increasingly let his dissatisfaction show, and had kept company more and more with the suspect tavern revellers. He would never know the truth, but his hatred would grow.

It was a sorry day for many prisoners in February 1803 when the word came around the scaffolding at Woolwich that Despard and six associates had been executed. The chief executioner had held Despard's head up before the angry and compassionate London crowd with the announcement, 'Behold the head of a traitor'. In his final address Despard had claimed that he was innocent and was to die because he was a friend of the poor and oppressed. The press had feared that, if Despard and his associates were taken through the streets to be hanged at Tyburn, there would have been riots and an attempt at rescue. Instead, they were hanged at Southwark. With them died the last hopes of a democratic revolution in England and any chance of a new order that would set men like Buckley free.

Buckley now lived on a curious and desperate mixture of feelings. Anger and resentment sustained his heart. His youthfulness in the face of despair, and the fact that he still didn't know the length of his sentence, kept his sanity.

Several weeks after Despard's execution word came that a new colony was to be founded at Port Phillip on the southeastern coast of New Holland. This time Buckley's physique undoubtedly served him well, as did being a 'mechanic'. He was selected to sail on the *Calcutta* under Captain Woodriffe. Buckley only knew that a place called New South Wales had been settled on this new continent, and that it was on the other side of the world from his poor country. His chance for freedom had to be there.

3

The English had founded the Colony of New South Wales, forming a settlement at Sydney Cove, for a complex of military, commercial, and penal reasons. But the French were also showing a keen interest in the area and had been busy mapping it. The English were now obliged to protect the southern approach to their new colony. Colonel David Collins, whose career had seen many famous actions, including sailing on the First Fleet with Arthur Phillip, was given the task, being appointed Lieutenant Governor of the new Colony.

The expedition sailed in two ships. The *Calcutta,* a fifty-six-gun frigate, carried Buckley and 306 other convicts, some of their wives and children, a detachment of fifty Royal Marines, and Collins and his civil staff. It sailed from Spithead on 24 April 1803 and joined the transport *Ocean,* which carried a few free settlers and the settlement's stores. Three days later the two ships left Yarmouth Roads, their last sight of England, and sailed south. They made a brief stop at Teneriffe in the North Atlantic and then began the long forty-day run to Rio de Janeiro. After nearly three weeks in Rio, during which the privileged few disported themselves with great pleasure, they finally dragged themselves away to continue their mission.

Details of the journey come largely from the journal of the Reverend Robert Knopwood, who started the journal on his first day on the *Calcutta.* 'Old Bobby' Knopwood had been a man of wealth, educated at Cambridge. He managed to squander an inherited fortune of £18,000 in the company of the Prince Regent and his hard-drinking and gambling friends. Debts finally forced Knopwood to sell his lands, and he used his influence to secure a job as Navy Chaplain which led him to sail with Collins. He was fond of a drink, well liked, and not known to neglect his parties for religious duties.

Among the children on board was the ten-year-old John Faulkner (later John Pascoe Fawkner), whose father was being transported for robbery. Referring to relations with the women on board, Fawkner later wrote that 'even the parson was compromised'. Certainly, at some stage Collins, who had left his American wife in England after an unsuitable marriage, took Mrs Hannah Powers, the wife of a prisoner, as his mistress. The acquiescent Mr Powers received favours and eventually a pardon.

Buckley, who was determined to make the best of a bad situation, tried to make himself useful where the opportunity provided. His stature and resourcefulness marked him out, and he was made a personal man-servant by Collins, thus gaining some freedom of the deck where he was allowed to assist the crew.

They lost sight of the *Ocean* on 31 July in thick weather. It sailed direct to Port Phillip. Late in August, the *Calcutta* had a brief stay at Cape Town, where one convict drowned attempting to swim ashore. At length they entered the Indian Ocean. Unbeknown to them it was a typical early spring in these latitudes; for an entire month they battled a continuing series of squalls, gales and high seas that created the biggest waves in the world, apart from tidal waves.

Buckley was unperturbed, being one of the few who seemed immune to seasickness. After the dreadful rigours of his months at Woolwich the voyage was like an adventurous holiday. He quietly enjoyed the way the winds and lightning and waves reduced all souls to the same rank before their inmost fears of the unknown. At twenty-three he was too fascinated with what lay ahead to look back, and too ignorant of danger to worry. They began to see big herds of whales. Dolphins sometimes played about them, mocking their turbulent progress.

On 29 September they had their first day in over a month when Captain Woodriffe and his distinguished guests could sit steadily at the table to eat. The sea stopped raging and the sun poured a dreamy, humid warmth over damp decks and cramped muscles.

Apart from a few clouds on the horizon Buckley could see nothing but a boundless expanse of water. He leant over the railing near the bow watching the foam surging below him. He looked ahead for a long time, thinking how utterly alone they were; and yet he found something so attractive about these southern seas. The whales and the dolphins seemed to beckon them on to hidden pleasures, and he began to lose his presence of mind, feeling like a drop of water in the ocean. His thoughts had just begun to reshape themselves around a lonely sea-bird skimming the waves when they were sharply returned to him by an armed marine ordering him back to his duties.

The bad weather continued, and on 6 October many of the weatherbeaten passengers spent the whole night out on deck anxiously looking for land in spite of the strong wind and high seas. The next day the first happy sign that the long journey was over appeared in the form of a butterfly. Then they saw a gannet heading steadily north–east, and in the evening a small bird landed on the deck. On the 8 October they sighted King Island in the east and, at five o'clock in the morning of the 9th, they saw the coast near Port Phillip. They entered the Heads and anchored at a quarter past ten. There they found the *Ocean* which had arrived on 7 October. The convicts were kept below while preparations were made to land. For a final night they were kept from sleep by a gale that blew up about ten o'clock.

The following morning a beautiful sight greeted the weary eyes of the people as they made their way on deck. There is no more eloquent testimony than that of Lieutenant Tuckey of the *Calcutta,* who wrote:

> The nearer shores along which the ship glided at the distance of a mile, afforded the most exquisite scenery, and recalled the idea of 'Nature in the world's first spring' ... The face of the country bordering the port is beautifully picturesque, swelling into gentle elevations of the brightest verdure, and dotted with trees as if planted by the hand of taste, while the ground is covered with a profusion of flowers of every colour.

It was spring in the new land and the country was indeed like a vast parkland in a new coat of green grass.

For the convicts it had been a merciful voyage by the standards of the day. One man had received thirty-six lashes for a theft, and several people had died from ill-health. But on the whole they had been well treated. Collins was a liberal man, especially considering his position in the era of Captain Bligh, when the lash and the rope were often thought too good for convicts. In fact, his ideas would have been considered an incitement to mutiny by most of his contemporaries; allowing convicts to live without continual extra punishment was considered too merciful. However, after his experiences at Port Jackson, Collins knew the value of a fit labour force when settling in the wilderness.

Over the next few days Collins, Woodriffe, and Knopwood scouted both shores on the south side of the bay, and on the 13 October Collins chose a spot not far from their anchorage. He called it Sullivan's Bay*, after a friend in

* Sorrento

the Colonial Office, and the settlement was begun.

Three days later the convicts were landed; the settlers followed the next day. A tent village called Hobart Camp was created overnight, trees felled and roads made. A press was set up under a tree to print the orders of the day. Livestock were landed and gardens planted, Collins himself having a two-acre patch. Soon the ancient patterns of human activity emerged. Death, birth, baptism, marriage, adultery, theft, and punishment were all noted. Young Johnny Faulkner had his eleventh birthday. Food supplies began to be augmented by local game from land and sea, although the first kangaroo was not shot until mid-November.

Yet somehow the settlement seemed to lack a sense of reality, of purpose. Virtually from the beginning Collins displayed a complete lack of interest in the place, which was never fully explained. It seemed he just wanted to go somewhere else; and the fact that his commission guaranteed him a payment of £500 in the event of his having to move did not give him much incentive to stay.

Although the decision was his, he was anxious for Governor King's support, and sent a boat to Sydney in early November. Thus, even as the settlement was being built, preparations were being made for departure. This dampened morale as the realisation filtered through to the colonists' minds.

Collins did have problems, the most immediate being the lack of fresh water near Sullivan's Bay. Yet he was slow to make any effort to look for a well-watered district, even though he was supposed to have known of the previous discovery of fresh water further up the bay. The settlement survived on the contents of six perforated casks, sunk like wells in the sand on the edge of the beach, that had to be guarded to stop the users polluting them.

Collins may well have felt that the northern shore was

too far from the sea lanes to be strategically useful, especially as he disliked the way the temperamental 'rip' was inclined to trap ships for days. In the meantime, he went through the motions and began constructions designed to secure the settlement against a possible appearance by the French, or any mass misbehaviour by the convicts. A gun battery was erected on the shore. The three men erecting it ran away, but were recaptured and lashed as a deterrent. This strategy was not effective, and other attempts to abscond were made.

Later, Collins wrote: 'The cause of this desertion I can no otherwise account for than by the operation of the restless disposition of men, which is ever prone to change, for the convicts are well fed and clothed, and are not overwrought.' But Tuckey, on observing the convicts labouring in the hot sun, had understood, quoting a poem:

'Tis liberty alone that gives the flower
Of fleeting life its lustre and perfume,
And we are weeds without it.

The first buildings were a bomb-proof magazine and a storehouse built of stone cemented with lime. Collins released Buckley from his personal service and put him on this project, it being his trade. It was this that first brought Buckley into the bush. The organisation of the camp was such that the mechanics were allowed to but themselves outside the line of sentinels who kept the general labourers under close guard. This was necessary because the nature of the work required them to go in all directions. The lime-burners gathered limestone found in abundance between the camp and the Heads. The sawyers went in parties miles up the peninsula to cut timber for a multitude of purposes, and the brick-makers and builders went to nearby rock outcrops where they quarried the stone for building.

The new freedom of movement in such a splendid

environment was a true joy. Buckley loved the brightness of the country and welcomed the excursions to their little quarry, for it was especially then that he was able to experience for the first time the uncanny, quiet stillness of the forest and marvel at the beautiful coloured birds that seemed to abound. There were parrots, big cockatoos and little wrens, and a black and white bird erroneously but lastingly dubbed the magpie because of its superficial resemblance to the European bird of that name. During gang rest breaks, and even better when he could wander off a few yards to piss, he felt the drudgery of his labour begin to drain from his body and his mind yearn fiercely to fulfil his desire for liberty.

4

After about two months of this tantalising situation, when spring had become summer and the sun had made work feel even more repressive to the now tanned and taut bodies of fit and frustrated men, Buckley determined to escape to Sydney. He knew it was about six hundred miles away, although his grasp of the direction was negligible and his mind chose to ignore what he knew his fate would be if he actually got there. Escape was his one obsession, and he knew his strength and health were such as to give him a good start. He would worry about survival when the problem confronted him.

The weather certainly did nothing to discourage these feelings. They had struck a particularly warm season; fresh from the old country the settlers chafed under the rising temperatures. From the second week of November many began to fall sick, and Collins had to temporarily reduce the number of sentinels. The military, allowed half a pint of spirits a day, were frequently drunk on parade.

On 19 November, 400 hundred blacks massed on the nearby mountain, which the first explorer of the bay, John Murray, had named Arthur's Seat, and threatened a party of woodcutters who were forced to run to their boat. Earlier in October, Tuckey had met the tribe on the opposite shore.*
At first friendly, their encounter had turned into a bloody skirmish, with the whites shooting and running.

*Corio Bay

These factors aggravated the low morale and strained the flimsy social relations between the different sections of the population as they waited to see what Collins would do. They even found the tools supplied to them by unscrupulous merchants to be shoddy and nearly useless.

In late November the *Calcutta* was sent to the top end of the bay, where it took on timber and fresh water. Yet nothing was said about the fine country there. On 11 December, Tuckey took a party exploring over to Western Port. On the 12th, the turning point came for everyone. The *Ocean* returned from Sydney with news of Lieutenant Bowen's encampment at Risdon on the Derwent River in Van Dieman's Land, and Governor King's authorisation for Collins to move there. The next day Tuckey returned with glowing reports of the soil, timber and water he had seen at Western Port, but no-one wanted to know. Feverish preparations for departure were being made by everyone, not all of them for Van Diemen's Land.

Among the convicts was George Lee, an educated young radical, very popular among his fellow prisoners. He had begun to gain their loyalty at the expense of the officers, and Buckley was sympathetic to him. Collins was afraid of a rumoured mass desertion, and his fifty besotted marines would have been useless against any such action. In fact their own loyalty was suspect; several of them had been involved in a mutiny on Gibraltar.

Collins decided to break Lee on a work-gang among the labourers, taking him from his privileged position hutted with the mechanics. But before he could move, the *Ocean* returned and Lee decided it was time to go. That very day he went to Collins' gardener and got a fowling-piece from him by stating he had an order from the Governor. He left immediately with a friend, William Gibson. Others began to follow suit over the next few days. Some returned; others, like Lee, were never heard of again.

Being close to Collins' circle Buckley was well aware of these events, and of Tuckey's discoveries. He knew, like Lee, that the departure to the island of Van Diemen's Land would set a seal on any hopes of getting to Sydney. If freedom was ever to be had the time would have to be seized soon. It would take several weeks for the settlement to be packed up. They were building a simple wharf to ease the job of loading. Buckley and five of his friends — Dan McAllenan, George Pye, Jack Page, Michael Warner, and Charlie Shaw — hatched a plot to run for it. They decided to wait until after Christmas in order both to enjoy the meagre celebration it might bring and to take advantage of the unsettled routine to make their preparations. In the meantime they could begin to salt away a few provisions.

On Christmas Eve the officers and a few other select members of the expedition held a party to celebrate the occasion. They dined on fish and crayfish caught during the day by the Reverend Knopwood, and were able to enjoy the first fresh peas and beans from the Governor's garden. According to the general orders, the population at large celebrated on a pound each of raisins rationed out especially for Christmas to all men, but not to the women and children.

That night the Commissary, Mr Fosbrook, slept more soundly than usual. Dan McAllenan slipped into his marquee in the dead of night and managed to get his gun and also his fine boots from the bedside. A few items of food were also acquired from the hospital tent. This booty was cached by the quarry.

On Christmas Day Collins dined with Mrs Powers and other leading 'citizens', and the first baby was baptised. It was a beautiful summer day, the temperature at one o'clock being recorded as eighty-two degrees.

On Monday, 26 December at about nine o'clock at night, when the southern sun still cast a dull glow in the western sky, and with the meagre festivities of Christmas behind them, the six men made their move. It was a stifling hot night, fairly clear but with dense black cloud building up across the bay. Under the pretext of cooling off while cray-fishing from the jetty, they cut loose a dinghy and rowed to a spot further along the foreshore, ran to the quarry to collect their gear, and began to move away from the settlement. Somehow they lost Page and Warner, Page being recaptured within minutes. Warner just disappeared. Apart from the gun and food they had also taken an iron kettle and some pots.

In the diminishing light, the pale sandy soils and sparser vegetation of the foreshore allowed a man to see where he was going well enough to keep running as quickly as he could. But the thunderstorm nearly foiled them. Lightning began to flash, and before they were clear a lookout party led by Corporal Sutton spotted the four and challenged them. Not receiving an answer, one marine fired, and Charlie Shaw dropped to the ground. Buckley thought he was dead, but he survived to be carried back to the camp on a cart by the assistant surgeon Mr Bowden, where he was healed and obliged to make a statement.

Buckley, McAllenan, and Pye ran through the night with their ill-chosen goods. Within an hour the lightning had become frequent enough to guide their progress, and draughts of cool air laden with ozone fired their groaning muscles to greater exertion. There was a cool wind for a short while and then the rain began. It poured down but soon eased off; they ran for nearly four hours until, exhausted and no longer afraid of apprehension, they allowed themselves to take a short rest. They had certainly passed the point of no return. Pressing on, they came to a small river, some distance inland*, where they rested until daylight. The rain had stopped.

* Cannanook Creek

Early in the morning Buckley had his first encounter with the blacks when, unseen, he scared away a large party armed with spears by discharging the fowling-piece. They were headed toward the settlement but apparently kept their distance. The three then decided to make for the hills they had always seen across the bay, in order to spy out the land. After waiting about half an hour they crossed the river. Favoured with height and some ability to swim, Buckley virtually carried the other two, and the clothes and provisions, across in several trips. The iron kettle was sensibly dumped (to be found some thirty two years later by some men clearing a paddock). Moving at a more leisurely pace now, the day's march brought them within a few miles of a large river,* where they again rested for the night.

The following day they crossed on the rocks of some waterfalls and marched south–west over a long-grassed plain to the hills.† From the peak they could see a hazy panorama of the vast bay. Open plains stretched all around them into distant hills covered in forest. Here they spent another night under the trees, and finished the last few mouthfuls of their rations.

In the morning Buckley, now the acknowledged leader, suggested they head straight for the nearest beach to look for food, as starvation otherwise appeared inevitable. They marched to a large sandy bay,‡ where they got shellfish and spent another night. The next weary day they followed the coastline, barely able to sustain their protesting bodies. Several sturdy, dome-shaped huts were spotted along the way, and they hourly feared attack from their inhabitants. At the end of the four days' march they struggled on to a little island at low tide and halted for a rest. Here they added to their diet a kind of gum which, when heated over

* The Yarra River
† The You Yangs
‡ Corio Bay

fire, was soft and palatable.

From their retreat they discovered to their amazement that they could see the *Ocean* lying at anchor on the opposite side of the bay. McAllenan and Pye, now desperately afraid of starvation, leapt at the chance of rescue, preferring to suffer any consequences less severe than slow death. Buckley was not ready to give in yet, but assisted them in making fire signals at night and hoisting shirts on poles. Knopwood recorded seeing their fires.

After two days of desperate hailing and anxious cursing a boat was seen to leave the ship and begin rowing toward the island. But about half-way across it appeared to have difficulty sustaining itself against the current and turned back. Pye and McAllenan gasped with despair, their faces gaunt. They kept trying more and better signals without result. The misery of Buckley's comrades deepened and he too became very subdued. But in his heart something held firm, if only because the others spoke with such grief.

After another week of fruitless efforts to attract the boat again, McAllenan and Pye decided to go back the only way possible — by retracing their steps around the bay. They implored Buckley to return with them, needing his company as much as being concerned for his fate. He remained resolute. Although not feeling his best, he was still far from beaten; his propensity to see himself as different from others had allowed him to avoid their excesses of despair. No amount of persuasion could even tempt him to return with them. He spoke of liberty; of flying free and clear like a bird. Dan McAllenan replied that he was almost forty, and men like himself were probably only good for another few years anyway. He had always believed in liberty or death, but now it wasn't worth the risks. George Pye was scared out of his wits.

On the final morning they all returned to the mainland and scrounged one last meal from the rocks. Little was said.

Finally, Buckley said again that he would have his right as a free-born Englishman, and bid goodbye to George Pye and Dan McAllenan. He watched the pair slowly shrink from view on the beach. On the 16 January, a roasting summer's day, McAllenan surrendered himself and the fowling-piece in the Governor's garden at one o'clock. George Pye was never seen again, at least not by white men.

Collins had sent out a party to search for them, but it had returned unsuccessfully on 30 December. When the launch had failed to cross the Rip a couple of days later the escapees were left to their own devices. A few runaways were the least of Collins' worries. On 29 December, fearing an insurrection, he had felt obliged to form the civilians into a vigilante group for night patrols. Crayfishing was banned. On the following day some soldiers were shot at in their tents by other deserters in the bush, possibly Lee; and on 31 December two soldiers were locked in the guardhouse, accused of mutiny. Loyal men could not be spared.

At the same time another heat wave came, with temperatures up to a hundred and ten degrees recorded. The roar of the surf on the back beach made many uncomfortable. An overwhelming obsession with packing up had gripped them, and most couldn't wait to leave. The *Lady Nelson* came to assist with the move, taking most of the settlers. The *Ocean* was loaded with convicts and stores. By 27 January they were ready. They cleared the Heads on the 30 January, leaving a small party with the remaining livestock and stores under Lieutenant Sladden, and sailed to the Derwent. Thus Hobart Town was built there instead of on the shores of Port Phillip.

In April the *Ocean* returned for Sladden and, despite a request by King, no-one was left behind. The *Ocean* sailed out of the Heads on 21 May, carrying the last official visitors for the next thirty-one years. Buckley could not look back now. He was the freest man in the world.

Part Two

5

Buckley immediately discovered something unpleasant about this freedom. Without the company of others to temper his feelings he fell rapidly into deep melancholy. Wandering some distance along the shore, he sank face down on the sand. He had crossed the narrow little peninsula separating the bay from the ocean, and the surf pounded in his ears. The breakers pushed his mind further and further back. With his body fragile from a spartan diet, his mind began to follow its own path. Vivid images of his past tumbled through him, his heart sinking with sorrow that it was all gone forever. It was a kind of death. He remembered his old friends in London and Macclesfield and running across the sand dunes in Holland; his family, he saw as never before, bringing within him the greatest yearning, and then the slavery of his convict labour and transportation.

It was only this latter memory that sobered his thoughts and made him begin to concentrate on the reality of his situation. After some hours he forcefully pushed his body up and wiped his face of sand and tears. Never look back, he had always said; but what groundless self-willed hope would he now have to find in himself to be able to look forward? He sat for some time with his chin on his knees, staring across the water, knowing he could as easily drown himself now as do anything else.

After a while these thoughts and memories began to drain

away and he found himself reflecting on what he was seeing; the sweep of the ocean and coastline, the clouds rolling in from the horizon. He was hungry. Food would not appear here miraculously, so he felt he may as well die looking for it as sit mulling over the same things. He got up and began walking along the beach, recalling the other famous forty days and forty nights in the wilderness he had been taught about, acknowledging with a curse the insignificance of his own fate. Even so, a small part of him still clung to the idea that he could get to Sydney, even though he really knew it was ridiculous. He would be detained if he did get there; and if he really made himself think about it he knew he was going in the opposite direction to Sydney, anyway.

McAllenan and Pye had left him with only a fire-stick, just a length of a small branch kept smouldering by constant movement. Bearing this last link with human society he walked for several miles across some flat marshland, following the coast. After a few hours he suddenly stopped and dropped to the ground in fright, a few yards from the bank of a substantial river. Several hundred yards upstream he could see a group of perhaps a hundred blacks moving about some huts built from tree branches and bark. A detachment of them were moving in his direction. Fearing an attack, he ran straight into the river and made for the other bank. In his panicky attempt to flounder across quickly he let the fire-stick skim the surface of the water. Cursing, he clambered out on the other bank, but too late. The fire-stick was extinguished. His clothes were soaked and he knew that he was going to be very cold. Slipping into the scrub he surveyed the land in the direction of the tribe. They had withdrawn from the river bank and were obviously not in pursuit. He felt relieved at this at least and made his way to the beach, stopping just past a lagoon at the mouth of the river.

It was late in the evening and Buckley prepared for what he knew would be a miserable night, in spite of the apparent loveliness of his surroundings. The weather had become cold and cloudy. Isolated clouds dragged skirts of rain across the ocean beneath an extravagantly beautiful sunset. Strong pinks and yellows reflected in the waters of the lagoon. Wishing he could relax and enjoy such things, he removed his cold, wet clothes and attempted to cover his hungry, shivering frame with leaves and rushes he had gathered, nestling in the thickest patch of scrub he could find. Mosquitoes added to his miseries. The only positive thing he could think of was that, not having a fire, he did not have to worry about being spotted at night.

In spite of the extreme discomfort, his physical and mental exhaustion at last brought sleep. The night began to pass, bringing its own desperate adventures. He dreamt he was at his grandparents' house. Colonel Collins was there and he was afraid they would find out his true relationship with him. They ate and chatted nervously about the strangeness of the forest. Afterwards the house was a ship and they sailed to London. Buckley wanted to go to the Flying Horse Tavern in Newington but was afraid he would be forbidden. They wandered the streets aimlessly. He met his brother but the conversation was far away, as he sought a means of eluding the forbidding presence that stopped him going to the Flying Horse. Eventually he was alone, walking on a country road, perhaps outside Macclesfield. But it was a bright land. Parrots and magpies appeared. He knew he was far from London. Yet he was determined the Flying Horse was ahead. It was true. There it was among the trees up ahead.

Even as he felt happiness within his grasp something was wrong. He awoke slowly, his mind trying to draw back into the dream. It was light and a breeze rippled through the scrub. He groaned 'No' to himself, his heart sinking. The depression of the previous day was immediately on him. He wanted to cry, and drew his stiff and aching body closer into itself, closing his eyes. But it was no use. He forced himself up out of his rough bed, quickly looking around. There was no sign of the tribe, so he dressed and stalked awkwardly down the face of the big dune that bordered the beach, and began to stumble through the sand. The pain of moving his body tore his mind away from its inner retreat. He moved further down the coast away from the river and lagoon, and began to look for food.

After wading a short time within the littoral he found some muttonfish. He could prise these univalve shells much more easily from the rocks than actually eat them in the raw state. Nevertheless they sustained life for another day. He tied a few in his shirt and trudged on.

He felt like the lowest scavenger in creation, just crawled from the sea on the shores of an unknown and hostile earth. March flies bit at him and little bushflies bored into his face, but he clung to life and kept moving. He crossed several streams but they were all salty or brackish, and thirst became his most immediate problem. The next day, all he had were the dew drops he licked from the leaves of small bushes growing on the dunes. The day after, he found a few shellfish and fearfully saw wild dogs following him. The next he went entirely without food or water. At nights he slept in terror of being discovered and slain by blacks or attacked by the dogs.

Towards the end of these three miserable days, marching ever further along the coast, he crawled exhausted and feverish between two large rocks on the beach below some high cliffs, hoping to find in sleep some relief from his agony. He dreamt of a world of abundant water in which he alone seemed to be forbidden to drink. As he began to plead with the indifferent people the incoming tide washed over him, a wave slapping up his nose. More instinctively than consciously he crawled, coughing and spluttering, up on to one of the rocks, and lay there exhausted and bewildered.

The tide swirled in and trapped him there for the night.

He lay face upwards looking at the sky. It was clear, and the grandeur of the Milky Way swept over him. The weather was warmer now — becoming hot on the very day he could find no water. Apart from this mixed blessing, his condition was the worst he could imagine. Trapped on a rock in the sea, starving and exhausted, it appeared the next and final step down the road of misery had to be death. Buckley wasn't ready for death. Twenty-three was too young to die. Yet the fact of it stared at him steadily, day by day, now hour by hour. He prayed hard.

The following morning, dazed and heartbroken, he left the rock. Going through the motions of being alive, driven by some will remote from his own mind, he scrounged again for food. The abundant birdlife he had observed along the coast, especially in the vicinity of swamps and lagoons, continued to impress him — particularly as the birds always remained so tantalisingly beyond his reach. Just one seagull, let alone a swan or one of the other larger varieties, looked a real feast. He noticed a number of birds appearing and disappearing from behind the cliffs a little further along the coast and walked on, hoping to find something.

Soon he came to a point where a rock island that had once adjoined the cliffs stood out in the water some yards. Scrambling through the gap he stumbled into a small inlet* where the cliffs gave way to a long sand dune. A stream emerged from a swampy area behind the dunes and opened into a small lagoon that stopped at a sandbar on the beach. Here he found an area of perhaps fifty or sixty acres which had recently been burnt, evidently by the local inhabitants. A few magpies and a crow were picking around the ground. He hobbled over in the hope of finding fire. The crow flew off lazily, uttering its mournful cry. The magpies moved silently back, perching on a nearby tree and watching him.

* Airey's Inlet

At last, among the piles of ash and the blackened trunks and branches of shrubs and small trees, to his great joy, he found a tree still smoking. He rushed to it as to an old friend and tore off a fire-stick for himself. Useless as this treasure was without something to cook, its effect on his spirit was immeasurable. From being a lost cause on a rock to the possessor of fire, within hours, had to mean there was abundant reason for hope. Food and water would come.

After a few hours he found a high shrub bearing a kind of wild raspberry*. The fruits were rather dry and insipid compared with the cultivated variety, but they grew in abundance on dense thickets. Buckley ate cautiously, for fear they may have been poisonous or at least might make him sick in his fragile condition. This apprehension proved groundless. The berries were very refreshing, and he could feel energy begin to flow through his body. He scouted around further in the scrub behind the dunes to see what else he could find. Within minutes his luck proved itself again. This time it was a well, dug in the bank of the stream not far from the beach. The water was excellent and he drank in long cool draughts. After days without food or fresh water, he found this the most memorable ale he had ever drunk. For the first time in about two days he had a piss; it was dark, salty and stinging. His body had begun to work normally again. With rising optimism he searched the rocks around the point and found plentiful supplies of shellfish. These he cooked on sticks over a fire.

It was a beautiful summer evening. The sun set behind the hills, casting a soft pink light over the little feast on the side of a dune. In one day Buckley had passed through the final stages of despair and become a man cursing as he burnt his lips on hot tasty muttonfish, periwinkles, mussels and limpets, with fruit for dessert and fresh water to wash over the aches and pains in his body. He stoked up his fire

* *Rubus rosifolius*

and made himself comfortable by it in the sand. He slept soundly all that night and almost to the middle of the following day.

He awoke quietly, his mind as fresh and calm as he had ever experienced. No dreams tried to drag him back. He couldn't remember dreaming. The sea too was calm, with only small waves breaking lazily. A pleasant on-shore breeze caressed his skin. Seagulls were picking among the shells he had strewn around the previous evening. As he lay there he reflected on the great fortune he had enjoyed. If there was a God who knew or cared for people then yesterday must have been his turn. He wasn't sure what he felt about this, but thankfulness was part of it. There was indeed hope for him now.

These thoughts turned over in his mind as he looked at the white clouds lazily rolling across the sky. Just then a seagull hovered a few feet over him. He lunged for its feet, but his body was stiff and unresponsive still. Although he missed easily, it got him up and smiling at his own mischievousness.

He ate some berries while rekindling the fire. The rest of the day was spent gathering and eating more berries and shellfish, and making occasional visits to the well. He dragged a few branches and tufts of grass together for a very crude shelter, for the clemency of the weather made anything more quite unnecessary. The only source of anxiety was the need to watch for the blacks should they chance to visit their well.

Buckley spent several days in this manner. His strength returned, although his body had many infected sores over it from bites and scratches. These he could only treat by bathing in salt water. Doing this several times a day he began to enjoy wallowing in the surf and then lying out on the sand to dry in the sun, which became quite fierce in the afternoons. He was thankful for the tan of his skin that he had been able to acquire by degrees, unlike most convicts, on the voyage from England. His face, neck, arms and feet were able to withstand exposure but parts of his shoulders, back and legs, previously unexposed, soon became burnt and required him to remain dressed for a day until the soreness passed.

During these days his sense of time began to come adrift. He couldn't remember how long it was since his escape, although it must have been about three weeks.

After a week of recovering in this little paradise, a day came when the wind turned it into a most inhospitable place. It was a hot, dry wind from the north, not just blowing but blasting everything. Trees, scrub, sand, birds, water; all shook for nearly two days. Buckley lay in his windbreak endeavouring to sleep as much as possible, going out only rarely for food and water. During the evening of the second day he could see dark clouds gathering in the west. Rain was coming and he moved camp to a small cavern in the base of the cliffs at the point. It wasn't very comfortable but at least it would he dry.

The first showers came with sundown, a spectacular show of colours forming a canopy over an ocean darkened by black rolling clouds spitting flashes of lightning across the water. At first the rain was brief and sweet. The sand was wetted down and the air smelt fresh and enervating. The wind dropped so that, despite the storm rolling in, the atmosphere felt mercifully still. Buckley watched the display over the ocean until it grew dark, then returned to his nest in the rocks. Later that night it began to pour heavily. It rained all the next day and the following night. He sat it out, sleeping and eating when he could, amusing himself trying to get fresh rainwater to drink where it gathered on the rocks. On the second morning the rain had stopped but it was cold and damp everywhere, the sky overcast and the sea breeze cool.

He couldn't remember how many days he had spent in this spot, but felt it was time to move on. The changed weather, his greatly recovered health, and the ever-present fear of discovery combined in an irresistible urge to go. He took a fire-stick, a few berries and shellfish and began marching further down the coast.

After two days the country had become increasingly mountainous, sometimes dropping quite sharply down to the ocean where the seemingly endless golden beaches were now more and more giving way to rocky platforms. At times progress became difficult for his infected and aching legs, and he feared it might cripple him to persist. When he came to a large rocky hill about a mile long*, he decided to make a long stop in order to try and recover his health more completely. The weather had grown hot again and the high mountain provided shade and shelter from inland winds and, to some degree, from prying eyes. At the base of the hill the ground formed a small ledge, then dropped ten feet or more down to a rock platform just above the water. He camped under this ledge so that anyone coming his way would have to come right down on him to spot him.

A pretty stream of fresh water gushed from the rock ledge above, so the tide was no threat to this resource. Indeed he soon discovered the tide movements here were smaller due to the steeper coastline. This was a safe and comfortable place in the warm weather. It was also quite strange and interesting to sit there. The bedrock forming the small cliff face behind, and the platform extending out to the water, was a pale greyish colour, setting off the other rocks embedded in it. They were mostly dark brown and rounded like balls. They appeared to grow like eggs from the maternal bedrock, eventually falling free from the action of the weather.

* Mt. Defiance

For food, Buckley found ample shellfish and pigface, a succulent weed that reminded him of watermelon — rather insipid and salty but refreshing — and two kinds of currant-like berries, one white and one black.* He built his first little home here, labouring steadily and happily, despite his ill-health, for four days. He dragged great quantities of branches and seaweed to the spot where the creek emerged from the bush and erected a sturdy but that kept out wind and rain.

One day, while he was working on this hut, he went to the stream for a drink of its cool and sweet water. As he bent down he noticed a particularly attractive stone in the water. He plucked it out and examined it. It was one of the ball rocks no doubt dropped from the nearby rock face, about as big as his fist. The shape was rounded and smooth, rather like a flattened egg. Its colour and texture contrasted with the predominantly dark tones of the other rocks; it was white with black spots and brownish speckles and a few larger dark lumps in it. He supposed it to be a kind of granite. Wanting in decorations for his hut, he thought this stone would be good. The ancient Celts had venerated things like stones, wells, and trees, his grandma had told him. Perhaps he would make this stone something special for himself. Later, he set it by the doorway on a large flat rock. It was something to look at, something undeniably his in possession and manner of display. As long as he could see and pass by this stone, something in his world remained stable. When his spirits began to rise high in reaction to his days of melancholy he even began to say good morning to it and to call it names according to his mood.

He remained there some weeks; eating, sleeping, and paddling in the sea, especially enjoying this early in the morning. If it was sunny he would sit for hours among the

* *Carpobratus rosii, Leptomeria aphylla* (currant bush), *Coprosma hirtella* (coffee berry or rough coprosma) respectively.

ball rocks watching the sea and the mountainous coastline, feeling his body heal. His strength of body and mind grew rapidly until he was almost back to normal. He even began to become a little bored, although he was still exceedingly thankful for his situation. He began making brief excursions along the stream and up the mountain above him or further down the coast, gathering food and more objects to decorate the but and augment his stone. All the while he was careful not to be seen, by who or what he was never sure.

But it was not enough. After some weeks of this existence, which only a short time ago had seemed utopian, he had to confront the fact that he was becoming miserably lonely. He had achieved what Robinson Crusoe, whose tale was well known to him, had achieved. He had fire, food, water, shelter, and some clothing. They had all received a new suit of clothes two weeks after landing but in these conditions it wasn't going to last long. Basically, he could continue this existence for as long as he liked, but he began to yearn for some kind of company. A stone was not a very useful friend. His return to normal digestion and bowel habits had intensified his craving for better food, and so too had his sex begun to make its presence felt, and felt sharply, for the first time in weeks. If there were people, there were women, however perilous the contact. There was the incessant niggling in the back of his mind that he was an easy prey for a surprise attack. Whichever way he looked at it, Buckley knew that the solitary existence of a Robinson Crusoe was not for him. The future had to lie with human society, 'be it ever so humble'.

6

One day while sitting near his but watching a reef heron gracefully snatch its food among the rocks, and thinking about the possibility of approaching the tribes, Buckley felt a chill of fear shoot through him like lightning. He suddenly heard the distinct tones of human voices over the sound of the sea somewhere above him. 'Amadiate', he heard. Freezing, he just turned his head around and saw three black men wrapped in fur skins, each carrying two or three long spears. They looked right down on him. He slipped into a crevice behind him, somehow trying to persuade himself they hadn't really seen him.

To their sharp eyes his excursions up and down the stream had left an obvious trail. They were soon down on him, calling to him to come out — or so it sounded. In terror of sudden death Buckley surrendered. There was no alternative.

For the first time he stood face to face with his future friends. They appeared to answer his terror with an equal degree of amazement. His height obviously impressed them, being a foot over theirs. They touched both his hands, seeming to want to test the substance of his flesh. Some satisfaction appeared to pass among them and they beat their fists against their chests. This they repeated on Buckley's chest, while he just stood, hoping it would all go away in a minute. His alarm was heightened at the peculiar noises they made during this encounter, a high-pitched 'nyaah' sort of sound. After some minutes of this chaos they pointed to his hut and moved with questioning motions towards it.

He motioned toward the doorway, pleased to do anything to avoid being speared. The three men needed no encouragement to go in, and they immediately made themselves at home. While one made up a big fire, another threw off his furs and ran into the water. A few moments later he came back with two large crayfish which he dropped into the fire.

As the crayfish cooked the three visitors sat looking at Buckley, their faces impassive. He searched their eyes with casual glances, his mind racing with the stories he had heard of cannibalism in the South Seas, fearing the extent of their hunger. To his amazement, when the crayfish were cooked he was promptly given the first and best portions. He took his time eating, even though it was a delicious treat, afraid of what was next. But when they had finished the three got up and went outside, beckoning him to come with them. He hesitated at first but soon relented as there seemed nothing else to do. They proceeded up the hill, two going ahead of him and one behind, obviously ensuring he kept with them.

He thought constantly of running away but that could have been a fatal move. After a few hours clambering up the hills they came to two small grass huts just as it was getting dark. They were only big enough for two people to lie down in full length side by side. Buckley was assigned one hut, sharing with one of the men. He thought this would he his chance to escape but his companion lay awake all night muttering to himself some strange incantations. Added to these distractions were numerous mosquitoes, so he did not sleep either and lay awake all night watching and listening and swatting.

In the morning, exhausted and itchy as he was, he felt it was time to make the situation clear. When they motioned that they were going further and wanted him to come, he shook his head vigorously. There ensued a brief and rather strange heated discussion by means of signs and noises. But they relented and shrugged their shoulders, again exchanging mischievous looks among themselves. Then they indicated that they would like him to stay until they returned and that — to Buckley's indignation — they would like his stockings. This demand he also declined, even daring to show a little anger at this suggestion. After a few more rounds of stamping feet and pounding chests they left him alone.

Buckley watched until they were gone and sat down to think over his next move, as he had lost his bearings the previous evening. Before he could decide what direction to take, one of them returned bearing a basket made of rushes in which was a load of the berries he knew. This the man wanted to barter for one of his stockings. Buckley refused adamantly, feigning indignation, as it was becoming hard to take the situation seriously. He felt he had to impress them with his resoluteness on this matter in case more important confrontations arose. Soon the disappointed bargainer left, and Buckley wasted no time in departing the little camp.

Having made a rough guess at the direction of the coast, he was relieved to reach it without difficulty in a couple of hours, at a point that was unfamiliar to him and away from his camp. He walked along the beach in the direction of his hut, musing over the hopeless failure of his first meeting with his fellow beings. Soon he came to a high rock on the water's edge. The sea was becoming tempestuous and pounded the rock with great thumping breakers. As he sat on the sand and watched, the clash between the unyielding stone and relentless waters seemed to reflect his own feelings. He felt exhilarated but also saddened to know that such conflict could last forever, even in himself.

While he puzzled this over, his heart aching, he noticed

a small rock platform some distance from the shore which was covered in the strangest creatures he had ever seen. They were fur seals, which, unbeknown to Buckley, were at that time being slaughtered in their tens of thousands in these very seas. It was soon after the end of the breeding season and he could see their young pups frolicking in the water. In this harsh place they had some society. As each one arrived, perhaps from distant and lonely stretches of ocean, it struggled to mount the rock and be with the others.

Buckley knew he had to go back and try again. The day was wearing on and he was again without food or fire. He traced his way back to the grass huts but they were deserted. Whether he was disappointed or relieved he wasn't sure, but he waited for some time and prepared a fire from the coals left there. When they did not arrive, he impetuously felt that having started this effort he should continue it. Taking a fire-stick he plunged off into the bush in the direction he had last seen them vanish.

With night falling, Buckley found himself alone in the forest of a strange land for the first time. Until now he had always been in company or along the familiar, universally known environs of the coast — sea, sand, sea birds were all easily understood. But now it was different. The forest here was dark and mysterious even in the day.

When it became too difficult to keep a sense of direction and low branches threatened his eyeballs in the dark, he was fortunate to notice a huge tree, which by its very size had created a slight clearing around itself. The base of the tree was half as wide again as Buckley was high, and quite hollow inside. The discovery pleased him greatly. He would have a good place to sleep, he thought. Making a fire at the entrance, he reasoned that at least he would be warm and relatively comfortable, the smoke keeping the mosquitoes at bay.

But this night held something far different for him. Before he was asleep he suddenly heard a terrible piercing shriek, then a ringing scream like a loud whistle. Alarmed, he peered out, but could see nothing. Shortly there followed a harsh, cackling laugh; this time much closer. He became afraid, imagining that the three men he had sought had now found him by the light of his fire and were practising some cruel joke on him, perhaps prior to his execution.

The unearthly shrieking and cackling continued, sometimes sounding like over-excited children. Now in the trees some yards away, now in the branches above him, now right outside the entrance to his hideaway that had become a prison. He called out half in fear, half in anger, 'Who is it? Who is it?' No answer. The cries ceased. The next sounds he heard were unmistakable; they were the howls of wild dogs. These howls also came closer until he fancied he saw one or two of the dogs move in the scrub beyond his fire. He kept a burning branch within easy reach in case of a direct attack. It was as if the menacing cacklers had summoned them. Whatever these creatures were they were totally strange; their powers were frightening and probably superior to his own. He was in their world and at their mercy.

Before long the shrieking and cackling started again, accompanied by more howling from the dogs. This continued throughout the night. At first Buckley gave an occasional cry of 'Stop it!' but the effects of this were brief and finally nil. He could only bury his head in his hands and cry miserably to himself, waiting out the endless night of fear and anguish. After a long time during which he thought he would go mad, he listened harder, for the cries seemed to be receding. They had stopped. A strange, expectant hiatus came — the night was over but the day not yet begun.

Suddenly he heard a beautiful thing. Deep in the mountain gullies, in the dense forest high above the fern glades, at the first light of dawn the first birds on the wing are the grey fantails. As the wombats sleepily return to their holes the fantails pipe their merry song down the mountainsides, calling all the other creatures out. Buckley listened with immense relief.

He looked out through the trees and could clearly see their outline against the sky. Dawn was coming and no man welcomed it so joyfully. He left the tree immediately, snatching up a fire-stick as he went, and resumed the trail he had been following.

Within a few hours the futility of the chase was impossible to deny. Worse, he had become completely lost. Everywhere he looked were rugged hills covered in dense forest; beautiful forest too with tall timber, great varieties of small shrubs and trees, some bearing flowers. In the damp gullies were numerous ferns of all kinds, some as big as trees. They were quite unlike anything he had ever seen. The whole place was often like a vast garden and somewhat tropical in atmosphere. Mosquitoes and leeches abounded, and he saw a number of deadly-looking reptiles.

He remained lost for three days, again with almost no food, the occurrence of berry trees and succulents being very haphazard, and the creatures of the land, unlike those by the sea, almost impossible to catch. Despite the lush growth he couldn't find running water, but occasionally he was able to relieve his thirst a little by slurping muddy water from some finger-sized holes in patches of wet clay. He saw only one of the inhabitants of these holes. It was a land crab, a tiny pale lobster-like creature that tried to crawl shyly away on its spindly legs, and made such a poor meal that Buckley did not risk delaying his progress to dig for others.

At nights he was beset by the same eerie noises. The dogs howled some distance off, probably having followed him during the day. After the second night spent in the open he was able to ascertain that the source of these noises was not human but came from some creatures in the trees. Whether bird or animal, or what their intentions were, he could not tell, but he certainly had great respect for them. With this threat and the dogs, and the arduous days of walking, his mind remained under great stress. He began to feel unsure of what he was seeing, even during the day. Frequently he would fancy that he saw from the corner of his eye a man standing in the undergrowth watching him. Looking again, it would always be just a couple of tree trunks or the stump of a fallen tree. He found it harder and harder to think about what he was doing and why he was doing it. He wanted to just sit down and look at the bush and perhaps sleep a little.

These wanderings continued until, one morning, as the sun began to clear the trees on top of the hills above him, he slumped down for a rest. A golden whistler cracked a sharp note from a small tree nearby. Startled, he looked up, wiping the sweat from his eyes. Through the trees and scrub he could see a lake. It was a beautiful sight and he could hardly believe that it wasn't a dream. The water stretched out in perfect serenity among the trees for several hundred yards along a small valley. Scores of swans and ducks swam gracefully together and wild fowl could be seen in the reeds.

After refreshing himself from the waters he found a river flowing from the lake, as he guessed, towards the sea. That afternoon he tumbled down to the coast at a place where he could see, to his great relief, the rocky islet with the seals on it. From there he easily traced his way back to the grass huts, arriving late that day. He crawled straight into one of them and slept soundly all through the night, untroubled by animals or spirits. Waking late the next morning, he found, to his great fortune, a well-laden berry tree. After gorging himself he made his way down the hills to his own but on the beach.

His old place was still there just as he had left it, with

his stone by the door and the view out to sea. Resigned to spending another indefinite period there recovering his strength and settling his mind again, he tried to persuade himself it was home. But his dreams continued to remind him of the strangeness of the forest.

He is in the hollow tree staring through the fire. Hideous man-beasts are in the trees. He can never see them; only the shadows of their movements and their terrible voices. They laugh scornfully at him, taunting and scaring him, taunting him to come out through the fire. He runs through the forest and plunges into still cool waters. The swans are not there. He is a seal in the ocean looking at his but from the water. He is alone and tired.

He remained for some weeks, but this time it didn't go so well. Not nearly so well. Winter was setting in and the weather became increasingly tempestuous. It was hard and miserably cold battling in the waves among the rocks for shellfish, and for some reason these seemed to become scarcer and scarcer. His health was suffering again. His clothes were falling off his body; his shoes were worn out, and so was his spirit. He had not had to contend with a winter in the wilderness yet. Before, no matter how had the storms, he had survived; it had always become warm again and he was able to recover his equilibrium. But now cold and rain persisted. Having failed again to survive alone, and failed at contacting the local inhabitants, there seemed to be only one other course left to him; one that he had all but forgotten in the months since he waved goodbye to his friends on the beach. He decided to try and return to the ship, even though he felt too weak for such a long march.

He had no idea how long he had been gone. Apart from following the rising and setting of the sun his sense of time was now quite gone. Judging by the seasons in an upside-down corner of the world it could have been anything from six to nine months. He could not afford to tell himself that the settlement had probably long been abandoned, the *Ocean* sailed to Van Diemen's Land, and he himself believed to be a dead man.

He was reluctant to leave his hut. He held the stone in his hand. It had been something of a home here. A free man's home; something he had never had anywhere before, and could not expect to ever have if he returned. He didn't even know where he could expect to sleep that night. At least he had a familiar and comfortable bed here. But he looked down at his tattered body and felt the wind howl over him. He contemplated taking the stone, but that seemed silly, and anyway he couldn't try to carry anything except his fire-stick.

He tossed his stone to the back of the hut, sighed goodbye and began to retrace his old route back along the beach.

7

The journey was painful and slow. He could only travel in short stages, a few hundred yards at a time. His legs hurt, and his failing strength was buffeted by cold winds; his body showered by salt spray. His fire-stick went out one night as he slept, too exhausted to build a fire. Again he was living on raw food.

One night, as the last glows of colour drained from the sunset, he was stopped by a wall of rock stretching out from the cliffs into the sea. He couldn't even remember passing it before. Unable to continue, with the tide coming in fast, he was forced to climb up the rocks, thereby stumbling on to a large cavern just above the high water mark. Panting heavily, he staggered into the cave and sat down. When he had caught his breath and commenced to make a meal of shellfish, he heard a peculiar noise. Looking up towards the entrance he realised to his horror that the cave was being invaded by seals, who evidently reached there at high tide.

After the initial shock had abated and he was wondering what to do, he dropped a shell. It clattered across the cavern floor, startling the timid animals. They tumbled over one another back out the entrance and down into the waters running in below. After some time they still showed no sign of returning. He ate his shellfish and sought out the most comfortable corner of the cave, and settled down to sleep. Many weeks before it had been his observation of seals that had sparked off his search for the three blacks again, only to land him in further perils.

That night he had the strangest dream. In the dream he is lost in a forest looking for the sea. A nameless fear of doom is upon him. There are some trees. One of the black and white magpies he had been aware of since the first days at Sullivan's Bay is perched on a branch. It is very close. He looks hard at it; apprehensive. The bird appears to look back in the peculiar side-on manner of its kind. A voice says distinctly: 'In a land of bright skies a black and white bird is pleasing to the eyes.' He is relieved. The fear is gone and he feels happy and befriended.

In the morning Buckley awoke feeling confused but refreshed. The tide was out and he was able to get around the rock wall and continue along the beach. He marched slowly, blindly, for another three days, suffering numbing cold through the nights, eking out an existence on shellfish and a few handfuls of pigface and berries. His resolve to go on was all but broken.

One evening he came to a stream,* one that he had crossed before. He went behind the long sand dune that snaked many miles along the beach and made a rough shelter in the scrub. Looking inland he was amazed to see a huge gathering of large black birds he took to be crows or ravens. They were all gathering in a patch of trees perhaps half a mile away. Within minutes there appeared to be about three hundred birds all gathering, rising, and turning and resettling in four or five trees and making a great noise, almost frightening, with the hundreds of 'aah, aah, aah' sounds.

As he watched this strange meeting he saw, floating effortlessly high in the sky above, the most magnificent bird he had ever seen. It must have been huge to be so big at that distance. It was certainly a bird of prey, an eagle, and it glided around without seeming to flap its wings at all.

* Spring Creek, Torquay

54

Buckley found this spectacle most interesting despite his state of exhaustion. The eagle circled the area above the crows for some time, maintaining its altitude. The crows continued to flock around the trees. Then, suddenly the eagle swooped in an awe-inspiring dive. It soared right down through the crows, but made no attempt to attack any of them, simply tearing through the middle of the huge flock and back up into the sky again. The crows let out a tremendous cry and rose together into the air, circled around and then, apparently realising they had merely been done some mischief, again settled in the trees. Buckley had needed to laugh and thought this amusing. He slept with some ease of mind.

The next morning he crossed the little stream and, as he approached the beach to resume his journey, came upon something that, unaware though he was, would change his whole life.

On the bank of the stream near the sea was a mound of earth. It was a grave, and stuck in the top of it was a spear. Buckley stood and looked at this spear and grave for several minutes. He was afraid of robbing the dead, but the spear would be a very real asset to him. A weapon with which to hunt, or perhaps to defend himself, was something he had needed all along. In his immediate situation it was so easy to grab and use to lean on as he dragged himself along the beach. He took the spear and marched on, using it as a walking stick.

The next day at high tide he came to another stream.[*] Instead of going inland to ford it at a safe point or even down to the surf where it flowed across the sand, he tried to wade straight across. He realised too late that he had underestimated its depth and the strength of the current. In his weakened condition he nearly drowned, being carried some distance downstream; but he managed to find a

* Bream Creek, Breamlea

55

footing just before he went under. He crawled out on to the beach and looked over the dunes for a sheltered spot. To his horror he saw some dogs drop from sight as he looked up. He gasped in fear, panting into the sand. Then he realised he still had the spear with him, and this gave him courage. He made his way up into the scrub, crawling on his hands and knees.

The day was nearly done and so was he. The dogs began to howl as he crawled under a bush whilst endeavouring to keep the spear at the ready. The howling continued all night. During this night of fitful sleep he truly imagined he might not see another morning, that the dogs would attack him in his last hours. This was the worst exile of all. Even the night on the rock months ago was not cursed with wild dogs howling impatiently for his corpse. Again he prayed hard for deliverance.

Another morning came. It was a day that appeared to offer nothing to a man more dead than alive, yet it was to be the turning point in his fortunes. The dogs were mysteriously gone and he forced himself to get up and walk. It took him until mid-afternoon to cover the next five miles. He came to a swamp not far from a substantial river* that opened out to a lagoon a couple of miles before the sea. It was, he realised, a different place on the same river he had once fled across at the loss of his fire-stick.

This lagoon was surrounded by scrub and timber, and the whole area was rich in birdlife. Pelicans were abundant in the lagoon, and there were swans, ducks and others in the swampy areas. Buckley was in no condition to try spearing any of these alert creatures. He plucked his way through the swamps looking for anything he could easily gather, but nothing seemed to come his way. By the lagoon the trees looked rather familiar from what seemed a lifetime ago when he was on the island with McAllenan and Pye. He

* Barwon

began to search for the gum some of the trees exuded, in the hope of getting a mouthful of something.

Unknown to Buckley, as he was picking his way around the tree trunks and limbs, knocking pieces of bark away, two pairs of dark eyes watched from only a few yards away. Before long he sat, or rather fell, down for a rest beneath a large and beautiful tree, again in a state of complete exhaustion. The owners of the eyes, two women, slipped quietly away in the direction of their tribe.

Several minutes later Buckley was startled from a semiconscious state of dreaming in which he was endeavouring to picture his welcome and food at the Sullivan's Bay settlement. To his fear, amazement and even curiosity, he found himself surrounded by six dark-brown bodies, all wrapped in animal skins and paying him the utmost attention. Just as in his previous encounter, they beat their chests and his, and held him by the arms and hands. Most of them were making loud, and to him, hideous whining noises and tearing their hair. The meaning of this behaviour he could not grasp and it added to his fears. But he was in no condition to do anything about it, being too weak to do more than stand up and that only with help. They pulled him up off the ground, motioning that he was to have food. A group of the women helped him to walk, the men still wailing and tearing at their hair. Whether this was rescue or capture for a terrible purpose he had no way of knowing. He could only go along with them for the present.

Shortly, the strange procession arrived at a little group of huts near some waterholes they called Yan Yan. His fears seemed groundless when they brought him a bowl made of dry bark containing a quantity of the gum he had been seeking, which they seemed to call 'gurring'. They added a little water and mixed it to a pulp which he ate greedily. They apparently assumed he was craving foods found around the base of trees. For the next course they all went away for a short while, motioning him to remain. They came back with handfuls of large fat white grubs. These they apparently called 'milork' and they were found in decayed trees, especially about the roots, and to him they were delicious.

Night came, but despite his weakened condition Buckley was unable to sleep. He was still anxious about the intentions of the tribespeople. His life could have been ended at any moment as far as he knew, and he thought of escape even though it was impossible. During the night the women continued their wailing and lamentations. It was still a frightening mystery — all the more so when he saw in the morning the women's dreadful self-inflicted wounds. They were covered in blood from deep lacerations on their faces and legs, the edges of these cuts having been burnt with fire-sticks.

Soon after dawn they all sat around sharing more gurring and milork. They smiled upon him, their faces lighting up, incongruously so on the part of the women who a short time before had apparently been in mortal distress. One of the older men held out the broken spear that Buckley had taken from the grave two days previously. Looking at him and the spear, the man said 'Murrangurk' and repeated it several times indicating, Buckley thought, that this was his name. The reason for this was obscure for some time, but Buckley later learnt that the man in the grave was a relative of theirs who had been killed in a fight in which his daughters had also been speared.

Still in ignorance of their beliefs about death, Buckley anxiously accompanied his rescue party to rejoin the rest of their tribe which they had left in order to collect the gurring abundant around the lagoon. After walking sonic miles through the scrub they crossed a river,* and entered a broad expanse of reedy marshes on the edge of a vast lake.

* Barwon

This place was pleasant in spite of the cool weather. Black swans and other water-birds could be seen, and the grasses around the edge of the marsh teemed with small larks and pipits whose constant twittering chatter added much to the friendly atmosphere. To the north he recognised the hills he had once climbed with Pye and McAllenan in order to spy out the land. He was told they were called Yawang. He was then quite close to Port Phillip.

Looking across the marsh he could see a number of black dots spread amongst a section of the reeds. At first he thought they were crows, but as they came closer he realised that the dots were the heads of many people. In a few minutes about a hundred men came forward to meet them. The women seemed to continue as before. They were gathering roots.

Soon most of the tribe had accompanied Buckley and his friends to their huts. These were very simple structures — a few branches and strips of bark thrown together on the shores of the lake which they called Kunnawarra. They gathered around fires in the middle of the camp, and Buckley's presence now attracted the attention of the whole tribe. They were eager to explain many things, often pointing and naming objects. Some things he could understand, but others took time. Later he grasped that these people were called Norngnor, meaning wombat-people, and were part of the Wothowurong tribe that occupied the country south of the Yawangs, and over to the west and down along the ocean coast.

About two hundred people of all ages crowded around him. Some of them beat their heads and chests with clubs, and women tore their hair out in handfuls. These displays frightened him again, but the people seemed to understand and tried to reassure him that no harm was intended.

He began to realise that these were their customary means of displaying grief. But he would never become used to their lack of concern towards their own bodies. Wounds that were self-inflicted, or gained in combat or by such accidents as rolling over a fire in the night were treated matter-of-factly and, he would observe, usually healed with remarkable ease.

After perhaps half an hour of this milling around they dispersed to their huts to eat a meal of the various roots they had gathered from the marsh and a little of the gurring brought back by Buckley's party. Two men stayed with him. They all ate at a leisurely pace and the camp was quiet for some hours, everyone relaxing in their huts until evening drew close.

Then, to Buckley's alarm, there began a great commotion in the camp, with dozens of people running backwards and forwards, shouting, laughing, and yelling.

As night fell the children — boys and girls about eight to eleven years of age — commenced to build a huge bonfire, a task they obviously relished. Buckley still had visions of South Seas cannibalism and watched all this intently. It was impossible for him to escape, as he was still very weak. Soon his fear was mixed with more pleasurable and positive feelings: The bonfire blazed high into the air, the sparks shooting skyward to mingle with a few stars that appeared between dark clouds. The flames cast an erratic and exciting orange light all around the camp.

Into this scene marched all the women. They were naked, carrying their skin cloaks in their hands. His two guardians brought him forward and the women circled around him. He was torn between disbelieving delight and fear that he may have been cast into the flames at any moment. In due course the women seated themselves by the fire. They rolled their skins up tightly and then gripped them between their knees and proceeded rhythmically to beat them like drums. One of the men sat in front of them and sang.

The rest of the men came forward bearing long clubs.

Their bodies were painted with streaks of fine white pipeclay taken from the shores of the lake. Lines were drawn around their eyes, down each cheek, along the forehead and down the nose, others converging on the chin, and long ones from the middle of the body down each leg. They advanced in a close column beating their clubs, which they called worra-worra, together in time with the women's drumming. The white lines stood out in sharp contrast on the dark bodies and even darker night background. In the flickering light of the bonfire they often looked like ghostly stick-figures moving in a manner that seemed to defy normal space and motion.

The man who sang also appeared to he the master of ceremonies. His song incorporated sharp commands at which three groups, the men, the women and the children moved backwards and forwards in various formations, sang choruses and beat their skins and clubs. The corroboree lasted some hours. It was an intense and exhausting experience for Buckley. He experienced a wide range of emotions. Alternatively excited, sexually aroused, frightened, curious, amused and saddened, but always in suspense over when it would end and what his fate would be when it did, be approached a state of hypnotic, emotional numbness in which he only watched those whirling white stick-men. His emotional trial was well rewarded. When the dancing ended the entire congregation gave three cheerful shouts, the men pointing to the sky with their worra-worras. Then each member of the group came up to Buckley, shook his hand and heat his chest as a sign of friendship. He glanced into each face, anxiously looking for some indication of their feelings.

As they came by his suspense turned to relief and from relief to joy, and he smiled to the point of tears. Such a welcome was beyond his wildest imagination; his fate was too good to be true.

The night's celebration drew to a close and the people melted away to their huts, leaving him again with his two guardians. They gave him some roots to eat and escorted him to their hut. In spite of, or perhaps because of the disturbing and exciting feelings of the entire day, he slept soundly that night, his sleep unruffled by dreams of either the past, the present or the future.

8

The next morning Buckley arose feeling greatly refreshed. He was pleased to find the camp almost deserted apart from a few older men and women. This gave him the chance to arise slowly and gather his thoughts. The rest of the tribe were out gathering roots and spearing Boonea, or eels. He began to move about the camp, nodding good mornings in a rather sheepish way, for they seemed amused by him. As he did so a messenger departed in the direction of the Yawang mountains. This was pointed out to him and something was spoken to him about it, but he could not understand, other than to guess that it was of interest to him.

Shrugging this little mystery aside he decided to make himself useful, as nothing could be gained by sitting around waiting to see what happened next. He spent the rest of the morning gathering wood and piling it up by the fires and bringing water in the wooden bowls called 'tarnuk'. These were fashioned from rounded lumps of wood that grew like great warts on the sides of trees, and were cut away and hollowed out.

By midday he was quite hot and tired from his labour. The sun was out and the weather not unpleasant considering how cold it had been. He went to the Barwin for a bath. Soon those remaining at the camp noticed he was missing and the alarm was raised. They called out to him everywhere.

Drying himself in the sun, in a sheltered spot by the river, he had begun to daydream about the events of the night before. Parts of the corroboree had left a great impression on him. He felt that he had seen something ancient, almost timeless. But it also enveloped great mystery, as though it belonged to a world of both the living and the dead. Just then a flock of the most beautiful parrots he had ever seen swooped gaily across the river into a tree close by. Partly blue as the sky, partly of the richest crimson, their call in flight was a shrill tweeting sound like some happy and boisterous gang of knockabouts. In the tree they made a delicate tinkling sound just like a bell. As he watched he became aware of faint cries from the distance. 'Murrangurk, Murrangurk', he heard from the voice of a child. He clambered back into his rags and looked again at the parrots, wishing he could fly with them, then began to walk back to the camp.

As he returned, the messenger who had left in the morning jogged into the camp, followed by a young man he had not seen before. Buckley was led to believe that this man was also Wothowurong but of another group, the Kumbada (or treefern-people). He invited Buckley's people to visit his own, and they all set off the next morning.

The Kumbada were only a few miles away at some water-holes they called Geewar, and Buckley and his people made camp a short distance from them. Soon after arriving the young man led Buckley to this group and brought him before an older man and woman. Their names were Torraneuk (meaning Heart), and Wombalano Beeaar (meaning Beautiful Stream). They were the young man's parents, and Torraneuk was the only brother of Murrangurk, the dead man. The young man was called Tro wernuwil (meaning Foam of the Waterfall), and was their only son and so now became Buckley's nephew, as Torraneuk had become his brother. As Buckley was to learn, all people were related in kinship. Everyone was a 'brother' or suchlike, and was treated accordingly. He was quite amused at the idea of having a nephew. At least he would not be held accountable for any profligacy displayed by his young relative as was often the fate of unfortunate uncles in his homeland.

He took Wombalano Beeaar to be a few years older than himself. She was solid and strong and wore the pleasant traces of early lines on her face. She had a headband made of twisted animal fur, a necklet with pieces of reed strung on a sinew and a fur cloak. Torraneuk was perhaps ten years older than she. His physique was near perfection and his skin was a glistening coppery colour. His dark hair and beard were greying, setting off the magnetic black pools of his eyes. He also had a headband and necklet, a fur armband, and through his nose a bone with a knob on one end that he twitched with expression.

That night Buckley's new friends treated him to another great corroboree in the style of the previous night. This time he was far more relaxed, and enjoyed the spectacle. His attention wandered from intently watching the women and wondering about the possibility and advisability of making advances to any of them, or whether any of them would be interested, to again reflecting on the mysteries of the ritual. When the dancing ended in the three loud cheers the people came forward to shake his hand and beat their chests in friendship. After this his new relatives took him to their but for a little feast. They gave him roots, gurring and, joy of joys, the first meat he had eaten since his days with the men from the *Calcutta*. It was possum roasted in hot ashes, and was absolutely delicious.

As he ate, it suddenly occurred to him that it may well have been possums that had terrified him when he was lost for three nights in the bush. He paused, looking at the chunks of meat in his hands, wondering if he was eating the body of an animal whose powers were far greater than reason would allow. Torraneuk and Wombalano Beeaar began to nudge each other and mutter about Murrangurk's peculiar behaviour. He finished his reverie, prompted more by his stomach than self-consciousness, and continued to eat heartily.

At the conclusion of the meal a sweet exchange took place. Wombalano Beeaar gave Buckley a rug made from possum skins. It was worn with the fur inside, the outer skin displaying an intricate diamond pattern carved into it with great patience. He presented her with his old jacket — her desire — and tattered as it was she tried it on, laughing at its strangeness. Her friends joined in the fun, admiring her. He stood in his new rug looking at her, and she and her husband and son looked at him. They all smiled and nodded. On this night Buckley became family for them, and they for him. It was to be the start of many years of warmth and closeness, and a night he would never forget.

In the morning he arose to find a quarrel had broken out between the two groups. He had assumed that being all of the one tribe they were friends, but they soon demonstrated that serious disputes could still happen among neighbours. The argument became quite heated and spears were suddenly flipped out of the grass by the toes and brandished. Abuse, challenges and much blustering continued for some time as both sides worked themselves up for the confrontation. Buckley noticed a tall and strong-looking Kumbada man who was being particularly aggressive towards the Norngnor. Suddenly he felt a tug on his arm. It was Wornbalano Beeaar, and she led him away from the camp to watch from the seclusion of a grove of trees.

This was to be the custom on all such occasions during his stay with the Wothowurong peoples. It was to shape his experience of their life in a curious way. Not only would he be excused from doing battle, but he would also be excluded from the secret religious life of the men. Initiation and other ritual practices would not be his to know, except for the less important public parts. Apart from the hunt he would spend much of his time with the women and children.

Soon the fight began in earnest. The two parties began hurling spears and boomerangs and swiping at each other with a variety of clubs. Spears flew through the air in profusion, and men and women were dodging around trying to avoid them or ward them off with canoe-shaped spear-shields cut from the woody inner bark of gum trees. One man was speared through the thigh by a long shot from about fifty yards away, the spear landing with such impact that the head passed right through his flesh. He was pulled off into the scrub and the spear drawn. After several minutes of intense and noisy combat a Kumbada woman was felled by a spear which entered her torso under her right arm. She died instantly, and this seemed to take the heat out of the fight.

Peace was restored and the parties separated. Torraneuk had defended himself ably as usual. The big fierce fellow was still angry. About twenty people from the Kumbada made a large fire and placed the dead woman on it. More wood was placed over the body and it was burnt to ashes. These were raked together and her digging-stick stuck upright at the head of the still smoking pile of embers.

Everyone left now except Buckley and his relatives and one other family. Soon they too were on the march, penetrating deeper and deeper into the bush. Walking through the forest brought at once relaxation and exciting distractions that soon began to place the violence of the morning in the past. The women carried food and implements in their woven net bags and rush baskets (or 'beenak'). They also carried the fire-sticks and the infant children. Under these heavy loads the march was slow and many rests were taken. The older children and dogs scattered around as they went, looking to flush out reptiles and small animals. The men had their weapons and scouted ahead in search of game. They also had large bags made of kangaroo skin tied up with grass string. They could hold game and various tools. This day they only had time to go about three miles — rarely did they do more than six — and made camp as usual about an hour before sundown. This gave them time to set up mia-mias, light fires, and cook food. They stopped by a small stream in an isolated gully. The country was timbered but not so densely that it couldn't be walked through fairly easily. There were mainly stringy bark and gum trees with many she-oaks, but the undergrowth was sparse. They stayed in this place several weeks, peacefully hunting and gathering food and spending many hours together. They lived on roots gathered by the women, with an occasional possum dragged from the trees by the men. Several times they also speared kangaroo. These were skinned with sharp stones and mussel shells. Buckley was taught how to do this and how to dry the skins and trim the tail sinews for use in sewing. He mightily enjoyed gorging himself on these kills, as they were the best feasts he could remember in years. This greatly increased his hope for the future and his return to health. He became more confident and began to take lessons in hunting and the art of battle from Torraneuk and the other men.

They had several kinds of spears. The nandum were from eight to fifteen feet long and usually barbed on at least one side. The barbs were made either by carving the wood or by glueing sharp chips of stone and shell in grooves down the side with gurring. A wound from one of these could easily retain the chips and result in a fatal infection. Bone and fish spines were also glued and bound on with sinews made from the muscles of kangaroo tails. A spear called the 'mongile' was jagged on both sides and considered the most deadly. The other important spear was the tark. This was six or seven feet long and consisted of a sharpened length of dry hard wood plugged into the end of a long reed. A manoeuvrable and deadly weapon in war or hunting, it could be used at close quarters but could also kill at ninety yards. Its deadliness came from its being thrown with the 'marriwan', or spear-thrower, a leaf-shaped piece of wood about twenty inches long with a rounded handle for holding at one end and with a hook carved into the other. The tail of the spear sat in the hook and the shaft rested along the flat body of the thrower, held by thumb and forefinger at the handle until the moment of release. Then the thrower swept forward like an extra length of arm, giving the spear a substantial extra thrust.

It was now that he was made to understand his hosts' startling beliefs about death and his own appearance among them. They held that death was never accidental or natural except in the case of young children (who they thought were soon reincarnated) or the very old. Generally, death was seen as murder, either by direct physical violence or by 'mung' — evil magic. In this region it was held that upon death the deceased went to the ancestral land beyond the sky, where they became white men or amadiate. White was naturally the colour of death. After this period of transformation and sojourn in the sky the dead would return for a new life in this world through various sacred centres. Thus it was that in many cases where they had killed white men it was in the belief that they were former enemies or, in the case of friendship, that they were former comrades and relatives. Buckley now understood the reason for his warm and emotional welcome, and why he had been led away from the fight. A man who had already died once in battle and had returned should not be submitted to the same ordeal again.

They were completely patient with his ignorance in these matters and others relating to food, language, and customs. In fact, his ignorance seemed to greatly amuse them, as they assumed that it was all the result of his death and rebirth having made him white and foolish. He learnt later that in certain initiation ceremonies the boys, on becoming young men, were regarded as having died and been reborn in a state of ignorance, so that their vocabulary and all other knowledge they had acquired in childhood had to be re-learnt under instruction.

He did not succeed in spearing anything during this period, but he enjoyed the situation a great deal. Secure in the knowledge that he could return to the camp for food when he needed it, he could go each day with the spears and a wooden tomahawk they had given him and roam through the bush. On these excursions he greatly increased his knowledge of its ways and those of its inhabitants. He learnt to know the animals and birds: 'Ko-im' the kangaroo, 'Wimba' the wallaby, 'Ka-warren' the spiny anteater, 'Murrinmooroo' the platypus, 'Wollert' the silver-grey or brushtail possum, 'Bemin' the ringtail possum, 'Eurok' the goanna, 'Gnurnile' the white cockatoo and 'Gnurnan' the black cockatoo, 'Gean-gean' the currawong, and 'Kaan' the tiger snake, and many others.

He developed a feel for the mood of the place — the weather, the streams and the sheer presence of the trees. Especially he loved the evenings when golden sunlight streamed through the boughs bringing out all the purple hues, and the wind would drop leaving him standing there in unimaginable quietness and stillness. Time would stand still, not because the world was somehow dead, but so vital. The trees and shrubs almost seemed to glow with energy. The mystery of time here was as it was in the corroboree. The ephemeral and the eternal were but two sides of one coin. A man's life is to the forest a mere blink of an eye, the glint of a dewdrop on any old morning.

When a forest giant, like a great mountain ash which has lived for hundreds of years, falls to the ground it may take the lifetime of a man just to rot away. All that time it provides shelter and sustenance for a whole complex of living things. For example, there were insects which flew out with millions of their kind some afternoon to live for one glorious spring day when the first hints of summer hung in the air like warm breaths and which swarmed in the evening, to be gobbled up by little speeding birds like fantails and wrens which moved so fast and delicately they were hardly aware of humans blundering about them.

After some time Buckley's guardians decided to move on and they journeyed to the south, rejoining about fifty other Kumbada by a stream in another little valley where they had a corroboree, this time of a different and more playful nature.

Tro wernuwil now took a wife called Weeitcho taerinyaar, meaning 'Playful Leaves'. She came shyly with her brothers from a neighbouring group they called the Kurung. There was no ceremony. When the time came she went with him to his own mia-mia and her brothers left, perhaps never to be seen again. She looked about thirteen and had through her nose a little ring of bone from Kururuk the brolga.

The next day they journeyed to meet another band on a rise not far from the creek. Within minutes of meeting there was a quarrel, and a savage fight broke out in which two boys of the other band were killed. Buckley was aghast at the inexplicable brutality, but could only watch and trust that he would not be attacked. The Kumbada were the victors in this skirmish and they made camp, the others retreating into the bush. But during the night they were driven off by a surprise attack. The enemy moved in and cut the legs and thighs off the bodies of their two boys and fled.

This action further mystified and sickened Buckley,

especially when Tro wernuwil explained that they would eat them. Buckley confronted in this another aspect of a totally different attitude towards the body, a more extreme aspect and thus even more impossible for him to accept. He would see and learn much more of cannibalism, but remain opposed to it despite his adaptation to so much else.

He was to learn later that these tribes were not cannibals in the same manner as certain other South Sea peoples. In fact they were against it, except for two ritual purposes. One was, as with these two boys, a sign of respect for the dead. The eating of the flesh was an expression of sorrow and affection; they wished to make the deceased part of themselves as an act of love. Parts of or even the entire body could be eaten in this case, but only if it had belonged to one who was healthy and in the prime of life. Even so many would only take a ceremonial mouthful, like the taking of a sacrament, or perhaps just smear a little fat on themselves, considering this to be of sufficient power. The other reason was in the case of an enemy. Only certain parts of the arms or legs were then eaten, or sometimes the blood drunk, as a gesture of contempt.

In the early hours the Kumbada burnt the remains of the two bodies in the usual manner and left at the first light of dawn. They crossed the grassy downs and entered on to the great open plains of the country they called Iramoo that surrounded the lofty Yawangs. After a couple of days they reached the shores of the great bay Buckley had once led his friends to in search of their salvation from starvation. It was called Jillong, and they made camp at a place called Kooraioo, meaning sandy. It was often their practice to seek out sandy places to camp for obvious reasons of comfort, and here they settled down to a life of fishing and gathering roots.

9

After only a few days on the tranquil shores of Jillong a bihar or messenger was sent off to another tribe. He was dispatched with great seriousness bearing a number of marks chalked on his arm, time being measured by rubbing one of these marks off each day. On his return a few days later there was a brief conference, and then all the men made obvious preparations for a fight. They painted their bodies and prepared spears and other weapons and were soon on the march.

Wombalano Beeaar kept Weeitcho taerinyaar by her side. They chatted together, fast becoming friends. Buckley walked at the rear with them as usual, but kept a sharp eye out for fear of ambush. However, this was not in the air.

After three days they came to the battleground, a natural clearing in the bush in the hill country of the north–west.

Five different groups or tribes were gathered ready for action. Some of them were strangely marked and adorned and were of the Wurunjerri tribe or Woiwurong language from the Barrern river valley on the north side of the bay. Wombalano Beeaar explained to Buckley that all the people who lived around the bay and up in the high country to the north were called kulin, meaning that they were men, or people. They were a language grouping with similar customs and vocabularies, unlike others such as the Kurnai. They lived far in the east past a land called Marin-e-bek, meaning 'Splendid Country', ruled by a spirit called Lo-an. They were called berhera, or barbarians, and were regarded as less than human. Communication with them and others was mainly by sign language and the skilful mimicry of birds and animals.

The tribes of the kulin included the Bunerong, who lived in the country on the north and east shores eastwards to the borders of Marin-e-bek, and therefore owned the territory occupied by the Sullivan's Bay settlement. It had been a party of Bunerong whom Buckley had frightened with the gun on that first morning of freedom. The others were the Woiwurong; the Taungurongs from the north of them; the Jajowurongs of the north west country; the Kurung, a group speaking Woiwurong from between the Wothowurong and the Bunerong; and the Wothowurong themselves.

A tribe consisted of several groups or bands based on their own localities. A hand consisted of some twenty to sixty families, but was not a tightly organised unit. The families and bands were headed by senior or headmen and would come and go as they saw fit. Thus the bands constantly scattered and coalesced and mixed with other groups of their own and other tribes according to the business at hand. The most able men — fighters, song-makers, men of knowledge — by their natural personal influence came to be headmen and make decisions among themselves, with the women and other men free to lobby and argue. A very influential man could become the headman of a band but this was not necessary, and depended on the individuals concerned at the time.

This fight was thus one among the kulin and was one of a series of battles between the Woiwurong and the Wothowurong during these years. There was a continuing dispute over Wothowurong access to the karkeen or axe-stone quarry the Woiwurong controlled in the north of their country. There were nearly three hundred fighting men assembled and the fight commenced immediately.

Buckley could not make out who was allied with whom but, despite the frightening proportions of the battle and the large number of wounds inflicted by spears and clubs, only three people were killed and somehow they were all women. It was now that he understood the reason for most of these quarrels and battles. They were not fought over territory, as each tribe was only interested in its sacred lands and had no motivation to expand and conquer those of other tribes, although access to something like axe-stone could cause conflict. They were primarily struggles over women, with many revenge killings resulting from the continuing feuds. Marriage by capture was practised and celebrated in ritual dances. Feuds could begin by the breaking of promised betrothals and by eloping lovers. This state of open conflict between the sexes and between the men over women would plague Buckley during his whole time among the kulin. He could never adjust to the futile tragedy of it. It seemed the one flaw in an otherwise harmonious way of life.

He began to notice that the women were never allowed to have a weapon more dangerous than their kurniang, or digging stick. They showed no propensity to use spears or boomerangs, having been taught from an early age that these things were for boys only. There was a good reason for this. The women were not merely chattels of the men, but the precious source of life itself. It was they of course who bore and nursed the children, but they also kept up the supply of vegetable and other gathered foods when game was scarce. As it was the women who brought forth life it was the men who struggled with death. Thus it was always the unwritten law that men had to he prepared to fight to the death at a moment's notice, to save their families from attack. If a man wanted a wife he had to be a good hunter and fighter to provide for and protect her, or no father would want to give a daughter to him.

In the world of the kulin everything took place in

an environment of manifested spirits. Everything was connected in different ways and so the relation between cause and effect was different from anything Buckley had understood before. Events could be influenced by sympathetic arrangements of things called magic. By this logic the bringers of life could not touch the bringers of death. It was bad magic for a woman to even touch a spear as it would clearly destroy the power of the weapon.

Betrothed mostly from birth and, like Weeitcho taerinyaar usually married at puberty, these women still asserted much independence of behaviour, and conflicts were inevitable. Their marriages were often to old men, and so illicit affairs with younger men were common. Buckley knew that before long he would find no reason to resist taking advantage of this situation. However, for the present he was cautious, as he still had reason to fear for his life.

During this battle he had seen various warriors in the different tribes pointing to him, and he was worried lest he would be sacrificed as a peace-offering. The Kumbada separated from the others and came to him. Forming themselves into a guard they marched him back to the centre of the arena. All three hundred men stood in total silence, their eyes on Buckley. He feared yet again that this was his sacrificial ceremony. Murder had only just taken place. Suddenly they began talking rapidly, and strange verbal rhythms swept through the crowd. They jumped and stamped and shook their spears, excitement mounting. But again it ended with three loud shouts, and they dispersed to their camps in the bush laughing and chattering. He had been welcomed back from the dead once again.

In the morning the other tribes had gone. The Kumbada returned to the country between the Barwin and Kooraioo where they remained for some time. The weather became warm again. The wattle, or moiyan, was blooming and wild flowers of all kinds began to open in welcome to balmy days.

Buckley was vaguely aware that he had now survived a winter in the wilderness and that it must have been a year since he had deserted the settlement. Yet he did not articulate this in his mind, for he no longer thought of time as something to be counted up. His mind was filled more and more with his hosts' words and thoughts, and he infrequently thought of such things in the concepts of his native English. He had all but forgotten the existence of the settlement in the rapid changes of circumstances he had undergone since the day he had found Murrangurk's spear. He was not content to just stay where he was, but for the time being he found his situation preferable to any desperate attempt to march around the bay. There were women here, and at least he seemed to be safe from assault. He had begun to understand their language now, and his health was much improved from his varied, if sometimes meagre diet. He would stay for a while yet.

One day a bihar came from the Jajowurong. He bore his message on a stick or kalk that was passed around for inspection. They followed him, travelling five days, climbing into the hills of Ballark, the inland country. The purpose of the visit was to hunt Ko-im, and when they arrived a great many people were assembled from the tribes. In the evening a grand corroboree was held, lasting far into the night.

Buckley had now begun to think of himself as one of them, and so in the morning he joined a hunting party with Torraneuk. They set off in good humour, everyone enjoying himself. It was his first big hunt and he was eager to participate and try himself out.

The advantage of large co-operative hunting groups was made obvious. Some men would surround an area where a group of Ko-im had been spotted, and would calmly manoeuvre them into a corner of a gully. There the others would lie in wait with tark and marriwan poised. A little Ko-im blood was smeared on the shafts of the spears for luck. In the scrubby places dogs were used to chase Ko-im out. These strategies were worked out with respect to wind direction, and the men who moved in for the kill smeared their bodies with mud in order to suppress their smell. Every precaution was taken, as Ko-im was no fool. To hunt him down by stalking was a real art. He could hear the crack of an ankle bone at one hundred and fifty paces. Torraneuk said he had seen big greys, when chased into a stream by the dogs, calmly wait in the water. When the dogs swam out to them they were grabbed, pushed under and drowned. Flies preferred the smell of Ko-im to that of humans and would fly to them. Variable wind was a danger. They could snatch a fly out of the air, sniff it, and know if it had just buzzed off an unfortunate hunter stalking nearby. They also made their young keep watch; one had to be very careful as they would lie in the grass looking like logs.

Their party killed several large Ko-im that day. Buckley was pleased to land one spear, although not the fatal one, in one of these animals. He was given the usual apprentice's task of carrying it back to camp. Gasping under the load he staggered in to be greeted by great compliments and jesting about his progress. They roasted their catches together with roots in mirrnyong, large stone-lined pits in the ground. The meat was considered done when their hunger became uncontrollable. Like all the animals, Ko-im was shared out according to custom. Each person had a right to certain portions because the animal ate the grasses of the tribal lands that belonged to all. Even the dogs, provided they earned their keep, were given a share.

A great feast and corroboree was later held and for Buckley it became his first night of love for about three years. The kulin showed little concern for privacy in these matters, so his frustration had become intense.

After the dancing had subsided the young men began to throw their spears about and amuse themselves by scaring people. Buckley knew this would end in mischief, and all the women obviously felt the same as they retreated to their huts. He expressed this sentiment in faltering dialect and smiles to a young Kurung woman who seemed to be alone. Her name was Woymber Myrrnie, meaning 'Warm Wind'. They walked together into the bush. The night was warm and light from a clear sky. Finding a place in the leaves they sat and looked at each other. Buckley hardly knew how to approach her; it had been so long and she was so strange to his ways.

He reached out to her, placing one hand on her shoulder, the other on her thigh, still wrapped in Wollert skin. She laughed and pulled her rug away and sat looking at him as much as to say 'Well?' He took off his rug then and laid the two on the ground. After another pause and more smiles he tried to push her down and lie over her, but she protested he was too big and pushed him back into a sitting position. She sat astride him and he leant back on his hands, his eyes becoming moist with the immensity of his pleasure.

In the morning Buckley awoke alone. At the camp he found that he was not the only one who had got into mischief. The Pootmaroos, a band of the Bunerongs, had taken two women, who had not shown much resistance, from the Yawangis, a band of the Kurung. A fight broke out but was for once settled without bloodshed, although not forgotten. Buckley and Woymber Myrrnie were wary of openly acknowledging each other in case the violent jealousy was turned on them. They parted; he would hardly ever see her again, nor the daughter of his that she would bear.

The tribes dispersed to their own localities. Buckley and his kinfolk now joined the Bengali, another band of the Wothowurong, and went with them to their hunting ground around Beangala on the shores of Port Phillip.

Soon after this Weeitcho taerinyaar made Torraneuk and Wombalano Beeaar proud grandparents and Tro wernuwil a father when she gave birth to a girl. They called her Koronn, meaning Feather, because she was so light. Upon birth the tiny baby, or hooboop, was rubbed down with clean ash from the fire to dry her and wrapped around with paper-bark. Weeitcho nursed her and the new grandparents fussed about. Buckley, ignorant of his own impending fatherhood, looked on wistfully. Out of one world yet not in another, he began to feel something that would nag at him one way or the other for the rest of his life; a feeling that he was missing something.

During this period they continued to hunt Ko-im and Karwer the emu, which Buckley found very tasty. He was always given the best portions and developed great respect for the kindness of his family. This style of life had now made him more fit than he had ever been and his diet had returned him to full health. His sores had cleared up, along with the other aches and pains. Ko-im gave strength and vigour.

At length winter approached again and the supplies of game began to diminish. The band moved to a new locality closer to the Barwin. Their diet now centred on Boonea (eel). Buckley became quite proficient at spearing them although they were often pulled in with a line and bait like Tarluk-purrn the freshwater crayfish and yabbies. At times they would go to the sea in the hay near Kooraioo or to Connewarre. He was taught how to spear Tu-at, the fish at night by attracting them to a flaming torch. They were cooked by baking them in a small pit. A thick layer of green grass was put on the coals, then Tu-at laid on this and covered with more grass and another layer of coals. They were juicy and delicious when cooked. Life began to roll by in an agreeable way.

10

After a long time their harmonious existence came to a terrible end. They were camped on the north side of Connewarre when they suddenly saw a large tribe of about three hundred people advancing across the plain near the reedy marshes. They were all men armed for battle, and identified as Waarengbadawa from the Taungurong tribe. Being so far from home and in such strength they were obviously looking for a fight over some old grievances. Only a handful of the Kumbada and Bengali were there — their numbers barely a quarter of the enemy.

The men ran to the lake and quickly smeared their bodies with clay while the women and children rushed into the bush, Buckley with them as usual.

The Waarengbadawa were painted hideously with red and white clay to give a frightening appearance. The fight began with a shower of spears from both parties. Then one of the Bengali advanced as a champion and proceeded to dance and sing, challenging the others and boasting his prowess. He and all the other warriors then sat down in silence.

Shortly, he rose and performed his song and dance again. Seven of the enemy then rose one by one and threw their spears at him. With great skill he dodged them or warded them off with his 'guram' (spear shield), and broke them all without a single wound. Next they threw their 'barngeet' (war boomerangs) at him. Made of hardwood with sharp edges, some of them were bounced off the ground with unpredictable rebound. Yet he dodged them with ease. Then a champion came from the ranks of the enemy, stood about three paces away and hurled a barngeet straight at him. The Bengali dodged it by dropping to his hands and knees and immediately springing up again, shaking himself like a dog. The enemy shouted 'Enough!' and the two embraced each other before proceeding to beat themselves over the head with clubs until blood ran down over their shoulders.

At this point Buckley could no longer understand the ritual. But this was a mere preliminary, as a general fight now started. After a fury of bashing, hurling, and yelling a Bengali fell with a spear right through him. His comrades raised a battle cry. This was a state of emergency. Their very existence was at stake now. The women threw off their rugs, seized clubs and flew into the fray beside their men.

Wombalano Beeaar remained with Buckley, Weeitcho taerinyaar, and Koronn, insisting that he stay out of the fight. He felt gripped in a terrible moral dilemma. He thought he should help his friends but could not see any sense in begin killed in such an affray, which was nothing to do with him. He could see Torraneuk and Tro wernuwil fighting furiously just to stay alive. His experiences in Holland were certainly useless to him now.

After a long time the exhausted fighters separated with a number of injured on both sides. Two Wothowurong women had been killed. The Waarengbadawa withdrew, sensing their foe would fight to the death of the last of them. Messengers were exchanged and long disputations entered into over many grievances.

At night the invaders retreated in the direction of their own territory. The kulin were never happy at leaving their own country and venturing into that of others where unknown dreadful spirits and dangers were sure to await them. This night, however, they would suffer a very basic form of terror. The big, fierce fellow Buckley had noticed when he first joined the Kumbada went around the camp urging a counter-attack. His name was Wuruum kuurwhin, meaning 'Grass Burning', and he was probably the best fighter the Kumbada had. With the reluctant support of Torraneuk and others they got together a raiding party and slipped away into the blackness.

The Waarengbadawa were ambushed as they lay asleep. Three men were killed on the spot and others wounded. They fled dropping their weapons, leaving the wounded to be beaten to death.

In the morning the bodies were mutilated and dragged back to the Wothowurong camp where the women beat them with their kurniang. To Buckley they all seemed in a frenzy of bloodlust, but then they had just won a desperate fight for their very existence. Limbs were hacked off; flesh was cut away and baked on stones and then used to grease down the bodies of the children to impart the strength of the enemy to them. The bones were smashed and given to the dogs or placed in trees for Waang the crow who flocked around the terrible scene.

The two Wothowurong women who had been killed were buried with more ceremony than simple cremation, which was usually only done when danger or urgency pressed on them. Mostly a proper burial was made. In this instance they dug two round graves about waist-deep with their sticks, coiled the bodies in them, lying them on their sides and tied up in their rugs. Boughs were placed over and the holes filled in. Their kurniang were put in place and fires lit in case they were needed to dig and cook roots when they came to life again. Sometimes a few days' supply of roots would be buried as well, and the fires relit each time the tribe passed by. The bodies were bound in order to ensure that the spirits stayed with them. Sometimes leg bones were broken or removed for this reason.

After remaining another night by the graves the bands separated. The Kumbada travelled several days inland to the shore of a large shallow lake called Murdeduke in the middle of an open plain dotted with extinct volcanoes. It was very bare here with little cover from the weather. But to look out over the plain for invaders there was, on the west side, an excellent vantage point provided by a solitary cone-shaped hill called Mookatook. They built solid mia-mias from stone and reeds; there was no wood, as it had to be carried a long distance even for the fires.

They remained here a long time, spearing the plentiful Boonea, and the women and children and dogs had many funny times catching Beruke the kangaroo-rat who abounded here and was considered a delicacy.

Buckley had completely resigned himself to this life, and was living in a state of perpetual astonishment. To his own amazement he was fairly contented. He felt at home in the daily life of his tribe. His old clothes were gone now and he lived as they lived; naked much of the time, wearing a skin rug when it was cold; sleeping on the ground in all weather and only occasionally suffering the slightest poor health. It was to him quite miraculous. He had not only gained his freedom and survived; he had done it so well. He could laugh really, especially when he thought of the slavery of his shipmates or, worse, those still in England. One day Torraneuk told him he had heard that the settlement had long gone from the other side of the bay and one or more other amadiate had been speared in the Barraring country by the Bunerong for being too free with the women. This news saddened Buckley at first. To know that he was now completely alone in the wilderness without any chance to go back made him realise he would have to learn to accept things. Fortunately the pleasant time he was having now made it much easier than it might have been. He wasn't really alone.

By now he was quite proficient in the language of his friends, and was becoming a respectable performer with the hunting weapons. He usually had the best fire and most comfortable hut, especially in the cold weather, and so had become popular with the young children who loved to sleep with him. They spent many hours at play together. He learnt as they learnt. He would tell them stories. Koronn and her friends would lie by the waters or around his campfire and listen to his tales about England. He told them about the big ships and the great cities where many, many kulin lived and died and laboured to make many, many things; where men, women and children were kept prisoner; where some could do what they liked and most were not free to hunt or gather food because the land was taken from them. They loved these stories, but it wasn't their idea of the land beyond the sky.

Buckley's feelings of contentment were especially reinforced when he was occasionally able to enjoy a brief sexual liaison. But even during long periods of celibacy he found plenty to do, hunting and exploring and learning what he could of the tribal lore. The disadvantage of his peculiar status with regard to secret rites and knowledge left certain gaps in his understanding. Nevertheless, he absorbed enough to begin developing his own understanding of the world he lived in. Much of it came from Torraneuk during the many hours they spent together making, decorating and mending their weapons. At such times Torraneuk gradually explained the basic arrangement of the universe as he knew it.

First, there was the higher power, Bunjil, the wedge-tailed eagle. Although not all-powerful, he was the Creator who had made the world in the Dreamtime. He had fought and beaten into submission a giant snake called Mindie who had ruled a world of terror and chaos. Now Mindie lived at a place called Bukrabanyule in the north–west and was greatly feared by all the tribes as he could and did sometimes come forth to punish them by disease or other disasters, but only on Bunjil's wrathful orders. Having subdued Mindie, Bunjil made the land and the trees and grasses. He made the animals and taught them how to behave. He made men and taught them their customs, and how to hunt, fight, and make weapons. After finishing his work he got Bellin-bellin the black-faced cuckoo-shrike to open some bags of wind and blow him and his family up to the land in the sky, where he retired, seldom interfering in the ordinary affairs of kulin. He became the star Buckley knew as Altair,* the two stars on either side being his two wives, Kunnawarra the swans. His son is Brinbeal, the rainbow whose wife sometimes appears as the second bow.

Bunjil also has six young men as his messengers or aides. They are Djurt-djurt, the nankeen kestrel, and Thara, the black-shouldered kite, two brave and cunning hunters whose stars were Centaurus, the two pointers to the Southern Cross where reside Yukope, the king parrot, and Dantun, the crimson rosella, the colourful and jolly messengers. Finally there is Tuan-tuan the ferocious little tree-rat whose star is Achernar, and Turnung the acrobatic and playful little flying mouse.† These six are all powerful wizards in their own right. It was Tuan-tuan and Turnung, the creatures of the night, who had come with their friends Wollert and Bemin, Poorool the sugar-glider, and Yundool the fluffy glider, and struck fear into his soul that night in the tree. Yundool especially loved to make blood-curdling

* The word altair derives from Arabic and means 'flying eagle'. It is the brightest star in the western constellation, Aquila the Eagle, which has been the location of several supernovae.
† Probably the star Canopus.

calls as he dived through the air. This was part of their defence against Kokurn the powerful owl and other owls that could swoop on them out of the darkness. Turnung often carried her babies on her back as she soared through the trees in the fearful blackness.

One day Torraneuk was teaching Buckley how to make fire (weing). There were various ways of doing it, but it was mainly a matter of rubbing a dry softwood against a dry hardwood. A weenth-kalk-kalk (fire-stick) could be bowed rapidly back and forth in a notch of an old fallen tree trunk. But the usual method was to find a stick of softwood about thirty inches long — the stem of a grass tree was ideal — and twirl it rapidly around in a hole bored in a flat piece of hardwood that could be held in place with a foot or knee. The edge of a malka, the solid club-fighting shield, was suitable. The stick was twirled by rubbing it backwards and forwards between the palms of the hands. Downward pressure was applied so the hands tended to slide down the stick, whence they were quickly shifted back to the top and the twirling continued. The hole was drilled right on the edge of the flat hardwood, with a groove running out of it. The hardwood was tilted at an angle so that as the hot black dust of the softwood began to build up in the hole it would fall out through the groove and on to some dry tinder already in place. Some frayed bark fibre would do, or dry grass; sometimes dry banksia cones were carried in damp weather. Provided the wood, especially the stick, was properly dry the procedure only took a minute or so.

Weing, Torraneuk explained, was one of the kulin's greatest assets. It had come to them through the activity of Waang the crow. Waang was the lower power; not the underworld, but the opposite to Bunjil. He was crafty and wise, and highly respected by all. His eye was sharp — he could tell a spear from a stick — and was almost impossible to catch even should they want to get him. He was only ever eaten in the most desperate circumstances of hunger. Bunjil and Waang were locked in eternal conflict. Sometimes Bunjil would attack and eat Waang. At other times Waang would steal the food that Bunjil had hunted. In the Dreamtime they had fought over the possession of fire. It happened like this.

Once there were seven women called the Kururuk. They possessed fire in their kurniang, with which they dug roots. They only gave Waang raw roots to eat. One day they dropped some cooked ones and he snatched and ate them. Thus he found out how good they were and what he had been missing. Determined to have fire for himself he placed some snakes in an ant hill and told the Kururuk there were some nice roots there. When they dug in the ant hill the snakes came out. They beat and killed them with their kurniang, but this caused hot coals to fall out the ends. Waang stole the coals and flew up into a tree and out of reach. Bunjil came down and demanded Waang return the coals but he refused. So Bunjil gathered all the kulin and they mobbed Waang. Frightened, he threw the coals down. Kurok-goru, the red-browed firetail, seized some, which it still carries to this day. Djurt-djurt and Thara got the rest and started a fire that swept across the country and burnt Waang black as he is today. Djurt-djurt and Thara then turned into stones in the mountains.* The Kururuk went up to the sky and became the seven sisters constellation.† All the people of all the country were divided into two halves or moieties. Most of them were Bunjil or Waang, but some in the west were Krokitch, the white cockatoo, and Kaputch, the black cockatoo. Among the kulin the moieties were the tribes and were thus associated with localities. The Wurunjeri and Kurung were Waang. The Bunerong and the Wothowurong were Bunjil. Marriage was always between

* On Bald Hill, Clematis, Victoria
† Pleiades

Bunjil and Waang and thus outside the tribe. This helped unite the kulin. The moiety also helped determine the roles each played in various rituals like corroborees.

On initiation each person was assigned a totem, who was special to him. This was usually an animal, but sometimes it could be a natural phenomenon, such as the sun, moon, lightning, clouds, or wind. This totem became a close friend to him; it was revered as a brother or sister and great attention was paid to it and its wellbeing. If a person was close to his totem it could, for example, warn him of danger, or tell him news of his family if he was a long way off on a hunt or journey. Sometimes, Torraneuk said, if the time was right you could ask for a sign and one of the totems would appear and indicate the situation. But this was very difficult to practise.

Torraneuk's totem was Karbor the koala. He was a wise and influential old one; the only animal that spanked its young like people. Buckley knew Karbor well; his screeches and grunts had often kept him awake at night in various places they had camped. He was almost as bad as Yundool. Torraneuk told him the story of Karbor.

He was once an orphan boy, neglected by his relatives. They wouldn't give him enough water. One day they were out getting food and left their tarnuks behind. He put all the water in the tarnuks and hung them in a tree. He climbed the tree and sang a magic song that made it grow very high. When the people returned hot and thirsty they found all the water was gone. They saw Karbor high in the tree with the tarnuks and angrily demanded he return them. He said it was their turn to go thirsty, and refused. They tried to get up the tree, but without much luck. At length two medicine men, Tuan-tuan and Turnung, reached him and threw him to the ground and retrieved the water. The shattered body of Karbor changed into the koala and climbed into the top of a tree. There he lives today and never needs water. But he made a law that, although the kulin may kill and eat him, they must not break his bones or skin him until he is cooked. If anyone disobeys then he will take the water again and cause such a severe drought they would all die of thirst.

When he had told this story, Torraneuk drew Buckley aside and said that soon he would tell him the name of his totem; when the time was ripe. It had not occurred to Buckley that he could have a totem, and he became very interested in the idea. It gave him much to think about.

II

One afternoon he was alone, wading the waters of Murdeduke on the opposite shore from their camp. It was early summer and a warm wind blew across the lake. He was naked and felt the air ripple across the water between his legs and flow over his skin. His hair was growing long, and like the reeds, it streamed in the sun. His body felt so vibrant that he began to stroke himself and think of Woymber Myrrnic. He was still wondering if he would be able to remain standing when he came into the water with his eyes closed. Shuddering slightly, he half submerged himself and looked around the lake.

Kunnawarra watched him from the reeds, gliding away a little as he saw her. She was said to be the wife of Bunjil the Creator, who made all the mountains, lakes and rivers. She was found with her sister Kururuk the brolga in the mud of a river by Balayang the bat when he was playing there, slapping the water with his wings. Buckley's immediate reflex was to freeze and begin to slowly bring a spear into position. But in his peaceable frame of mind he let it go, sitting back in the water, just watching. Waang called far in the distance; so mournful and so far away. Kunnawarra drifted further away into the reeds. As a current of air swept through the reeds he realised that Kururuk stood among them watching the sky.

Lark the cloud drifted overhead, silver and grey in the blue depths. He had once roamed the earth. A lonely man, he searched everywhere for a girl to marry, but because he was always searching he was always a stranger wherever he went and no-one would give a daughter to a stranger. After a long time he stopped one day for a drink. Seeing his face in the pool of water he realised he had become old and grey. It was now too late for him. In his despair he grew angry and vengeful and poured all the water in the country into a big tarnuk and fled to the sky. Woonduble the Thunder Man boomed his alarm through the land and the men of many tribes rushed with their spears; but none could get to the soaring Lark, except for one. He was Moorinno the Lightning-Man, and best spear-fighter in the country. His spear shot up like a flash of light. It couldn't hurt Lark, who was now a cloud, but it did pierce his tarnuk and cause a big rain. Nowadays Woonduble lives in the sky too and calls to Moorinno, who has joined him, to spear the tarnuk whenever it is full.

Buckley looked back at the reeds. The birds were gone. 'Am I like Lark?' he wondered. The thought darkened his face as the cloud itself crossed the sun. He returned slowly to the camp feeling unsettled again in a way he had not felt for a long time. He wanted a woman, a companion; but what hope was there for a stranger from the land of the dead?

He sought out Wombalano Beeaar and asked her if she had a totem. She said yes, her totem was Murrin-mooroo the platypus. Murrin-mooroo was a very special totem because it was related to all the other animals. When the first men became animals the country was so thickly populated with birds, reptiles and animals that they were all fighting each other for food. Life was dangerous and fraught with conflict. In the end they remembered the corroborees they had held when they were men and once again came together for a great debate about their troubles.

Kaan the snake spoke first, complaining about being eaten by the bird people like Kooring-kooring the kookaburra. But they retorted angrily about Kaan and

Eurok raiding their nests for eggs and fledglings. The animals attacked the birds and reptiles about their constant preying on them, especially their helpless young who lived in terror. After much argument Kaan told the others they would have to leave, as the land belonged to the reptiles. A chorus of derisive laughter came back from the birds and animals, led of course by Kooring-kooring.

The argument raged on and on until Narrut the frog grew impatient and decided to give them all a fright. Narrut called up a big rainstorm and soon it was teeming. It rained a steady downpour for days. The ground started to become waterlogged; runnels grew into streams, streams into rivers that filled lakes to overflowing. The birds fled and the animals and reptiles hid miserably in caves and under soggy trees, or climbed the mountains to escape the floodwaters. After three days of this misery the clouds finally rolled away. The sun came out and the land steamed under its warmth. Wet and bedraggled creatures crawled out to dry themselves. They searched for their friends among the fallen trees and swampy grounds. Everywhere they found the bodies of the drowned, the greatest number being Murrin-mooroo. They had been too slow to escape. Once numerous, they were now seemingly wiped out.

Years passed and the tribes recovered from their ordeal. But no Murrin-mooroo ever appeared until one day Tutbring the flame robin, who had gone far up a stream into the mountains, saw the tracks of Murrin-mooroo in the mud along a ferny bank under a grove of golden wattle. Someone asked what totem Murrin-mooroo was, that their relatives might seek them out. The birds pointed out that because Murrin-mooroo had a bill and laid eggs they must belong to the birds. But the reptiles explained that they too laid eggs. The animals pointed out that Murrin-mooroo had fur and a tail like them and so must belong to them. The fish claimed Murrin-mooroo as theirs because they all lived in the rivers together.

At length it was agreed to send Tutbring to bring Murrinmooroo to speak to them. Tutbring went and returned in a few days with an old and venerable Murrin-mooroo. The tribes gathered excitedly, the young astounded to see this strange creature. A hush fell and a space was cleared amid the throng. Murrin-mooroo stepped forward with dignity and spoke in a voice that at first was low and unsteady, but soon grew stronger.

'My friends, you have asked me to tell you what people we belong to. Ever since the great flood we have been isolated. We felt unwanted but will be glad to return if you are all our friends. We come from an ancient race of great wisdom. We claim kinship to you all. Our first ancestors were reptiles. Later we were birds and then animals who chose to live with the fish.'

Murrin-mooroo then called forward Tchingal. The crowd buzzed in bewilderment as Karwer the emu stepped forward. Karwer said to Murrin-mooroo, 'You have called me by my ancient name, given to my ancestors and known to no-one but myself for a long time. Such is your great wisdom. My totem is Kaan. What is yours?'

Murrin-mooroo replied, 'I am Boe-ung the bandicoot.'

'That is my uncle,' said Karwer.

'So here you see we are all kin,' said Murrin-mooroo.

They all begged Murrin-mooroo to stay. But the one who belonged to all would stay with none, and Murrin-mooroo returned to live alone on the land and in the water.

Buckley was moved by this story. But he was unable to find solace for his own sharp loneliness. He asked Wornbalano Beeaar how Torraneuk would know what totem to give him. She chuckled and reassured him he would know and not to worry. The time would come; he would have what he wanted.

*   *   *

Wombalano Beeaar was reluctant to tell Buckley too much yet, for there were things about her husband that should not be gossiped about. Torraneuk was a wirrarap or medicine-man.

As a young man he had passed through the usual initiation. Among the Wothowurong this was not drastic physically, involving mainly a period of withdrawal, a ceremonial plucking of hair from the face and body, and eventually a ritual reintroduction to tribal life. This procedure was carried out under the guardianship of Tutbring, whose brothers watched over each novice to see he completed the ordeal with success. On his return to the tribe he was taught their ways anew, so as to give him a rebirth. They did not knock out a front tooth as was common among many more distant tribes of the hinterland and even the Wurunjerri. Nevertheless, it was enough of an ordeal to make a great impression on the new man. And a new man he was, because this initiation created for him an identity as a certain member of the tribe. This creation was to the young man indistinguishable from a revelation. His true place in the world and relation to it with respect to the totems and the Dreamtime that existed in all eternity were revealed. His totem was given, and Torraneuk's was Karbor.

Some years later when in his twenties, Torraneuk felt what is usually named 'the call'. By his interest in magic he had already attracted the attention of certain of the elders. Sometimes men became wirrarap by heredity, but this was not so in his case. He was one who seemed to have a destiny that marked him out, before he was even aware of anything himself. After suitable preparations and arrangements had been made for the care of his young wife Wombalano Beeaar and their little boy Tro wernuwil, he was taken away for initiation. This initiation was longer and much more rigorous than that to manhood. There was no comparison. This one really was a death and rebirth that would shatter anyone not ready for it.

A small group of the old men took him to a remote gully in the mountains. Here they left him to sleep on a certain grave. Later he walked through the forest. Djurt-djurt hovered above. He looked and the bird was gone. Yukope and Dantun flashed past screeching into a tree. Excited, he looked up into the tree but they were gone. Then he saw Kaan sunning himself on a rock in front of a small cliff face that rose above the gully. Kaan slithered away. He followed. There was a cave and Kaan led him inside. He saw a magic passage that opened and shut in an instant. He knew he had to go through even though a touch from it meant death. Kaan waited. Torraneuk plunged through like a flash. He was in another glittering cavern covered in rock crystals. He walked in astonishment, bathing in the light that seemed to pierce his body.

Suddenly they appeared from nowhere; moorup, shades, the souls of the dead. They took him up into the sky. They flew up and up. At last they landed in Bunjil's country; the land in the sky they called Tharangalk-bek, the gum-tree country named for the manna-gum which always thrived along the banks of beautiful streams where life was easy and happy. Under Bunjil's instructions the moorup seized Torraneuk and struck him down as if dead. Then they performed an operation on him. They cut open the side of his belly and inserted some of the rock crystals and then healed him up without a mark. Then they flew him back to earth and placed him on the grave.

He awoke three days after the elders had left him. He returned to the camp somehow, in a mentally deranged condition. He staggered about and muttered unintelligible words. The elders smoked him by burning the branches of Poo-lyte, the native cherry tree, annointed him with red ochre and greased him with Karwer fat in public, and then taught him his name again. 'Torraneuk; Torraneuk,' they intoned into his tortured face.

Everyone knew what was happening and behaved normally. They knew that soon he would return to 'normal', but now he was a wirrarap with certain powers that he could practise after about a year. These powers included the use of crystals to perform magic. These were quartz crystals called thundal, the most potent coming from high in the remote mountains of the far north–east. There the Yaitmathang tribe traded them to others, who brought them down the great river in the north called Millewa, until the Jajowurong got some and traded them to the rest of the kulin.

Along with thundal, Torraneuk's symbol and instrument was mooyum karr, the bull-roarer. A flat piece of wood with a small hole at each end, it was swung around the head on a long string threaded through one of the holes. It made strange sounds emulating the voices of the spirits. Other powers were the ability to steal marmbula, a man's kidney fat and the seat of his soul, without leaving a trace, and thus cause death to an unsuspecting enemy. He would be able to fly, to disappear for days into the heavens and converse with the spirits and souls of the dead and bring back news of them or even, when acting as a doctor, catch the soul of one just dying and return it to the body and restore life. He would have extraordinary powers of mimicry that enabled him to talk to the animals, and Kaan would be his new totem or 'familiar', like a pet with magical powers. He would never eat Kaan. He would resume a normal life, as a family man and hunter, with no special privileges, but he could be called on for special duties when the tribe or band faced a crisis.

12

Soon a bihar came from a tribe called the Koligon. They were part of the Mara language group, occupying the country from the lakes where the sun set, through to a more distant westward area bordering with another big tribe called the Wotjobaluk, which Buckley never saw. The Koligon tribe had the section incorporating the lakes and the mountains to the south. They were neighbours to the Wothowurong. The message invited the Kumbada to come and visit them for the swan-egg season.

Kunnawarra was a benevolent provider in the autumn and winter. They were pleased to move on after the long period at Murdeduke, although there was some anxiety at travelling into the territory of another tribe. All weapons were put in order before departure and they set off. The journey took seven days, and covered some thirty miles across flat and open country. They passed several smaller lakes and reached the rocky hills that overlooked a beautiful expanse of water about twenty miles long and several miles wide. The shore was irregular, forming a number of inlets and promontories; the country on the other side being a lightly timbered plain expanding towards distant hills that poked up from the haze in isolated cones. This was a salt lake called Corangamite, and Kunnawarra abounded. She nested on several areas around the lake, including a small island near the southern end.

They marched around to the nearest approach to the

island, which could be reached by wading on a submerged isthmus at a place called Pomborneit. The country all around was dotted with ancient volcanoes. The terrain they had entered consisted of a large area of hillocks covered in basalt boulders. These stony rises were covered in trees and scrub. An endless maze of mysterious little gullies and dips drew the wanderer into another world. The Koligon spoke of net-nets, fearful and hairy little people who could rush out of a hollow and steal a slain wallaby from in front of the hunters' very eyes.

Buckley was rapt in these new developments. Perhaps he would have a woman out of this meeting, as had happened to him before when they had congregated with other tribes.

They camped and made huts a short distance from the host tribe. Other kulin bands joined them. There followed several days of feasting and corroborees. The Kunnawarra eggs were a delicious treat, and they speared many birds as well, roasting them in pits. Buckley had his desire at least appeased, but only by the frustrating tactics of furtive meetings with a young woman whose old husband spent all his time talking.

One morning the Koligon left their camps in a hurry, which seemed suspicious at the time, but nothing eventuated. The Kumbada moved further up the lake where it was very narrow and many more Kunnawarra were to be had. A few days later their hosts rejoined them for a corroboree. It was one of the most exciting Buckley had seen. The women all separated from the men and painted their naked bodies with white ochre. The men were painted red and wore emu-feather skirts. They squatted on the ground cheering and beating out a rhythm with skin rugs and sticks while the women danced.

Eventually a fight broke out and clubs were wielded against heads without mercy. It was over a young girl who had willingly run off with one of the Koligon. The young man who had stolen her stepped forward and bravely offered to have the revenge taken out on himself. He began to sing and dance in preparation for the fight. The girl's father stood before him and the other men began to call out to him to let the young man have his daughter as her betrothed was unworthy of her. The confrontation ended in a compromise, the girl returning to her father.

After this dispute it was considered wise to leave, so the Kumbada and others departed, undertaking a long march through some densely wooded hill country. They hunted as they travelled, the men moving ahead in a reversed arrow formation. Those on the flanks moved in two prongs, up to a mile apart at the two ends, attempting to drive game back into the ambush set by the men at the rear. The younger men and bachelors travelled ahead covering the wider ground, while the older, married men — often the best marksmen with their spears — travelled towards the rear near their families. They looked out for Wollert while the women and children gathered gurring from the wattle in the gullies, knocked down birds, chased bandicoots, and dug for roots and grubs.

The most common big game they found on this march was Wimba who, although smaller than Ko-im, tasted much the same. He was usually chased out of scrubby gullies by the dogs and into the line of hunters. Wimba was Weeitcho taerinyaar's totem. Wimba and Ko-im had once been close friends, but they had fought over food. In the ensuing quarrel Wimba had heaped up the earth into hills and mountains, making the gullies favoured as home. Trying to sweep back Wimba's hills with that strong tail Ko-im, who preferred the open country, had created the plains. Thus the two had lived apart ever since.

Several days later the Kumbada halted in the vicinity of

another beautiful lake in a region called Gerangamete. The camp was set by a fresh waterhole, the lake being brackish.

Buckley loved this place. The bush felt good after a long time in open country, but they could still enjoy the waters of an excellent lake. They were in an extensive and open valley in the upper reaches of the Barwin, the country stretching out and gently undulating towards more distant mountains.

They made nets with strips of bark and caught freshwater shrimps — a real delicacy — in great quantity. Tortoises were plentiful and fun to catch, everyone diving around in the water. This was to set the style for their stay. They lived here sumptuously and in peace for a long time.

It was a good time for Buckley. Looking back in future days it would sometimes appear as paradise: the forest and lake, the good food and relaxed company. He began to think that if he was ever to feel really free, and therefore happy, this was a time when it had to be realised. Of course he still longed for a companion to join him in wandering the bush, and did not despair of finding one. He was free in a real sense; not in jail, not under the lash, not hungry, not old, not sick, not working for slave wages, and not totally frustrated by sex. Many days passed in contentment. Leisurely hours by the waters of the lake were combined with new learning in the arts of gathering the abundant food in the vast undisturbed gardens of nature.

The birdlife always amazed him with its beauty and variety. Yukope and Dantun, those happy wizards of Bunjil, would appear in chattering hordes and flashing the colours of the rainbow, with their friends the Gang-gang cockatoos, Yaar-rar the galah, and many others, all bringing joy to his heart with their cheerful antics. Wombalano Beeaar, many years after giving birth to Tro wernuwil, became pregnant and bore another son whom they called Burmbo Merio, meaning 'New Moon Now', as it was so at his birth. She thought Kunnawarra had played some happy mischief. Her granddaughter, Koronn, was now running with the older children, and was soon helping to show the new booboop how to find grubs and other food.

Each day the people sang and danced, beating out their ancient rhythms on skins and sticks. The girls especially loved to dance. The young men spent a lot of time in friendly wrestling matches and a certain ball game. Using a dirlk — the scrotum of an old man Ko-im stuffed with grass — two teams vied to keep possession of this ball by dodging and throwing, and drop-kicking with the instep and marking. The teams were usually made up of the members of various totems, such as Thara and Ko-im. Another popular pastime was playing with the wonguim, or returning boomerang, a source of great fun.

Yet in spite of all this Buckley could never quite lay to rest his dog of desire. His perpetual amazement at his life bred a burning eagerness. Contentment seemed to become a threat at the very moment it was approached. Even as he cursed his unstilled mind he could reject contentment as suitable only for the dead. But what could he yearn for here? His wanting focused on having a wife. It was the obvious lack. But at times he also looked for the love and respect of his kin. He liked to impress as a pupil in the hunt or with his efficiency as a man about the camp. To achieve skill and useful results was a manifestation of vitality. Like the waves of the ocean and the waters of the river he was alive because he had no rest. It was his very freedom from basic want that now made Buckley yearn to do something extraordinary. His curiosity about the sacred ceremonies grew. He wanted to explore the mysteries of the eternal realms that were denied him as a living corpse. But this would remain unattainable. He would live on and bide his time, awaiting his opportunity.

Perhaps Torraneuk had sensed these feelings in Murrangurk. He felt now that it was time to assign him his totem. Careful thought and observation was given to such an important thing. Not long before they were to leave Gerangamete they went together on a day's excursion around the lake and along the river bank. They hunted and fished, but didn't try too hard. In the afternoon they camped to eat some fish they had speared. Torraneuk explained that Murrangurk's totem was Barroworn, the magpie.

Buckley knew certain things about Barroworn. He was a remarkable bird; intelligent and able to learn — he had seen children keep him as a pet and teach him a few words — he was also courageous and rather pugnacious, especially in the nesting season. He would attack any intruders into his territory; native cats, dogs, and people could be subjected to diving strikes with bill and wings. Barroworn was also a rather self-contained bird. When not nesting he gathered with one or two friends — a small covey at most. Often he was content to just sit in a tree choralling away for the pure enjoyment of it. This was his greatest power. Barroworn was an outstanding songster, probably the best, and rivalled only by Geiwoorn, the grey shrike-thrush.

Intrigued, Buckley asked many questions. Torraneuk would only say that Murrangurk was the man who could get the best of both worlds and thereby be the survivor, the one who would always live. Then he told him a dreaming.

In the Dreamtime, the sky had been lying over the earth and everyone had to crawl about in the dark. The magpies, being intelligent, thought they could do something about it. They decided that if they all worked together they could raise the sky and make room for everyone to move about. This they did with long sticks. They struggled hard, gradually working it up on low and then higher boulders. As they struggled to lift the sky even higher it suddenly split open revealing the beauty of the first sunrise. They were overjoyed to see the light and feel the warmth of the sun's rays. In their ecstasy they burst forth into song. It was a beautiful melodious piping, and they sang as they saw the blanket of darkness break up and drift away like clouds. To this very day the magpies still greet the sunrise with their beautiful song.

They returned to the camp at dusk. As he lay down to sleep Buckley remembered his dream.

The band now moved to another lake, as food was becoming scarcer. This lake was called Moodewarri, meaning musk duck. It was full of Boonea, the water being perfectly fresh, and lay in a basin below a volcanic cone called Moriac, in undulating country at the head of a valley opening out to the sea in the south–east. They made camp on the north bank, looking across the lake and down the valley, and lived peaceably here for some time. Wombalano Beeaar became pregnant again. Soon Burmbo Merio had a little sister. They named her Mirri Mallo, meaning 'Sunshine Soon', as she was born just before dawn on a clear day.

Buckley did not dwell on his tendency for discontent, his yearning for the extraordinary. The days rolled by easily enough and he began to think in terms of recreating, each day, the best patterns of their life. Koronn, Burmbo Merio, and now Mirri Mallo offered plenty of diversions. There was always the gathering of food; the bringing of firewood and water; cooking and eating; feeding the children; tending to weapons; and singing, dancing and beating rhythms to accompany the movements of many hours.

Every few days he would have the urge to go hunting alone; at least that was the understanding he had with Torraneuk and the others. Mostly he had to be with his own thoughts and continue to extend his personal understanding of the bush. He would find interesting things — plants, fungi, insects and old bones — often bringing them back to show to Torraneuk and Wombalano Beeaar, and to learn of them.

One day he was on the far shore of the lake. It was late in the afternoon and the others lay at the camp. The day was dull and overcast. A sluggish blanket of grey cloud hung over the country and the water stood in perfect stillness. A few swans and ducks seemed to huddle down at the far end of the lake, and even the flocks of twittering little bush-larks and pipits that usually teemed in the grasses by the shore were strangely quiet. He walked along the edge of the water, half in the shallows, half on the shore. His mind drifted; his eyes wandered lazily across the landscape.

Without warning he suddenly saw a movement in the water about twenty paces from the shore. It was as though something had turned over in the water leaving a few quiet ripples fading smoothly away. At first he thought it was probably a cormorant diving for the bottom, or a musk duck he had scared. They swim low in the water with their backs awash. To escape danger they dive, with their young sometimes clinging on, rather than taking to the wing.

But, after waiting for a time, no little head bobbed up anywhere on that glassy plain. It may have been Boonea performing an unusual manoeuvre, but it didn't seem right. The movement, although subtle, was too big for any fish or even Murrin-mooroo. This left one other possibility he had been told of but of which he had no direct experience, and that was a bunyip. It was one of several strange creatures said to lurk in the hush and various rivers and waterholes. These were monsters who lived and did their terrible work quite independently of Bunjil. The descriptions Torraneuk and others of the kulin had given him of this fabled creature varied so wildly he had little idea of what to expect when he saw one. They lurked in waterholes; at least this much was known. Whether his friends had ever really seen one he had his doubts. He did not know whether it was covered in feathers or fur. Its size was generally thought to be in the Wimba-Ko-im range; but its shape, especially of head and tail, remained a mystery. One thing was certain, the bunyip was the one thing they feared the most. It was like the powers of darkness incarnate; to interfere with it was to risk disaster. Buckley had no concept of such a thing and so had no fear of it. To spear a bunyip, regardless of the taboo, would be something irresistible.

He waited until dusk, watching the water closely. His excitement grew while he crouched in the grass right by the water's edge. This was something he had not thought of, but he now realised it could be the opportunity he wanted. If it was a bunyip, and he could successfully spear it, his hunger for amazing adventure would receive just the kind of experience he sought. But his wait that day was in vain.

The weather remained calm for the next few days, the cloud still hanging listlessly. Each afternoon he returned to the same spot and waited with three nandum spears. He still doubted if it was worth the time, but would not have forgiven himself if he had lost his chance. Perhaps there was no bunyip. But, he reasoned, there are many spaces in this world rarely if ever looked on by human eyes. Who knew what might exist in them only to be glimpsed from the corner of the eye by an unwary explorer?

On the third evening the water surged strongly about thirty paces out, then settled again. Buckley set his face and rose to a standing position, his spear poised; waiting, praying. The water surged again only ten paces from the shore, exposing a grey hump — a back covered in a kind of fur impossible to discern in the dull light. He hurled the first spear at the surge but the hump had disappeared even as the spear left his hand. Cursing the panicky shot he searched the water desperately. The surge came again, longer this time, about the same distance out but further down the waterline. He ran along the shore avoiding the water in case the splashing of his feet alarmed the creature. The surge continued. He could really see it now, although its proportions were unclear.

Scared of missing his chance, he quickly drew level with the moving shape, aimed his second spear and threw. The barbed tip flew over the hump, missing it by inches. It pierced the water beyond its target, and the shaft struck the animal on its back. Buckley saw it leap sideways and lurch in towards the shore. He cursed inwardly at his second miss but thrilled at the chance now presenting itself.

With his last spear he was determined to make sure of a kill. He now saw it as clearly as the darkening water would allow. It was at least as big as Ko-im, probably bigger, with four limbs. The head and tail appeared rather stumpy but were not clearly visible.

Its threat to human life was quite unknown, but Buckley could pay no heed to that now. Half desperate and decidedly reckless, he plunged into the water, attempting to run out and circle the bunyip, blocking its retreat to deeper water. This he almost accomplished, but the bottom of the lake was very muddy and slimy to the foot. Even as he thrashed through the water, keeping his knees up like a soldier jogging on the spot, and drew level with his prey, it began to surge away down the shore.

In one last desperate effort he lunged forward with the spear, attempting to jab into the bunyip's side rather than taking time to aim and throw. This time he definitely hit something. The creature kicked violently away, and the spear was wrenched from his outstretched right arm. He'd fallen down into the water on his knees and groping left hand. The jerk pulled him forward flat on his face and into the muddied water.

He stood up spluttering. It was gone. His broken spear floated on the water. Covered in mud and disappointment, he retrieved the other two spears from where they still stuck out of the water and began to return to the camp. Walking slowly around the lake shore he cursed his luck. But he had to admit his own impatience had probably ruined his chances, and more skill with the nandum might have brought success.

He was still wet and muddy when he entered the camp and approached his hut. Weeitcho taerinyaar saw him first and called the others' attention. Wombalano Beeaar asked if he had been eating his evening meal with the Boonea. He muttered something about nearly catching some ducks. They smiled and began to laugh. Tro wernuwil called out the story to rest of the people, and soon the whole camp was laughing uproariously and chanting 'Murrangurk, Murrangurk'. Buckley could now laugh too. It had been ridiculous although behind his smiling face was a voice telling him that one day he would get one of those things and prove his point. But he never did.

13

The Kumbada began a long unsettled period of much wandering. A bihar came from a band in the mountains past Gerangamete who were offering to exchange roots for Boonea, at a place called Barramunga on the head-waters of the Barwin. They accepted, marching straight there in order to preserve the condition of their Boonea and Tu-at, which were carried in Ko-im skins.

They were a Koligon band — the Burnarlook or black-wood people — numbering about eighty men, women, and children, and they gathered on the side of a clearing opposite to their visitors. Two men of each party met in the middle and, after a brief discussion of the deal involving much sign language, they carried their goods across on pieces of bark borne on their heads. They made nine trips each, thus exchanging approximately the same quantity by volume of roots for Boonea.

Soon some other bands began to arrive and further exchanges were made. Among them was one of the most remarkable Buckley ever met on his travels, the dreaded Pallidurgbarrans. Numbering only a few dozen people, they came from the deep, dark gullies that disappeared into the rugged mountains. Conditions must have been very harsh for this band. Whether for their survival or for other reasons they had developed a taste for human flesh. They were reputed to kill and eat people whenever they could. Such notoriety made everyone else very uneasy. They stood out because their skin was a much lighter copper colour and they had large protruding bellies. They didn't appear to build huts at all, but just lay about in the scrub. The women appeared to be particularly ferocious and were said to favour the flesh of children. Tales were going around the camps of the increasing number of attacks they were said to have made in the time prior to this gathering. It was agreed that something had to be done about them.

Tro wernuwil had a particular interest in these negotiations. His totem was Ka-warren, the spiny anteater. In the Dreamtime there had been an old woman who lived alone and survived well — to the mystery of the kulin, who could not understand where she got her food. Once a certain boy went missing and they realised she must have taken him. Under Bunjil's instructions, Ka-warren was sent to the rescue. He saved the boy and killed the wicked old woman when he discovered she had been eating her captives. Thus, all the Ka-warren men of all the tribes felt a great duty to rid the country of the Pallidurgbarrans.

The morning after trading had ceased the cannibals were asked to leave. There were some heated arguments and threats made, but the outnumbered Pallidurgbarrans withdrew further into the bush. The Ka-warren men now put their plan into action. It was a well-known hunting technique among the tribes to use fire to trap game. If the winds were favourable and the bush dry, an area would be surrounded by a circle of hunters and the boundary fired all around. All the game would thus he burnt or cut down as it tried to flee through the circle. Buckley had once found a life-saving fire-stick from such a burn.

The Pallidurgbarrans had gone into a deep valley a few miles to the south. It was too large an area to surround completely, but men moved out along the two ridges on either side and covered the northern end. A strong northwesterly was blowing, and by mid-afternoon they had the valley ablaze. A wall of fire advanced deeper and deeper into it. No-one could see the Pallidurgbarrans. They would have had to be very lucky to escape, although there was some chance they could have climbed the ridge to the south and got out.

That night a great corroboree was held in celebration of this united action for justice. The Pallidurgbarrans were never heard of again. A legend later arose that the last of them had turned to stone somewhere on the far south coast where there was said to be a petrified life-like figure of a man; perhaps, as Buckley thought, the figurehead of a wrecked ship.

The Kumbada stayed on a few days to continue the feasting. Before they left, Buckley walked through the burnt-out valley. It was easy strolling, the fire having scoured out all the scrub and undergrowth. Great blackened trees with pale scorched leaves, the black skeletons of small trees and shrubs, big burnt logs still smouldering and casting a friendly warmth on the passer-by, and bare rocks and brown earth strewn with piles of black and grey ashes; these were what remained of lush forest. Yet after only a few days tiny shoots of green grass — feed for Ko-im and Wimba — already showed in the ash, and the first bulges of green leafbuds could be seen on some of the trees. The valley was alive with birds, all scratching and pecking among the ash and earth for the millions of insects, either cooked or exposed by the loss of their cover, that were evidently easy to be had. Weing was the transforming element. Violent and painful, it stripped away the superficial greenness and the accumulated rubbish of dead generations of vegetation. Everything started again, fresh, new and equal. New trees would spring forth, germinated by the fire. Within months the forest would be fully restored, provided it was not burnt again too soon.

* * *

At length the tribes separated in peace, agreeing to meet again sometime for trading. The Kumbada made a long march to join the Bengali at Beangala on the shores of Port Phillip. They hunted as they went, stopping at a number of their old camps by the Barwin, the reedy marshes and Connewarre. They sat out a winter at Beangala, hunting Ko-im when the weather was favourable.

Buckley was amazed to see the Bengali had some iron axes. They said several amadiate had left them on the banks of the Barwin some time ago when they had come up the river. He guessed they must have been sealers and found he had curiously mixed feelings about having missed them — more curiosity than disappointment, mixed with a certain relief, as there was no telling what trouble they could have brought. He asked that he be told if any of them came back.

In early spring the time came to meet the Burnarlook again for trading. This time they took Ko-im and marched many days to the lake country in the north–west. They met at a placed called Lib-Lib on the shore of a lake known as Bangeballa. It was a large sheet of shallow water surrounded by reeds and open country.

Buckley had a great shock soon after arrival. He saw Woymber Myrrnie. They were unable to talk as she was long since married to a Woiwurong man. The shock came from seeing with her a tall, graceful, light-skinned young girl. Just once Woymber Myrrnie met his questioning gaze and nodded in affirmation. He was distressed and confused but saved from complete misery by a strong sense of elation. He could hardly take his eyes from his daughter for the whole time of the meeting. He found out her name was Karrie Ael, meaning Summer Rain for the sunshower in which she was born.

The tribes soon got down to trading their food. Among them was a strange man from the great river Millewa. No-one could understand his speech but he had some fur armbands called yelum-keturuk. These were made from the fur of Tuan-tuan and were valued for the strength they gave. At these meetings it became apparent to Buckley that this trading was not the only reason for coming together. More importantly, they came to bring out their daughters, arrange marriages and generally exchange women.

Every man belonged to one sex totem — Balayang the bat, brother of men, and Bunjil. Every woman also belonged to one sex totem — Ngaribarmgoruk, the owlet-nightjar, sister to all women. Ngaribarmgoruk and Balayang flew out of the hollow trees in the evenings to hunt insects. While Balayang swooped through the dusk skies, Ngaribarmgoruk ate the bugs on the ground, flying prettily and playfully from place to place like a butterfly. These two creatures were never eaten but respected as guardians of the soul and the hours of love.

Marriage was regulated by complex kinship rules which served to prevent even a hint of incest. If a man wanted a grown-up sister of another he had to give his own in exchange. Bunjil married Waang, and the bands of various localities reciprocated and so forged unifying links with each other. The woman always had to leave her tribe and go with her husband. But his power was not absolute. In an extreme case of beating or even killing, her brothers would come in revenge. It was not unusual for grown sons to take up the cudgel against fathers who maltreated mothers. Wife-lending was common but a man could not give a wife away, being held responsible for her wellbeing. Women who sought out their own contacts were condemned, endangering themselves and their lovers with beatings and duels. If anyone was caught with a partner of the wrong skin, death by spearing was certain. These complex rules were aggravated by the way the exchanges usually worked across generations. Young men would inherit the wives of their fathers — other than their mother; old men would be given daughters of friends, sometimes promised years before the girl was even born. Such arrangements ensured that the aged usually had someone young to care for them, but inevitably meant continual intrigues, affairs and elopements based on physical attraction and passions.

Buckley was by now long familiar with the outcome of these affairs, and this otherwise happy meeting for trade and corroborees ended in another round of fighting, after which the Burnarlook parted, along with sundry other groups. With great remorse Buckley had to watch Woymber Myrnnie and his beautiful Karrie Ael leave, not knowing if he would ever see them again.

But he had little time to dwell on his feelings. That night Wuruum kuurwhin, who sported a new Tuan-tuan armband, stole after the Burnarlook and speared a man dead in his sleep, right next to his wife in their mia-mia. The victim had promised him a daughter some years before and then given her to another. On returning to their camp, Wuruum kuurwhin boasted of his cowardly revenge, causing great consternation. His relatives and close friends left immediately, fearing an immediate attack more than the terrors of night travel. Buckley and the rest of the band remained, and in the morning went to the camp of the Burnarlook.

The murdered man had been popular among his people. He was a beloved song-maker and his loss was taken very badly. His body was trussed up in a Wollert skin rug and placed on a platform about twelve feet up in a tree. It was then covered with bark and logs in order to keep off the birds of prey, and was set with the face upwards, inclining toward the setting sun, for this was the direction the man's moorup (shade) would go on its journey. First travelling to Ngamat, the dream-camp of the sun at the edge of the earth, it would then ascend on Karalk, the bright streaming rays of the sunset glow, to Tharangalk-bek.

Entry to Bunjil's country had nothing to do with any concept of sin. The only test on arrival was that Bunjil would examine the moorup to see it had passed through the proper initiation ceremonies. As this man undoubtedly had, he would be given wives equivalent to those he had on earth, and then be free to hunt in the hunter's paradise of teeming game and abundant water. After a time he would descend to his earthly totem centre to await rebirth. Death was like the dropping of a piece of bark into the river. It would bob up again somewhere downstream and so recreate the deeds of the ancestors; dying because they died, returning as a manifestation of their eternal presence. It was now, in learning this, that Buckley understood that Murrangurk, his name, meant soul returned from the dead.

The trussing up of the corpse and other practices were due to a vague idea of a second soul. The first went to Bunjil, but the second was inclined to loiter and make visitations and so had to be discouraged. The deceased was never, directly mentioned by name, at least not for a long time, in case this loose second soul should hear and come around. Thus whole tribes would drop certain words from their language after a death or have a second vocabulary to use during a mourning period.

The widow and other women joined in the most distressing lamentations and, the men joining them, cut their hair short with sharp shells and daubed themselves with clay in a prescribed manner. Fires were lit around the tree to warm the moorup and one word was said in great solemnity: 'amadiate' — gone to be made white but not forever.

Buckley, continually irked by these killings and the distress they caused, was particularly sickened by this event. Most of the Kumbada themselves were disgusted by its selfishness and pointlessness, especially considering the trouble it was bound to bring on all of them. The following morning a long discussion was held with the Burnarlook and these sentiments were expressed and understood on all sides. The Burnarlook also had to weigh their desire for revenge on the murderer against the fact that their man had broken an important promise.

As the Kumbada prepared to leave, dark clouds rolled in from the west. They could see Myerre the swift soaring in great numbers; they moved towards Bangeballa, drawing the clouds after them. A cool wind came, then huge spots of rain started to splatter faster and faster until a great hailstorm burst over them. The giant stones were sometimes bigger than eyeballs and fell like violent seeds, even stripping the bark from the trees. A terrible power had unleashed itself on the earth. The Kumbada huddled in their mia-mias unable to move until it ended. After the shock of it had passed they all began to laugh in amazement and play with the piles of hailstones. All except Torraneuk.

Later that day they rejoined the others on the way south. Angry arguments ensued over the killing and the trouble everyone was now caused. Torraneuk and Tro wernuwil were particularly angry, and Torraneuk even threatened to kill Wuruum kuurwhin himself. Buckley began to wonder if his mutterings about these killings had begun to change their ideas. But Torraneuk had his own reasons. The murdered man was a Murrin-mooroo man, and thereby a brother to his wife even though of a completely different tribe. This placed Torraneuk in a difficult position of divided loyalties.

The previous night he had sat and watched the tree burial. In the sky he had seen the Southern Cross above them: Yukope and Dantun. But suddenly they had been darkened. Kokurn the powerful owl had flown across the contellation and swooped over the camp. Few had seen it but Torraneuk felt the fear of death spread among them like a sudden chilly breeze. The cosmic anger of the hailstorm the following morning made him feel a great pressure on himself to act for the wellbeing of his people, but Wuruum kuurwhin was a principal man among the Kumbada-kulin with many relatives and friends. His totem was Garl, the dog.

Garl had always hunted everywhere without challenge until one day he met Yern, the little native cat. They circled each other warily, putting on bold postures but both a little scared. Garl had strong teeth but Yern was very sharp of claw. The most combative creature in the bush, Yern the tree-dweller would attack fearlessly and relentlessly and with ferocious speed.

As the sun rose and the day grew hot they settled under a tree and talked to stay awake. Garl pitied Yern for being confined up trees; Yern pitied Garl for running about all over the hot plains. Garl said he was the strongest and not afraid. Yern laughed and exclaimed that strength was nothing. He had the power to return from the dead. So saying he challenged Garl to cut his head off, lying down exposing his neck. Garl did not need to be asked twice and swiftly severed Yern's head. He swaggered away chuckling to himself.

A few nights later he was making camp at night when an ethereal voice greeted him from the darkness beyond his fire. Suddenly a bright glow shone in the sky, coining closer. Yern jumped lightly to the ground in front of a trembling Garl. 'Now it's your turn,' he said. 'Don't be afraid; all you have to do is believe. Let me show you.' Before the astonished Garl could think, Yern had pushed him down and severed his head. 'A pity he didn't have time to believe,' mused Yern.

It was Yern who taught men to bury their dead and the secret of reincarnation. Many believed the moon was Yern. Garl knew nothing of this, living out his days as an animal, hunting the arid lands, lacking the confidence he had when a man and without hope of return to earth after death.

Any move against Wuruum kuurwhin would be fraught

with danger for Torraneuk and his whole family.

These fearful developments were not without effect on Buckley, who felt a growing alarm over the direction events were taking them. He had also seen Kokurn. When they camped the following night he dreamt they were somewhere in the bush. All was quiet. They were spearing Boonea and Tu-at, but everything kept getting away. A great fear came on them. A terrible fire was sweeping around them. They began to run but it seemed hopeless. They didn't know whether to try and get out at the far end of the valley or hide deep down in the tree ferns and risk suffocation. They looked for a sign but all the animals were confused. They cried in terrible anguish. It must all be a mistake; it could not be. The fire raged so hot.

He woke up scared and feeling half-dead. He thought immediately of Karrie Ael. Remorse weighed on him doubly hard. He could not bear any more. He wanted to go.

In the morning Buckley made up his mind that this time he would leave the tribe. His friends were all shocked when he announced his desire. Everyone implored him to stay, making every oath to reassure him that whatever feuds befell them no harm would come to Murrangurk, especially under the circumstances in which he had returned to them. Their sincerity and kindness soon eroded his resolve. Hopelessly confused, he agreed to continue with them but still far from convinced of his safety, and still very afraid for them.

14

The fear of the Kumbada was so great they marched all the way to Godocut on the ocean coast near the southern limits of the Wothowurong country. They camped on a high hill that projected out into the sea, with cliffs and steep descents to the beach stretching out for several miles on both sides. Inland the country dipped into a saddle before rising again into forests of stringy-barks and gums, with grass trees and shrubs in the understorey. This site provided an excellent natural fortress against the expected attack from the Burnarlook.

Unfortunately, the only food to be had was shellfish, and this was difficult to get. After a few days, hunger and impatience with the siege situation won out and they moved several miles inland through thick scrub above the valley of a pretty river Buckley had not seen before. It was called Kuarka Dorla and it flowed from the mountains separating the upper Barwon valley from the coast. They camped by two freshwater wells and hunted Wollert and dug roots. After a few days they wandered on, moving down to an open woodland called Paraparap, where they had once camped when Buckley had first joined the Kumbada. They lived by hunting and spearing fish in the waterholes along the creek. All this time watch was kept day and night for fear of attack by the Burnalook.

Eventually the months of fear and loneliness were broken by the arrival of another band, the Ko-im (kangaroo people). At first they were spotted coming across the plain towards the Barwin, and the Kumbada all fled into a patch of rocky scrub where they were forced to remain all night without food or fire.

In the morning a party was sent to investigate and they did not return until the next morning, when great anxiety was felt about their safety. However, their return soon brought smiles of relief. They came with fire-sticks and good news. The Ko-im were friendly and extended an invitation to join them at a small lagoon in the Iramoo country where they were camped. They had found an abundance of Boonea there, and wished to share them with any kulin.

This gathering more than doubled their numbers, and they now felt secure enough to forget the long-held fear of attack. Once again they slipped into a long period of idyllic living. Apart from the commonplace family squabbles, nothing disturbed their peace and contentment the whole time they were there. The Burnarlook had evidently decided against revenge. Food was plentiful and easily acquired. Occasionally, they would make small excursions to different parts of the surrounding country to do some hunting or just for the pleasure of taking a walk around their beloved homeland. Their troubles seemed to be a thing of the past.

Eventually, they left this place for no other reason than boredom with the same diet and daily routine. Leaving the Ko-im, they returned to the hill country near Kuarka Dorla, moving slowly and hunting as they went, and stopping at a place called Boordek. The bush there was dense and rich in animal life. The Kumbada had come for Wollert and Poorool and they found plenty.

This time Torraneuk gave Buckley a good course in how to catch them. They were really playful creatures, somersaulting through the branches at night, and such good eating. He showed him how to look for scratches on the bark and how, by breathing hard on it, one could detect the hairs they left when ascending the tree trunks. A positive result on these tests and one of them would climb the tree by cutting toe-hold notches in the trunk with an axe and drag poor, sleepy Wollert or Poorool from their holes and throw them to the ground. There the other would knock them on the head. Each time Buckley learnt a lesson well Torraneuk would call out 'Merrijig! Merrijig!' meaning 'Well done', and his face would light up around those black eyes. They lived like this for some time, supplementing their catches with a delicious white root that, when roasted, was as sweet as chestnuts.

But Wollert could not last forever, and they moved on once again from an otherwise idyllic camp to new places in search of diverse foods and hunting experiences. This constant nomadism gave great variety of diet and did much for the health, as Buckley had found to his benefit.

But now another period of great trouble started, and Buckley's worst fears returned in force. In the volcanic hills of Moriac they hunted Poorool and set up camp. After some days the men left on a hunting excursion, leaving only half a dozen men, including Buckley, with the women and children. Later that day a strange band came and camped close by. They were the Galgal-bulluk (dog people) from the Jajowurong.

The next day they became aggressive and began to make it plain the wanted the Kumbada to be off. After a period of shouting and angry gesticulations, a shower of spears was launched quite suddenly by a group of men in the bush. A boy and girl were killed and the Kumbada prepared to fight for their lives. Now Buckley joined the fray for the first time. This group did not know him and were obviously prepared to kill him despite his formidable and strange appearance. With his height and reach he was no easy prey, acquitting himself well with malga shield and leonile, the long battle club with a hooked end. The brawl went on for some time. They began to tire, so the women joined in. Buckley smashed the sharp end of his leonile into someone's teeth, but there were no more fatalities and, faced with such fierce defence, the Galgal-bulluk withdrew.

The Kumbada immediately despatched a messenger to recall the hunters. They returned that night and at once began smearing themselves with pipeclay. Soon their preparations were complete. At the first light of dawn they set out in pursuit of the enemy, leaving Buckley and the women to bury the children. They returned two days later, some severely wounded but all alive. The mission had been a success, and stories were told and fights mimed as they proudly related the deaths of two of their cowardly opponents. Torraneuk and Wuruum kuurwhin had fought side by side against the common enemy as they had done many times before. There was no doubt Wuruum kuurwhin was a good not afford to lose men him, regardless of his selfishness.

They shifted camp to a small lake called Gherang near Moodewarri. However, their anxiety remained with them, owing to the presence of yet another band on the other side of the lake.

During the night there was a tremendous uproar from their camp. The Kumbada investigated in the morning, finding they had been attacked by the Galgal-bulluk. This small group of families were the Kawer-kulin (emu people) and they had been all but massacred. Dead and mutilated bodies were lying about. Others had drowned in the lake whilst trying to escape.

The survivors came forward timidly, eventually agreeing to join the Kumbada, and all withdrew from the scene without waiting to bury the dead. Another attack was feared at any time. They marched quickly through two miles of light timber to the east and came to their old quarters at Moodewarri.

The mood of the lake was the same, but Buckley was unable to settle his mind into it in quite the way he had before, and he had all but forgotten any wish to pierce the mystery of the bunyip. The events of the previous months had been too distracting. The repeated periods of anxiety and fear over fights and ambushes kept him in a continual state of wearying suspense. Added to this was his continual sexual tension, the conflict between his desire and the dangers involved in fulfilling it. The only escape from these pressures was to leave the tribe and be alone again. He knew he was free to go. He was no prisoner. It would be easy to 'go hunting' any day and not return. But then he had to think of the possibility of meeting hostile tribes when alone, perhaps one who knew him as Wothowurong. He would not have a chance of surviving such a confrontation. He still remembered the near starvation his first months alone had brought. At least now he had acquired substantial knowledge of hunting and the gathering of vegetable foods.

Day by day he weighed these factors. Across his troubled mind fell the shadow of Kokurn. He discussed it with Torraneuk. 'Might be something; might be something,' was all he would say. But they all knew what it could mean. Kokurn preyed mostly on tree-dwelling animals like Wollert and Tuan-tuan and even Yern. But he also took the occasional bird like Kooring-kooring, Waang, and Barroworn. Was it a sign they saw? And if it was, whom was Kokurn after? He was such an aloof one, living alone, keeping regular habits and taking baths in icy mountain streams before dawn. Who could tell the mind of such a bird?

These things Buckley had seen and felt in waking and dreaming seemed to press for recognition at this time of decision. Yet he had no way of judging them; no way of knowing whether they were mere fancy or important signs that told him how to live. He couldn't express these things to Torraneuk or Wombalano Beeaar without again raising the subject of his leaving. They probably knew more than he, but it was hard and language was confused in his mind; and things moved fast at times. The repeated assurances they made regarding his safety were sincere, he knew. But they gave less and less comfort and, finally, no real sense of security, especially after the massacre he had just seen and his recent bloodying in combat.

One day he did approach Torraneuk with some of these problems, asking what he thought the future held for them. Torraneuk just twitched his nose-bone and continued to carve his shield. 'Don't worry,' he said, adding, 'Whoever you are,' with a funny little smile on his averted face.

Buckley winced inwardly at the insinuation. Torraneuk was at least sceptical that he was Murrangurk. Maybe Torraneuk knew — he had some idea of the old Sullivan's Bay settlement and Buckley's connection with it — but it wasn't really the point for him. Perhaps others felt the same. Perhaps they also suspected or knew about the women he had been with and if they did, could he really trust them to defend him and go on protecting him forever? In spite of the dangers of fighting in the army and starving in the wilderness that he had lived through before, he had never lived for such long periods with the threat of sudden violent death. But this was his life, and to make a drastic change he would have to face other troubles — not the least being loneliness again. He was, he knew, not by nature a hermit.

These problems remained in a state of suspension in Buckley's mind for a season. Moodewarri was after all a favourite place, and decisions were not to be rushed. A time of peace seemed to settle over the kulin, and the problems of survival gained full attention. In the normal course of events there was little time for fighting and none for the concerted efforts called wars. The fear of sudden death abated for Buckley, if not always for his friends, who sometimes lived with the possibility of perishing by hostile magic rather than physical attack.

Mirri Mallo was a funny little girl. She had a friend who lived in the moiyan or silver wattle trees. It was Turnung, who came out at nights and glided through the forest, silent and delicate as a feather floating on the air. Whenever they camped at a place where there were moiyan trees, Mirri Mallo could be seen sitting under one of them. Sometimes she would talk to the tree and tell Turnung about herself. Other times she could be seen sitting and listening. Turnung was wise and knew all about the other animals, especially the ones of the night. She knew only too well the fright Kokurn could give. But Turnung would tell Mirri Mallo not to be afraid; one day they would all be safe whatever trouble would come.

Buckley laughed to hear Mirri Mallo tell of these conversations, but was not averse to hoping it was true. After some time at Moodewarri he again started to have the strangest dreams himself.

15

The trouble started again. Another band, the Eurok (goanna people), arrived and camped nearby. There was a dispute over a woman. She had been with a Eurok man for years and had a child by him. Wuruum kuurwhin's brother seemed to think he had some old right to her, and they went one night and took her away by force. The brother then brought her to Buckley's mia-mia, much to his displeasure as he feared trouble — and correctly so. During the night her husband came with his friends and took her back. Without warning he rammed a spear through Wuruum kuurwhin's brother, pinning him to the ground. Wuruum kuurwhin and Buckley tried desperately to draw the spear — a deadly mongile — but were unsuccessful. A woman finally succeeded, but he died in the morning and was given a tree burial with full honours.

By this time the Eurok had all fled. However, several days later the Kumbada accidentally fell in with them on a hunting excursion. Wuruum kuurwhin went crazy and reaped a terrible revenge. Unable to get the man who had murdered his brother, he killed his child and the man's brother and speared the mother through the thigh. The Eurok fought back. During the *mêlée* a huge barngeet whirred down on Buckley and almost killed him, splitting his guram in two. He reeled back, more shocked than injured. The barngeet had been intended for Torraneuk, who stood nearby. Despite the fury of the brawl the man who had thrown it came and apologised and accepted a bashing from some of his own comrades by way of punishment. Wombalano Beeaar and Weeitcho taerinyaar came forward crying and bound Buckley's bleeding left hand — now both had suffered in battle — with a piece of skin and some twisted hair-string from the pelt of Wollert.

Meanwhile, the fight continued until a Kumbada man was killed and the two groups separated. The Eurok took their victim, hacked most of the flesh off his body and carried it away on their spears, threatening to serve the rest of them in the same manner. That night they could hear them having a corroboree as they ate their trophies.

Torraneuk and Tro wernuwil were in a state of simmering fury. The dead Kumbada was a Ka-warren man; the second totem brother dead through Wuruum kuurwhin's ferocity. Again, Torraneuk was caught between two loyalties and felt obliged to act in spite of immense danger.

The Eurok left and they moved to Paraparap. They had been there some days, and were just beginning to settle down again, when a strange thing happened. Burmbo Merio had begun to sleep with Buckley in the little bachelor camp, set as usual a short distance from the main family quarters. One night he cried out, as Buckley thought, in his sleep. It was a strange, frightening cry. He let it pass, thinking it best not to wake the boy, but soon he cried out again and Buckley went to him. Burmbo Merio was not asleep but awake. He asked him what was wrong. Burmbo Merio explained he had seen visions. Buckley said it was only ye-yey-dyileen (dreams) and tried to reassure him. But Burmbo Merio was adamant; they were not dreams. He was awake and could see the visions with his eyes open. He saw them in the sky. Flaming green-gold images of Karbor, Murrinmooroo, and Ka-warren appeared above the treetops. He had to stay awake and watch them until they faded.

No-one could tell the meaning of these visions, but the Kumbada's fear grew. The next day they left and wandered about for some time until they came to a lake called Koodgingmurrah, named for a root that grew there. Here they camped until near the end of winter, when the season came for kalkeeth, the larvae of the wood-ant.

A long time ago Kalkeeth had been discovered by the ancestress Marpean-kurrk, who became the star Arcturus when she died. When she was in the north in the evening at about the end of July the kalkeeth were coming into season, and the Kumbada marched deep into the bush in their southern hills near Boordek. The kalkeeth were their main food for over a month until early September when Marpean-kurrk set with the sun in the evening. They were obtained by knocking on hollow trees with an axe. At this noise they would show themselves at their holes, indicating where they were concentrated in hives, which were then hacked open. In season they were as fat as butter and delicious after being roasted on sheets of bark over the fire.

The other great prize got from hollow trees was the honey of the native bee, or sugar-bag. Sometimes it was found by sticking a small petal or leaf to a captured bee with some sticky gum and following its struggling flight back to the hive.

This festive season in the bush helped to distract everyone from their worries. The getting and roasting of kalkeeth was a great collective adventure and basic common purpose for which everyone in the band — men, women and children — loved to come together.

At the end of the kalkeeth season a bihar came, summoning them to join the Ko-im at a place called Boonea yallock, the river of eels, to share the Boonea then abounding there. Torraneuk was delighted. They had enjoyed a successful stay with them before, and their strength and easy-going ways had led him to look forward to extending and strengthening the Kumbada's friendship with them. His pleasure was short-lived, for when Wuruum kuurwhin heard the news he began to threaten revenge on one of the Koim over an old grievance. Torraneuk was determined that relations with this band should not be wrecked. As well, the man in question was of Karbor, his own totem brother. He remained silent when they all decided to get a good night's sleep, eager to depart early the next day.

Only Burmbo Merio could not sleep. Again the visions came to him. Flaming green-gold images of Karbor, Murrin-mooroo, and Ka-warren appeared above the treetops, and he watched them until they slowly faded.

In the morning they set out in good spirits, but on the way a strange turn of events took place. A few days later as they were approaching the Iramoo country, Torraneuk and his family separated slightly from the rest of the hand, although keeping to the general direction. Soon they came to a small stream in a gully lined with beautiful manna gums. Karbor was sitting on a low branch just above a small clearing. Wombalano Beeaar, Tro wernuwil, Weeitcho taerinyaar, Koronn, Burmbo Merio, and Mirri Mallo sat down on the edge of the bush and motioned Buckley to join them. They remained still and silent for some time while Torraneuk stood and looked at Karbor, who nonchalantly continued to chew his leaves.

Then Torraneuk stepped forward across the clearing and stood quietly a short distance from him. To Buckley's astonishment he heard the distinct grunts and squeals of Karbor, but they were coming from Torraneuk. With uncanny feeling he mimicked Karbor through a series of phrases. Buckley's astonishment began to turn to agitation when Karbor started to grunt and squeal back to Torraneuk, as if in reply. It was in fact a reply, as Torraneuk began again, and elicited further response from Karbor. This conversation continued for some time until Torraneuk finally made gestures of gratitude with his hands and turned away. Karbor climbed away high into the treetops.

Buckley was still very excited and wanted to ask questions. But the serious manner of the others made him keep quiet. Torraneuk announced he would wait there for a while, and that they should go on. Buckley was perplexed, but Wombalano Beeaar and Tro wernuwil assured him that Torraneuk had business and that they should continue without him; and this they did. As they marched away Buckley looked back at him. He was just standing in the grove looking straight ahead, motionless.

Some time after the others had left, Torraneuk slowly crouched down and took his small net bag from the girdle around his waist and tipped his thundal into his hands. Fingering them, he began to make a low chant with intense concentration.

He rose and took the mooynm karr from his bag and began to whirl it around. Its strange voices swept through the bush, alerting all creatures. He softly repeated his chant.

As Buckley and the rest of the family approached the appointed meeting place low grey clouds gathered in the west. Narrut began to call up the rain, thousands chirping across the country as they approached the Barwin valley. It was a typical spring storm. The warm air became a vibrant blue and the tension in the air mounted until they could feel it on their skins. Soon a strong, cool wind ripped through the stillness and the first showers broke from the sky. They were near Boonea-yallock, a stretch of the Barwin.

The Ko-im were camped over on the far bank. Instead of

crossing to join them they decided to quickly make camp and take shelter until the rain cleared. It fell heavier and heavier and Woonduble made a deafening chorus. They quickly threw together some rough branch and bark mia-mias. The weather was warm, and the rain smelled as dusk began to settle over the valley. Having made a bed with some grass and leaves that were still reasonably dry, Buckley decided to sleep until the morning, as the camp was always inclined to become dismal in bad weather.

Karbor was sitting high up in a big gum tree. He looked up. Djurt-djurt soared across the sky and circled, hovering motionless in the air. In the manner of his species he could stop still on the wing in a breeze, moving neither up nor down, nor sideways, nor backwards or forwards. Thus he hung there, waiting for some unwary lizard or other prey to expose itself, then dropped like a stone out of nowhere with a quick and deadly strike. Djurt-djurt dropped into the scrub behind some rocks. Kaan slithered rapidly across the grass — he must have come from the rocks, stirring to life in the spring warmth. Garl came trotting by, his attention focused on some distant object. He frightened Kaan who lunged and bit hard, holding on until his poison went into the heart of Gad and he began to die. Djurt-djurt flew high in the air over a rainbow.

In the morning when Buckley awoke there was a great commotion in the camp. Women were wailing and men were muttering together in anger and consternation. During the night the heavy rain all along the Barwin valley had caused the river to become swollen. It had burst its lower bank at this place and flooded up towards their camp. Many frogs and snakes and other creatures had fled to the higher ground. One of the snakes had fatally bitten Wuruum kuurwhin as he had approached the river at dawn in order to ascertain whether they could cross to the other camp.

Buckley was trembling at the implications, and became very fearful. Torraneuk was still missing. He asked where he was, and they said perhaps he was in the bush some way further back where they had left him. Buckley took his spears and ran through the trees. His anxiety was unexplained but he had to find Torraneuk. After running several miles and calling to him, he came to a clearing that he thought he recognised. A rainbow crossed the sky among showering clouds above the tree-tops.

He couldn't see Torraneuk and half fell to the ground panting, resting his back against a tree. He began to draw his breath. Suddenly a Wollert fell from above him, its neck broken. 'Merrijig!' He looked up. Torraneuk was in a tree, laughing and indicating the rainbow. 'Brinbeal,' he said, and swung down to the ground, picking up the Wollert.

Buckley gasped that Wuruum kuurwhin was dead. Torraneuk was inscrutable and unmoved. 'I don't know,' he said. 'Might be something.'

They marched quickly to the camp and breakfasted on Wollert and some roots Wombalano Beeaar had gathered. No-one mentioned the situation of the band.

In the afternoon the river subsided enough for them to cross and join their friends, and this they did, leaving the family and friends of Wuruum kuurwhin to bury him in a tree and perform the necessary rites. Things seemed quickly to return to normal as everyone went through the exchanges of greetings and got down to the business of catching Boonea. They abounded here, as the riverbed was rocky and the eels tended to gather in the pools along its bed. They expected to do especially well this time as the river must have dropped plenty of food for them as it subsided. Buckley had always found they were perceptive and wary-wise creatures who would dart away into deep water at the sight of a falling star or the sound of a bare foot padding on a rock, and yet they would miraculously rise and be placidly taken under a fishing torch held over the edge of a pool in the night. By this method they caught scores of Boonea and feasted happily for several days; things were seemingly relaxed again.

At length a rather momentous occasion arrived. Koronn, now a young woman, was to be given in marriage to a man of the Yawangis. Her totem was Kooring-kooring now. Bunjil had needed a noise to wake the people from sleep when he had lit the fire of the sun. He appointed Kooring-kooring to laugh out loud when he put up the morning star as a sign, Weeitcho taerinyaar and the other women had been preparing Koronn for some months; teaching her the duties and skills of a married woman. Finally she had to say goodbye to them all and go with Tro wernuwil and some of his friends to the Kurung country further north in Iramoo.

How time must have gone by, thought Buckley; and he still without a wife of his own. They watched her go, then he went walking with Burmbo Merio and Mirri Mallo, feeling abysmally lonely again. He sat on the riverbank while the children scrambled around in the bush. His thoughts began to drift back over his life, but suddenly Mirri Mallo let out a squeal and came running back. She had been bitten by some bull ants — Collenbitchik. They went back to the camp. Wombalano Beeaar uprooted some bracken ferns. Splitting the roots open she rubbed the bites with their juice for it had a soothing effect. Mirri Mallo said that Turnung had warned her to watch out for the ants. 'How right she was,' muttered Torraneuk. He knew that the following days would see his fate determined; perhaps the fate of them all.

Several days later Buckley noticed a strange thing. The bulk of the Kumbada were now dispersing, but there was not the usual gathering and preparation to march together or meet at a designated place for the next camp. By the time they had had their fill of Boonea only Torraneuk's and three other families remained. He found it strange at this particular time, and was sure Wuruum kuurwhin's death had something to do with it.

Presently, the Kumbada said farewell to the Ko-im and promised to meet again for Boonea when the time came.

16

Torraneuk knew only too well what, was happening. The inquest into Wuruum kuurwhin's death was being held and all the men who were under suspicion were afraid, including himself. There were several methods the avengers might use to find the vital clue that indicated who his murderer was, for there was no question to them that his death was not an accident. They would clear the ground under his tree-platform and cither note the flow of his bodily exudations towards a line of sticks or stones laid out to represent the possible killers; or they would look to see if any animal trails — such as those of Collenbitchik — marked the ground so as to indicate the direction of their quarry. They would discuss the last statements of Wuruum kuurwhin — without ever mentioning him by name — to see if he had given any clue about whom he suspected, whom he may have dreamt of. The wirrarap in charge of the proceedings would check his own dreams for the vital information. Finally a decision would be made and the revenge party formed.

Torraneuk's and the other families marched to the northwest following a stream called the Yalloak so they could meet Tro wernuwil on his return from the Yawangis, and with a vague intention to return to Moodewarri. They were a small party and Buckley was anxious to move quickly and reach the lake. Perhaps other friends would be found there. However, the others seemed unhurried, and they hunted and gathered as they went, camping at any pleasant spots along the river — although careful not to stay too close as a monster called Moorabool was said to lurk there and snatch unwary passers-by.

After a few days they were rejoined by Tro wernuwil, who came alone. He said the Yawangis were not far away. But early one morning, before they had decided on their course, they suddenly saw a party of about sixty men coming in their direction. They passed them by at a distance, moving back up a rise on the other side of the river. They must have spotted the camp, if only because of the smoke from their freshly-stoked fires, so their evasive behaviour seemed odd.

Their intentions soon became clear when they could be seen applying ochre to themselves in preparation for a fight. Within minutes they were on the opposite bank shaking their spears and yelling for blood. They stormed across in quick attack. Wombalano Beeaar and Weeitcho taerinyaar and the children had little time to escape, scattering through the trees in wild panic. All the others ran off as the terrifying horde confronted Torraneuk. Pausing with their weapons raised, their leader drew his breath and cried out the charge that their brother — the dead one — had died by the agency of Kaan but the will and evil magic of Torraneuk. Among them were Wuruum kuurwhin's totem brothers from the Kumbada. They were with their new allies the Collenbitchik (ant-men), among whom were some with a grudge against Tro wernuwil.

Buckley stood his ground with Torraneuk and Tro wernuwil. If death had come at last, to flee such a party was futile. He had to stand by Torraneuk and that was no bad thing. He had half expected this charge, but was still reluctant to believe it. He looked at Torraneuk, hoping to find an answer; but his face and poise, his tark held ready, revealed only an utterly fearless resolve to kill or be killed.

He realised that he had never really known this man. He had never been initiated into the secret cult-life of the totems, let alone the even more obscure and secretive ways of the wirrarap.

Buckley's question would never be answered. Torraneuk fell with a mongile through his body. A barngeet knocked Tro wernuwil down, a man then driving a mongile through his heart while cursing him for giving Koronn to another. Even as Buckley knelt beside Torraneuk in the hope that his writhing body was not mortally wounded he looked and saw them dragging Wombalano Beeaar from the scrub. They clubbed her senseless and drove their spears through her. He tried to support Torraneuk and divert his attention. But Torraneuk saw it all and, in his last agonies, pushed Buckley away, telling him to run; and, tearing one of his spears away from him, hurled it at the nearest of the murderers, wounding him in the arm. A dozen men fell on Torraneuk with clubs, and he was dead.

Buckley screamed in outrage, tears rolling down his face. In the fury and terror of those moments he had forgotten his own fate. Yet again he, miraculously, was unharmed. He sat crying beside Torraneuk, ignored by the gang who now withdrew some distance in conference.

After a long time he rose from the body of his dead friend. He stumbled over and looked at Wombalano Beeaar, her face still twisted in terror. Then he went to Tro wernuwil, who lay on his back, pinned to the ground. He cried and screamed at the murderers, who ignored him, and raged at the madness of the land he was in. He gathered Torraneuk's spears carefully against a tree in the proper way Torraneuk had always done; his eyes throbbing, he sobbed at each spear and collapsed in front of the mia-mia.

Presently a tall and powerful man came across and demanded the spears. Buckley, reckless in grief, roared at him to go, refusing to surrender them. The man backed off a little, a fawning smile on his face. He then brought forward some fish, wrapping them in his rug. These he placed before Buckley, telling him he must go back to their camp and join his wife and family. He assured him of his goodwill and future friendship.

Buckley was torn with grief that no-one would replace 'his' family, and anger that one of their murderers could be so preposterous as to think he could now take him like a piece of property. He could have no faith in his assurances of friendship. He didn't want to go without learning the fate of Weeitcho taerinyaar, Burmbo Merio, and Mirri Mallo. Mercifully, they had not been seen since the attack, and he felt they were probably alive. Their safety was still in jeopardy and, in case their exposure proved fatal, he dared not seek them out. In view of the threatening presence of the man and his murderous comrades he resolved on leaving in the hope that he could return later and find them. He took the 'gift', and his and Torraneuk's spears, and left in the direction he was ordered.

After jogging dispiritedly for about a mile he stopped and broke down. In all his suffering in the wilderness this was the worst. His grief was agony in his heart and he cried again. Torraneuk, Wombalano Beeaar, and Tro wernuwil had been the most sincere and loving guardians; their kindness to him the most precious jewel ever bestowed on his life. They had always shown complete concern for his safety and wellbeing. Now it was over. He wanted to leave the whole nightmare, but there was no other world to awaken to. Certainly he would not be joining the Collenbitchik camp.

In the afternoon he sat with his head buried in his knees. His feelings subsided; his mind drained clear. He quickly decided to leave the area and head south into their old hunting grounds. Throwing the fish into the scrub, he put himself in light marching order, tying his spears together and rolling his rug into a tight bundle. He crossed the Yalloak and made for the bush, hoping to make some progress towards Moodewarri before nightfall.

His luck held. After about four miles he met the Yawangis. Koronn and her new husband were with them. They cried bitterly at the news, the whole band swearing vengeance. They directed him to camp at a place near the Barwin where they would meet him after seeking their revenge. Reluctantly, Buckley parted from them alone and reached the banks of the Barwin at nightfall.

In the morning he swam the river and climbed the beautiful hills called Barrabool. They were covered in lush green grass and lightly timbered with she-oaks, and provided an excellent view of the Barwin valley to the north, and where it ran to the east. He made camp and watched for the approach of whoever would return from the Yalloak, making a turf and bark fence around his fire so that the light could not be seen at night. The weather was warm, so he could live without it during the day when he spent most of his time gathering roots and venturing down to the river to spear fish. Thus he waited for three agonisingly slow days. In the evening of the third day he suddenly noticed a light approaching in his direction on the plain below and coming away from the Barwin.

He dowsed the fire. The food and his spears he hid away, to make the camp appear deserted, and withdrew among the trees. Obviously they knew where to come, as the light approached right to the campsite. After a few minutes a woman's voice asked where he could be, and others answered with certain suggestions.

Buckley almost wept with relief, and presented himself. They were five young women from the Yawangis and very pleased to see him. They told him that their men had ambushed and fought the Collenbitchik, killing three of them, before they had left the fatal camp by the Yalloak. They had burnt the bodies of Torraneuk, Wombalano Beeaar, and Tro wernuwil in order to prevent their mutilation. Weeitcho Taerinyaar and the children had been found hiding up the river and were safely with them. These women had left independently as they had been threatened with possible capture by the Collenbitchik during the battle. They were exhausted and hungry. He gave them his fish and roots and rekindled the fire. Their presence greatly lifted his spirits. They ate thankfully and slept the night in his mia-mia.

The next morning two of them left, anxious to rejoin their people who were expected to come their way at any time. The other three decided to wait with him. After the emotional and physical trials of the previous days he found this situation some consolation. They remained several days. He would go to the river fishing while they collected roots and a few lizards. The weather was sunny and cheerful, and the women were good company. One of them, Moonalelly, would slip away and meet him by the river.

In the end the others didn't come, and the women felt they had to go. They all bid a cheerful goodbye and left the lone figure of Buckley at his camp on the hill. As he watched them move off over the plain below he again felt the crushing loneliness of an empty world begin to swirl down on him, just as it had so long ago on the beach near the isle of Barwal as he had watched Pye and McAllenan walk away. This time it was a whole other family that his heart yearned for, conjuring them up until he began to feel the tears forming again. He could not go without paying his last respects. He broke camp and marched to the scene of the massacre by the Yalloak.

Late in the afternoon he approached the campsite, half hoping that this was a dream, but knowing all he could hope to find. Sure enough he soon saw the three piteous piles of ashes and bones. His heart so heavy he could hardly move, his eyes watering, he scraped each pile together and dug little holes for them with one of Wombalano Beeaar's old kurniang, and buried them as best he could. He stayed the night in mourning, dozing fitfully, half afraid of a visitation, half hoping for one.

In the morning he said goodbye to each grave and left. Returning to the camp at Barrabool, he met the Yawangis the next day. There was a joyful reunion with Weeitcho taerinyaar, Burmbo Merio, and Mirri Mallo. Everyone begged him to stay with them, swearing protection for him against the certain death that would befall him if he travelled alone. But Buckley was inconsolable. He could not picture himself in their society any longer. Much as he felt akin to this band, something within him, something he had not felt in years, urged him to strike out free of all ties, and to seek refuge or liberty or escape in some forgotten or unknown place. He begged leave of them, and they were reluctantly compelled to let him go. After a day they left, crossing the river and setting out for the north–west.

He watched them out of sight, then tied his spears together, wrapped a few fish and roots in his rug and moved off to the south. He wanted to feel the sea again, to try his luck along the coast, where the turbulent and isolated world of the land met the timeless and universal world of the ocean; and he knew just where he would go.

17

Buckley marched straight to the south past Paraparap and tumbled down to the beach at Kuarka Dorla, just south of Godocut, on the second day. By that evening he had reached his destination, a place he now knew to be called Mangowak; the one that he had stumbled on so long ago to save his life. Here there was the creek and beautiful little lagoon behind the sandbar, the long expanses of lonely beach stretching away on both sides of the cliffs forming the point. The waterhole on the hillside and even the wild raspberries or neram that once turned the tide against his thirst and starvation were still there.

It was now early summer, and the following day he built a sturdy mia-mia on the bank of the lagoon and began to settle himself in for a season of carefree living. He had never really explored this country before and there was plenty to do. The mountains behind him rose away to the southwest and there was always time for exploring the beaches on a beautiful coast such as this one. The warm days soon rolled by as he fell into a routine of fishing and gathering plants, and gradually made himself at home.

But the more routine took care of itself the more time he had to contemplate his loneliness. He wondered if his best years were already behind him. He could hardly look forward to things becoming better. So often he would be struck by memories of his tribal family and become sad and tearful when he let his feelings develop. He swore he would never look back, but at times the lonely isolation would begin to close over him like an impenetrable fog.

He would often look out to sea, hoping to catch sight of a vessel passing, but always without luck. There was little traffic around the coast in those days, especially through the Strait, and the Sydney-bound ships kept well off land. The cheeriest sights he ever saw out to sea were the wallowing schools of Barbarka the dolphin and Gandu the whale. The very hopelessness of rescue stopped it becoming an obsession. Much of the time he was quite content; certainly so when the weather was favourable and food easily come by. The one great lack, as always, was a woman, but now he was a little older and a little less desperate. His furtive sex life in the years with the Kumbada had at least taken the frantic edge off his desire. He was able to balance it against the trouble of seeking satisfaction by contact with the tribes, still feeling that greater unhappiness and real danger would come of further time with them.

During this peaceful summer by the sparkling ocean perhaps he was as free and happy as a lonely man could be. He was still young and, not threatened now with starvation, maintained his hope that something would turn up eventually.

The winter came again, bringing cold winds and heavy rain. He began to find his old friend neram and other foods scarcer, and was indeed becoming a little restless. He smiled to himself that he must have become like his old friends in their habits, and decided to shift camp at least for a while, moving about twenty miles up the coast. To go down further south would take him to the less familiar and more inhospitable country around his old haunt under the mountain. The wind and rain would be worse. Moving up the coast had several advantages. The country was familiar and food plentiful — there being a great abundance of roots, especially the sweet radish-like mirrnyong. The position also gave him a good view of the Heads at the entrance to Port Phillip. He had long known of the departure of the Sullivan's Bay settlement, but at least if any other ships did put in to the bay he stood a good chance of spotting them.

He chose a place on the south bank of the Karaaf, the stream that had been swollen and nearly drowned him the day he found Murrangurk's spear not far from where he was found by the Norngnor. It flowed fresh at low tide and there was a well on the other side, so water would be no problem. The but he erected was tucked into the base of a rise in the ground, with the door facing out over an expanse of sand, across the stream and along the coast to the Heads. This position gave him the best protection from the weather, especially the terrible storms that sometimes raged along the coast from the south–west. As for meeting the tribes again, it was still a relatively quiet area, out of the way compared with the much-frequented shores around the bay itself. The position of his but also gave him a view over the plain to the Barrabools so he could watch for anyone's approach.

For some time after he first arrived the days were taken up digging mirrnyong, improving his but and fishing in the stream with a crude tackle. The latter was time-consuming and often left him disappointed and hungry. He would watch the movements of the fish and, one morning as the tide was running in, he was thrilled to see a huge shoal of bream come into the mouth of the stream and make their way some distance upstream into a swampy area behind the large dune running between the beach and the inland. When the tide receded they swam back out to the sea.

This set Buckley thinking hard. If there was any way he could trap these fish his food problems would be solved. He worked the idea over in his mind the rest of that day and into the night. The next morning he was ready to try his solution. He selected a point on the stream a little way back from the beach where the movement of the tide was less than two feet in depth. He prepared a dozen or so large bundles of sticks and reeds, binding them together with grass thongs. At low tide these were placed in a row across the entire breadth of the stream, each one bulky enough to just protrude above the surface of the water. Long pointed stakes held them in place, pounded down into the sand with a rock.

On the next tide the fish came through, swimming over the weir and meeting it on their return, even though it was still submerged. But instead of swimming over it they were confused by the barrier and turned back upstream, meeting other fish and swimming down again. Many of them repeated this several times, and by then the weir was above water. Buckley patrolled along it to make sure none escaped over the top. Thus, in time, he trapped thousands of fish. Many of the bream, an excellent eating fish, were over three pounds in weight; and he feasted well, the pangs of hunger again becoming a memory. Within days he had far more fish than he could eat, and he felt compelled to remove a section of the weir in order to release the fish. This again put him in jeopardy of running short. Sometimes he put the weir back but the fish didn't come. After several weeks he realised that their movements were correlated to the phases of the moon, and he began to observe them and adjust the weir accordingly. When the moon was full the fish would come in great shoals on the high tide, especially with a fresh south-westerly blowing up the estuary. After some months of experimentation he evolved a system of fishing that gave him a continuous supply. In between catches he dried the surplus by hanging the fish in trees or spreading them out on the roof of his hut, bringing them in when it looked like rain. This proved an effective method of preservation.

In time he was able to add sea-bird eggs, Tooiyung

or crayfish, including Tarluk-purn or fresh-water crays, Kooderoo or mutton-fish and other shellfish to his diet. With food supplies more or less reliable he was able to devote time to improving his hut, making the most comfortable house in all his time in the wild. He cut turf from the dunes to cover the roof so as to make it rainproof. The walls he built up by stacking wads of turf on top of each other; and in the same fashion he built a chimney, ending up with a structure not unlike some he had seen in remote corners of his own native Cheshire. This was a task he most relished. As an old building man he relived some old times on this job, and chuckled to himself that he wasn't working for a boss either. These were happy days again and better than ever. Another summer came and went and so he was settled, quite resigned to living out his days in this lost world. The predictable feel of the sea gave him a stable environment, and he had more visits from Barharka and Gandu. The permanent presence of the Heads remained the fixed point on which all remote possibilities of rescue were contentedly fixed.

A long time passed. Once again his heart began to fill with the breathless longing that had once driven him across the world; yet he could not say what for. He began to toy with the idea of seeking out the remnants of the Kumbada, but was reluctant to leave or otherwise endanger his hard-won comforts.

One day the problem was solved for him. He was busy with his fish-drying when he heard a voice saying, 'Amadiater.' Knowing he must have been seen he slipped into his hut, grabbed his spears and leonile, and ran to the nearest point of concealment in the scrub. But he soon saw two men approach, slightly relieved also to see two women and several children with them. He thought they looked familiar and when they called out 'Murrangurk' he knew at once they were Kumbada. He came forward to meet them and a joyous reunion ensued, the women crying with joy to see him. After several seasons had passed without word of him they had assumed him long dead. One of the men, named Terragubel (Standing Up), handed him a Ko-im leg and some roots and gurring from his bag. Buckley motioned them to his hut, where he presented them with a selection of his Tu-at, and proceeded to explain his system of trapping them. They were quite overjoyed at his survival and these remarkable achievements, singing and dancing and capering about in a wild burst of fun. Terragubel said he deserved four wives.

Shortly the two men endeavoured to get the women and children to leave so they could party with Buckley by themselves. They forcefully refused to be excluded, to Buckley's pleasure, and so all made camp with him for several days of fishing.

Next they went on an excursion up the coast to the Maamart around the lagoon at the mouth of the Barwin, passing by the same big old tree Buckley had once collapsed under that fateful afternoon of his rescue by the Norngnor people. They camped by a well of good water and gathered various roots and gurring, returning to the Karaaf at the next full moon. Their success with the fish was so great that Terragubel went to fetch the rest of the band, their old friends the Ko-im, whom they had since joined. They came bringing heaps of Ko-im, and dug mirrnyong, or ovens, on top of the dune behind Buckley's hut. Great feasts were had, as they stayed on for some time.

Buckley soon forgot his fear of trouble at being among his friends again. The presence of the women aroused him, reminding him with gale force how long it was since he had been with a woman. He knew that if he stayed it was only a matter of time before he would find pleasure with these rebellious and independently minded women. His wish was soon fulfilled for he was now a man who had, after a long time, unintentionally impressed his people with his ability. They had no trouble, after some time living on fish, in persuading him to accompany them on a hunting excursion.

They marched to the Iramoo country around the shores of Jillong and made camp, hunting Ko-im and Norngnor with great success. Norngnor was caught by sending a child down the burrow, feet first. On feeling the animal with his toes the child would yell and bang on the roof of the nest. The adults listened above with their ears to the ground. Having found the spot the child was called out and they dug down, easily removing and clubbing the sleepy creatures, who were then gutted and roasted in their skins like Karbor. Although excellent to eat it was hard work getting them out. Only one was usually in each burrow, so digging for them was not often attempted unless from necessity or a particular longing for their taste.

Many months passed in peace at this camp. Buckley was enjoying the varied diet and the company of the people. But eventually the old troubles returned. A large group of strangers came, far outnumbering the Ko-im. They were Pootnaroos, who seemed to be in the habit of making excursions to the Wothowurong country, and a group of Woiwurong unfamiliar to Buckley. They camped nearby, peaceably for a while, but in the end the Pootnaroos surrounded the Ko-im and one of them speared a young man in jealousy over a girl. Being the weaker party nothing could be done but to break camp and move on, after giving the young man a tree burial. They moved to Nellemgobeet on a plain half-way between the Barwin and Yalloak where good water-holes were plentiful.

The father of the young man gathered a large force of fighters who ochred themselves and prepared for battle. They set off after the Pootnaroos but soon returned, reporting that their foes had fled back to their home territory. Some of them went to the tree and brought the lower part of the young man's body, which they roasted and ate, the mother taking the dried knee-caps for an amulet in affectionate remembrance of her son. As usual a portion was offered to Buckley, and he was again obliged to forcefully refuse, and try to explain his objection and reassure them he meant no disrespect.

The repetition of these old scenes repelled Buckley and he again feared for himself. He slipped away before dawn on the following day and returned to his beloved hut at the Karaaf, eager to resume his old routine.

This recent experience left him shaken for some time. He would never entirely accept such bloodshed even though he had come at least to an understanding of the cannibalism. He remained distressed, despite his return to his comforts, and despaired once again of ever knowing the companionship of his own loved ones around him.

18

Buckley lived in a state of great wariness. Now that the tribes knew where he was he fully expected a party of them to look him up. But after some time no-one came, and his tension and despair subsided under the demands of survival. He thought it strange they didn't come and wondered if they had developed some sense of understanding of his need for privacy. This could only be because they had always regarded him as being a little odd anyway, considering who he was. Privacy was not a great value among them, they being so in need of each other for survival and comfort, and finding intimacy so natural except with those proscribed by tribal law. Little did he suspect that the absence of his friends was simply due to their patience as they made arrangements to give him the things he wanted, for they understood him better than he thought.

One fine spring day they came, slipping down to his beach retreat with big grins in expectation of their reunion.

Buckley was stretched out on the sand in front of his hut, warming himself in the sun. He jumped up, startled, but relaxed and smiled when he saw who it was. His smile broadened into a joyous cry of astonishment when he saw who was among them. Coming behind with the children were Burmbo Merio and Mirri Mallo, now about ten and nine years old. He ran forward and clutched them to him, lifting them up all laughing, with one in each of his huge arms.

But even as he yelled with delight he stopped with the chilling realisation that something was wrong. Burmbo Merio was peculiar in his movements, and he held him out to look. He was blind; struck blind many months ago by an unknown malady. Mung — bad magic — some thought. A wirrarap could blind someone at a distance by burning the cones of the she-oak in a magic fire. Perhaps Torraneuk's enemies had still pursued their revenge. Buckley's joy was swamped with sorrow as he stroked the upturned and questioning little face. He took the children by the hand and led them all to his hut, sitting with them at the entrance. Mirri Mallo introduced him to their new friend and constant companion, a sleek young bitch with all the colours of the forest floor in her coat, that they called Yerao-bo (Joyful Bandicoot). She pranced all around them, enthusiastically licking at Buckley's hand and finally rolling down next to Burmbo Merio. The Ko-im gathered around and everyone talked loudly at once, Buckley asking for news of people and events and all the latest gossip.

Eventually Terragubel called for silence. When all fell quiet he announced to the astonished Buckley that it was now time for him to take a wife, and a young woman of about twenty years of age was ushered forward from the crowd.

She stood facing Buckley, looking at him and the others with a jaunty and somewhat defiant expression. She had been married before, her first husband being killed in a fight. He found her good-looking and, although of mild temperament, she was obviously self-assured and fearless in her dealings with men. Her name was Boorang, meaning 'Mist-in-the-Valley'. He was astounded. Suddenly, at last, he would have his own wife. No more furtive contacts; no more fear of revenge. Here was the companion he had longed for all the years. He smiled at her and gestured his friendliness with hands outstretched. She returned his look but would soon make it plain that this arrangement was strictly one of her brothers' and not her own choosing.

There was no wedding ceremony, no elaborate feasts or gifts or rings; no debts. Having presented her, Terragubel's family took Mirri Mallo — Burmbo Merio went with the bachelors — and they all withdrew, leaving Buckley with Boorang and some gifts of food, making their camp some distance apart. After a meal everyone settled down for the night.

Buckley pulled Boorang to him and caressed her body. She passively complied with his advances; lying back she let him move over her, hardly stirring as he made love to her. And so it was with their time together. She never resisted, but neither would she ever respond or take an initiative to give either herself or Buckley any pleasure.

After many days of this he understood that she was only complying with the situation because she had been forced into it by circumstances beyond her control. It even made him more fond of her. He wanted to please her. As a provider she could not deny his skill in acquiring good food for her. As a lover he tried his best, seeking to use all his experience and imagination to give her the tenderest pleasures. But it was to no avail, and she remained resolute in her disinterested passivity. Neither could he interest her in helping to mother the children. Even Burmbo Merio in his helplessness received little comfort from her.

They remained by the Karaaf together for some months. In time Buckley ceased all efforts to win her affections. Having spent too many years alone and frustrated he took the path of self-interest and used her body when he felt the need. He knew she resented this, and sometimes he wouldn't touch her for many days until his desire annulled his conscience, and his growing resentment, and he would reach out for her in the night. He would attempt to appease his conscience by giving her the best food out of respect for the value placed on fair exchange by the kulin. As time passed his resentment faded, along with any other feelings, except perhaps a little pity. He would be glad when she left.

Finally, the situation was resolved by the arrival of some men who knew her. One evening, when the other men were away hunting, they took her with a show of force. She, however, went willingly.

The next day Buckley went to see Terragubel on the hunt. With feelings of relief that it was over he told him of her departure. He had wanted to talk to someone, but soon realised he should have known better as Terragubel and the others quickly swore murderous vengeance on Boorang and her friends. Buckley instantly refused to be involved in any troubles, and attempted to play down the event. Cynically appealing to their feeling that she was only a worthless woman, he shrugged it off. This at least prevented any immediate and hot-headed action and they all continued to hunt together.

On their return Buckley was nervous. He dreaded both the possibility of seeing her and the probability of a bloody fight which could be a danger to himself. When they arrived at the camp it was a shocking anti-climax. Boorang had already been speared dead by a man who was jealous of her. But the matter did not end there. After several arguments a fight ensued which at least only resulted in broken heads. Buckley stayed out of the fight but on the defensive, threatening dire consequences to any attacker. As usual their respect saved him from possible injury. In the end the whole affair was settled amicably enough. After a grudging reconciliation, encouraged by Buckley's refusal to admit any insult to his honour, a great corroboree was held, releasing the remaining energy the fight had accumulated. Far from her people, the unmourned Boorang became a wistful memory after Buckley had seen to her proper burial in a mound grave.

The next day the campsites around Buckley's but were quiet as the people resumed their concentration on hunting and gathering. Small parties moved about laughing together, the events of the previous days forgotten. Buckley felt quite alone except for the soothing presence of the children. He could not forget his situation so easily, and began to feel melancholy. He tried to busy himself with his fish but his mind would not rest. He found himself resenting the invading presence of the tribes into 'his' camp, even though he knew that it was in their country and that they had every right to be there. In any case, there was no question that he could possibly offend his friends by asking them to leave. Terragubel and the Ko-im had meant well by bringing him Boorang, and he could not deny his deep gratitude to them for reuniting him with Burmbo Merio and Mirri Mallo. There was only one solution and that was to leave, at least for a while, and go well away from the Karaaf. He put the proposal in guarded terms to Terragubel, who agreed at once. With Terragubel's and another family, Buckley and the children left.

The small party made their way up the open Karaaf valley running behind their camp to the west, passed Paraparap and met the Barwin. They marched for some days, reaching Bearrock on the far reaches of the Barwin valley. Here there was a chain of fresh waterholes full of excellent Boonea, with roots abundant nearby. They made camp and settled in for a long stay.

Buckley now put himself into the role of being a father. Each day his energies were directed towards the feeding and general well-being of his family. Burmbo Merio and Mirri Mallo would come with him on many hunting and fishing excursions. Despite Burmbo Merio's blindness the children were little or no trouble. He had long been aware of the extraordinary nature of these tribal children. There were no whimpering or nervy little creatures among them. They were self-reliant, and used to looking for help from a wide range of kin when they needed it.

The kulin, although practising a practical infanticide in cases where children were deformed or when they just had too many, or perhaps when one arrived while its predecessor was still at the breast, were extremely kind and indulgent towards their beloved children. He had even seen them, when a child died, leave the body in a hollow tree until it dried and then carry it about with them for some time; such was the strength of their affection.

In the close living conditions of tribal life the children were astute observers of adult behaviour. Without formal teaching they learnt the ways of their people by direct contact with the facts and events of life. By the age of five they knew about copulation, birth and death, hunting and gathering, from personal observation. They instinctively sought out their own food as soon as they began to crawl. By the time they could walk they could almost feed themselves by digging roots and grubs. They began to help in the tasks around the camp such as gathering firewood. But there were no long arduous hours of work as among peasant farmers or industrial city folk. They were taught to swim as infants and, like jolly young Barbarka, romped naked for days in the rivers and lakes. They also shared fully in the terrible experiences of fear and danger when their people were threatened by attack or natural disaster; and Burmbo Merio and Mirri Mallo had been through the worst of such experiences.

Yerao-bo was a constant delight and source of good cheer with her antics. She was Kneerekeyan — a dancer. She would leap in the air and pirouette around, then race about them in circles, bounding in a zig-zag back and forth with the sheer joy of going for a walk. These displays of unlimited enthusiasm were made in constant interplay first with the romping of the children, and then with Buckley. Sometimes he would be brooding about the tragic Boorang, and Yeraobo would leap all over him, licking his hands and face with affection, and then would bound off with a dancing twist, and stop and look back at him as if to urge him to join her in some fun in the bush.

Garl the dog was probably the most important animal in the lives of the kulin. They were very fond of their pets, and a good hunter was well-rewarded. But wild dogs were hunted and eaten and considered a great luxury. Once Buckley was offered a choice leg and refused it, to their perplexity and amusement. They laughed uproariously as he traded it for a Ko-im leg; taking the worst of such a bargain again demonstrating the foolishness that death had brought upon him. Sometimes, in the late spring, known lairs were raided and pups taken. Some were always left to continue breeding, but the others were eaten or kept and trained as hunters. They were also good watchdogs.

Together Mirri Mallo and Yerao-bo were constant guides and comforts to Burmbo Merio. Mirri Mallo showed him places where there were roots and berries, making little digging sticks and baskets for him, so that he could feel out some of his own food. Buckley furnished the two of them with tackle made of bone and sinew, and they would creep together, up to the waterholes and, with the greatest of skill, catch themselves Boonea. Sometimes they would all go on hunting parties with the other men and look for Wollert or Karwer and other easier prey. Burmbo Merio and Mirri Mallo could not kill but they were willing carriers when it was time to return to camp.

Summer came again, and life grew sweet and content for Buckley. The cicadas sang back and forth to each other, sometimes with a deafening ecstasy, sometimes in harmonious groups high in the trees against the evening sky. He developed a great love for his adopted family. Everything he did now had a purpose far beyond any he had experienced before. As time passed he could see the children grow and learn under his care and guidance. He could hardly believe his good fortune yet again. To have survived so much and yet find such a complete existence as this was indeed miraculous. He came to love each day with complete abandon. He was exhilarated by the very presence of his young wards. Each day they plunged off into they knew not where. He seemed to find their energy and delight radiating into his own being; the feel of their lithe and strong bodies as they wallowed together in the pools and cuddled around the campfire at night made him move like a young Ko-im bounding through the bush.

If ever a man could be happy, Buckley knew it was at a time like this. The only shadow to fall across such a land of light could be the knowledge that it, like all else, would not last. To worry about when it was going to end, and how, was the only way it could be destroyed. He had suffered so many violent disruptions to his life that he was not sure if he was becoming immune to them or reaching the point where he couldn't bear one more disaster. He would have to be practical with his feelings now, enjoying this time thoroughly while it lasted. At least with the children and Terragubel and the others around him he felt more free of worry. Again his thoughts turned to the mysteries of the beautiful forest garden they roamed.

On a hot afternoon when Terragubel and the others had gone off to the Barwin laughing about some hunting story, Buckley lounged in the grass on the bank of a large water-hole. Mirri Mallo and Burmbo Merio were asleep under a nearby tree; Yerao-bo stretched out under a hush. The frogs and insects whirred lazily. All was slow and still except for an occasional draught of warm air up the valley. He loved these days, so soft and quiet they aroused him with their very tenderness. Kooring-kooring gave an occasional sleepy chuckle, and Buckley wondered where Koronn and

Karrie Ael could be as he himself hovered on the edge of consciousness. He felt like dreaming, and thought with pleasure of the things that could happen in a dream and how strangely they sometimes seemed to run parallel to and get mixed up with daily life.

Suddenly he started up, sure he had heard the distinct sound of a baby crying in the distance. He listened intently until he heard it again, but then was unsure of how far away it was. A breeze stirred a tree nearby, causing a branch to creak. Then he saw a pair of Gang-gang cockatoos flying high along the valley, unmistakable by the male's bright red head glowing like a coal, their curious lurching flight, and the almost questioning tone of their long rasping screech. He watched them out of sight. Perhaps his ears were playing tricks, perhaps not. It was said that spirits awaited rebirth in certain trees at certain places. Might be something, all right. Everything Torraneuk had seen or heard or felt he had regarded as only the superficial manifestation of an invisible and greater world; a world perhaps accessible by other means or revealing its meaning in ways that depended very much on how one looked at things.

In the bush it was easier for new ways to develop. In that stillness when his senses were straining to grasp at the strangeness of his adopted country, he wondered if the creaking of a branch and the distant cry of a bird, or the gurgling of a stream and the croaking of a frog might not be two tones his ears distinguished from a single voice belonging to some being existing in another place, another time. If the world was alive all things in it could be connected. Perhaps nothing happened by chance. Everything might be fraught with meaning and thus with great danger if one could not, as once his own ancestors had done, read the signs in the movements and calls of birds and other things. This was a terrifying prospect. He grew uneasy and kept looking distractedly about him. He could not regain his previous mood. Perhaps it was instinctual to keep watch all the time, especially when Kaan might be lurking.

The afternoon shadows had begun to stretch long across the water. He woke the children, and they returned to camp and silently commenced preparing an evening meal.

Sometime later, when the last rays of the sun were shrinking behind the hills under the western sky, his fears were crystallised by the sudden appearance of Barroworn. Buckley had to consider it a real possibility that this visit was no accident. Such an appearance of one's totem could be a warning of danger. Barroworn sat silently on the branch of a nearby tree, looking imperturbably in their direction for a little while, then flying away making the mournful cry he sometimes did. Buckley's peace of mind would not return now.

Terragubel's wife had gone to a nearby waterhole to fetch a tarnuk of water for the morning. As she bent down to the water she heard the bushes rustling, a short distance away, and then the sound of human footsteps. She ran and told Terragubel, and they both roused Buckley from his bed and warned them all they might have to run for their lives. The children were terrified and Buckley was ready to go anyway. Everyone quickly withdrew from the camp and hid in the bush. Terragubel and his friend went to reconnoitre, and returned before long with the news that they had seen a camp fire surrounded by several men who spoke in the manner of the Galgal-bulluk. The danger was very great.

Buckley ran back to the camp and placed some coals in a tarnuk, covering them with turf and throwing in a few roots and Boonea. He told Terragubel to meet him the following day on top of the hill called Banor across the mountains on the coast. With Burmbo Merio, Mirri Mallo, and Yerao-bo he struck out into the gloom, making for the distant ridge high above them, beyond which lay the sea.

19

The night sky was clear, the milky way bright and dense like a silver cloud. With his weapons in one hand, the tarnuk under his arm, Burmbo Merio on the other hand, and he in turn holding on to Mirri Mallo, the three of them made their way laboriously up one of the ridges between two creeks that fed into the Barwin far below. Yerao-bo scouted up ahead. Despite the dense forest the light was strong enough to allow them slow progress with frequent rests.

The kulin generally avoided night travel. Vulnerability to attack was aggravated by fears of various spirits and monsters. Buckley was sceptical about most of these, but after his encounters with the bunyip he could not disregard them entirely. The main thing he was wary of on this epic journey was the ngarangs. They were greatly feared and said to have heads like men, with long flowing hair and beards. They lived in large dwellings in the roots of old gum trees, going in and out by an invisible entrance. Roaming about at night they were reputed to snatch straying kulin with their long, hairy arms, and drag them down to their tree-root homes to devour.

He strained his ears to hear the reassuring sound of Yeraobo steadily forging her way ahead over the pounding of his ears and the panting of all three of them. Each time they rested and all fell quiet as Yerao-bo sat and waited for them, the mere falling of a leaf or the distant cry of Wollert or Yundool, or the delicate flutter of Balayang passing would make them nervously push on. By the middle of the night they had crossed the top main ridge of the mountains in the region of Boordek. There was a bright sky above and everywhere the dark forest rolled away below them as they began the descent to the sea. Tired and sore, they reached Banor soon after dawn.

From this vantage point Buckley anxiously surveyed the surrounding country. Early in the morning he saw people approaching. In case they had been tracked by the Galgal-bulluk he took the children and concealed himself, weapons at the ready. To their relief Terragubel and his party soon came panting to the top of the hill. They also had managed to avoid the Galgal-bulluk and to march through the night without incident. They began to consult each other as to their next move.

They were a small party and always vulnerable to a disastrous attack, or had to flee whenever other groups were encountered. Terragubel and the others argued that they should seek out the rest of the Ko-im by marching inland to the north, towards Moodewarri and the Iramoo. Buckley realised that this was a crucial decision but could not know just how important. He wished a sign would appear to give him guidance, but there was nothing to help him and no time for complex calculations. He was free to do as he pleased, and again the seductiveness of the beautiful coast in summer called strongly to him. He wanted to return to the beach, and knew that whatever he did now he would inevitably be drawn back to his beloved home on the Karaaf.

He therefore bade farewell to Terragubel and his party and reluctantly let them go, watching until they were out of sight in the dense forest below. Descending towards the sea he tried to cheer the children with talk of the good things they could do along the coast and how they would be getting fish again at his weir. With their usual spontaneity they soon fell in with the idea, and in the evening they all camped happily by a little stream at a place called Kirkedullim, under the hills and just in from the beach. The next day they reached Buckley's old place at Mangowak. The warm weather continued, and they stayed for some time in a relaxed manner, living on shellfish and a sort of wild grape from a vine that trailed over the sand-dunes.*

When the weather began to grow cooler they moved on and, after several days' march along the beach, reached the Karaaf. Buckley grew more and more anxious as he approached the stream. At first he was worried that some tribe, especially strangers, might be camped there, but these fears dissipated as they walked quickly over the last mile. The area looked quite deserted and he couldn't see any sign of smoke from camp fires. He was also worried that his but might have been damaged or even destroyed by hostile kulin or a bad storm. His heart was in his mouth as they finally rounded the corner where the big coastal dune came to a halt at the Karaaf; and, to his immense relief, there was his hut, outwardly still in perfect condition. He yelped for joy and ran, still anxious, to the entrance, wondering what the inside would reveal. All his hopes were fulfilled. It was just as he had left it many months before. There wasn't even a sign that anyone had been in it.

He sank to the floor with relief and joy. This was home and he inwardly poured out gratitude to the elements, to the spirits and to the kulin for respecting it so much. Mirri Mallo and Burmbo Merio entered cautiously and looked questioningly at Buckley. When they felt his happiness everyone laughed and danced, Yerao-bo leaping all around inside and out.

The next day he rebuilt his weir and, after several days of living on a few roots, the favourable tide came. Soon they had plenty of bream and mirrnyong and settled down to a most comfortable existence. But now Buckley

* *Cissus hypoglauca*, native grape.

found that his ideas of independence did not mix well with the responsibilities of rearing the children. There was love between them all, but they were hopelessly exposed to attack. He couldn't hope to protect them alone. If anything happened to him by accident they would be doomed. He began to worry but despaired of a solution. Even to go looking for the Ko-im would be fraught with great danger. He went through periods when he dreaded the approach of every night. A surprise attack after dark was not impossible, and he would find himself lying awake watching the pale rectangle of light that was his doorway, his ears straining for the slightest sound that may have betrayed the presence of a prying scout from an unfriendly band. Each morning he would go out alone at first light and survey the immediate area to make sure it was clear.

On one of these excursions he travelled back up the creek beyond the marshes to the top of the first hill that rose gently away from the coast. No-one was around for miles, he was sure of that. On his return he stumbled across the carcass of Bunjil. He rolled it over with his foot. The belly was full of huge white maggots. 'Too bad,' he thought. It could happen to himself any time, he knew. Even in the full blossom of life, decay and death were just around the corner. The world was a joyous thing with maggots at the centre, Wornbalano Beeaar had once told him. He returned to the camp but spent most of the day apart from Burmbo Merio and Mirri Mallo, who played in the stream around the weir.

Sometimes he dreamt that they were being chased along the beach by enemies, with no place to go except the water; but Barbarka and Gandu would not wait for them. Or that he was returning from a hunting excursion but could not approach his hut due to an unaccountable dread. Or that they were all happily feasting around the camp fire but the food was full of maggots. Torraneuk told him that Waang would eat them, but he thought there were too many.

The next day Buckley sat in gloom. Everything had seemed so good: the hut, the food, the children, even the dog. He should have been happy, but these demons seemed to be ever creeping in and he was at a loss to understand, let alone fight them.

The children returned from a walk. Mirri Mallo had been out gathering food, guiding Burmbo Merio along as usual. She had her own little beenak and sat before him to show what she had. She pulled out some roots and grubs and a few little skinks and, proudly, one blue-tongued lizard. Buckley was so cheered by her. Hoping for some good news he asked her if she still talked to the moiyan trees. She said sometimes but not for a while. He asked her why, and she said that last time she had talked to Turnung, she had told her all the trees were frightened. She had not been to any good moiyan trees since then.

Finally a man came with his family. He was Ko-im, but had left after a quarrel over some business he would not tell Buckley. His presence was certainly welcome. His three children were added company and protection, especially for Burmbo-Merio. The five of them were now an independent little band of their own. The man and his wife and Buckley shared the hunting and gathering, enjoying a greater variety of meat. Their very presence eased Buckley's mind. They helped watch the approaches to the camp and he began to sleep better. But his unease would not entirely go.

A few days later a young man came. He appeared without warning from the hinterland, alone and desperate. It was soon apparent that he was seriously ill, but they could not get any sense out of him as to where he was from or what was wrong with him. Buckley's friend suspected mung, but neither of them was in a position to know what could be done. Buckley had always been inclined to feel sorry for any of the kulin who were suffering either through ill-health, or through injury received in battle, even when they had probably got their just deserts. As an outsider, their prejudices and jealousies meant little to him and they each retained an aura of innocence in their respective plights. This was to prove a disastrous mistake in the case of this young man. Buckley took him to his own hut, which had now become the bachelor camp, and made a sick-bed for him. He tried to comfort him but, after two days, he and Burmbo Merio awoke one morning to find he had died in the night.

They cremated him straight away, but the whole experience had been very unnerving and Buckley suggested that they go away hunting for a time. This they did, but their fate dogged them. Near Paraparap they came upon a small group of Collenbitchik, most of them of the young man's family. They were desperately searching for him and feared the worst. Accosting Buckley's group suddenly, they questioned them aggressively. Unaware of the old trouble with the Collenbitchik, before long the other man had told the story. Within minutes they had reached a terrible frenzy, screaming abuse at Buckley and his friends, blaming them for the death.

They were outnumbered three to one in fighting men. To attack first or try to run with the children would have provoked a fatal assault. He could only stand his ground and hope they would eventually calm down. But it was no use. Whether by some twisted reasoning — perhaps they remembered Torraneuk his father — or by sheer cowardly revenge picking the weakest target, they advanced on Burmbo Merio. Buckley and his friend counter-attacked with their leoniles in a desperate attempt to show they would fight to the death. He grabbed Burmbo Merio by the arm as the boy groped frantically for safety in his terrible darkness. Before he could push the boy behind him Buckley was beaten savagely back by four men who cursed Burmbo Merio merely for having been in the same but as the dead youth, and accused him of being the agent of his death. Burmbo Merio screamed and cried his innocence. A heavy kudgerim knocked him senseless, and two spears pierced right through his little body. Death was instantaneous. Buckley roared with rage. He and his ally were held back against a large tree with spears at their throats. His friend's wife had fled with her children and Mirri Mallo, who dragged along the wriggling, squealing Yerao-bo to save her from certain death and devourment.

Buckley watched in dazed horror as the Collenbitchik made a fire and began to roast Burmbo Merio in preparation for their ritual. Before it commenced the two defeated men were released and chased off with a warning of death if they appeared again. Buckley's stunned mind could hardly think. The shock of Burmbo Merio's brutal death blanketed his need to find Mirri Mallo, to run, to seek revenge, to thank God that he had survived death once again.

They ran in the direction the others had taken, towards his old haunt at Moodewarri. It was less than five miles away and they expected some friendly Wothowurong to be there. Soon they found the woman and four children. They were hiding pathetically up a big moiyan tree and crying bitterly at the terrible murder they had witnessed. It occurred to Buckley that there must be friends close by, as that could be the only reason their lives were spared. Surely they too would have been slain, unless the enemy had feared certain revenge.

Shortly they reached Moodewarri and found there, to their relief, the Woorer-woorer (sky people), a band friendly to the Ko-im. Among them was a man called Waraduk (Stormy Wind), to whom Mirri Mallo had been promised in her infancy. When they heard the news they all swore vengeance and prepared themselves for a fight. This was one war party Buckley wanted to join. However, he was adamantly refused permission. They all insisted he was above such matters due to his resurrected status. A small party of their best fighters left on the run, leaving Buckley to his thoughts. He felt half cowardly, not taking effective action even in revenge, and became very melancholy. If only there was some way to act, to undo or somehow correct what had been done.

After two days the revenge party returned; and he was glad he hadn't gone, as they had simply killed two children of the Collenbitchik. By this time he was filled with remorse. He cursed himself for the mistakes he had made in protecting Burmbo Merio and Mirri Mallo. Instead of following his own urges he should have gone with the larger group for protection; he should have done it many months ago when he and Terragubel had parted ways on the misty top of Banor. His strange reluctance to leave the seacoast and accept the perils of the inland had been his undoing. His passion for personal liberty had been at a terrible cost to love and life. But then who could know whether he might not have been waylaid and the same thing happened anyway.

These bitter thoughts were soon tempered by more immediate problems. Other groups began to arrive and settle around the lake. Soon there were over two hundred people, and most of them were strangers to him. There was nothing surer than the advent of more fights, with great danger to himself and Mirri Mallo. Paradoxically, the wiser thing now was certainly to leave for a more remote refuge. In spite of all that had happened, the only place to which he could contemplate returning was his home on the Karaaf. This time he made sure he would at least keep the protection of a small group, with some good fighters around him. He persuaded Waraduk and his present wife of some years, and two other families, to accompany him and Mirri Mallo to the coast. Their party consisted of five men, three women, and seven children.

Within a few days they had reached Buckley's but and settled in with the usual diet of fish and roots, supplemented by the occasional hunting foray into the bush.

Buckley had things much as he wanted them again, but he remained deeply troubled. His remorse over the death of Burmbo Merio continued to gnaw at him. He became sick at heart over his growing realisation that he could never succeed at being a father to these children; that the task was too great for him; that he was going to fail with Mirri Mallo as well. Perhaps it was age; perhaps if he had been a bit younger; perhaps. In his mind, the gulf between himself and his tribal friends yawned greater than ever. He could see that it was no use to think he was going to keep Mirri Mallo, although he loved her and wanted her with a desperate longing. She was the only person left in the world he could feel to be his. In her was the only remaining link with his long-lost youth when he had run into the vast wilderness like a wild, young Garl and met and found succour with her father and mother. But he could not hope to raise her and teach her in the manner of her people. He could not deceive himself that there was any good in her growing up bearing the stamp of a man who was a ghost.

Within a short time she would be approaching a marriageable age. He was becoming greyer all the time; he could not contemplate her for himself, so young and so like a daughter to him. In any case, there was nothing surer than that he would have to confront the possibility of deadly fights over her possession. A large group could easily appear from a distant tribe like the Bunerong and kill Buckley and his friends and carry her off. Self-sacrifice was the rule of parenthood among the warm-blooded animals of the bush. Even if, like Karwer, it did not extend to a will to defend the nest to death, it was always done for the young for the future of the race. Buckley could not find it in himself to face this responsibility for Mirri Mallo. He began to drive himself to despair.

At length, cursing his own lack of courage, the bitter memories of all his dead and lost friends bearing down on him, he made up his mind to leave.

He confronted Waraduk, who was shocked and distressed. With adamant support from his wife he urged Buckley to stay, and was reluctant to take charge of the unknowing Mirri Mallo. He had enough to do looking after the family he had, and felt Buckley should take the responsibility. He was her uncle, after all.

Buckley, having made his decision, was feeling hard and merciless, determined to have his way no matter how bad the consequences. He insisted to Waraduk, and the latter had little choice but to relent. Buckley went and picked up Mirri Mallo, who now realised that something bad was afoot. Stroking her hair he told her he had to go, and put her down and said goodbye. He turned away before he choked, and gathered his weapons and fire-sticks. He walked off along the beach watched by two watery brown eyes and a heart that longed for the last of her family going away. Yerao-bo began to follow Buckley, but stopped and looked back at Mirri Mallo when she realised her mistress wasn't coming. The two of them stood and watched him.

Waraduk and the Woorer-woorer people had broken camp and stood atop the great sand dune waiting for her.

20

Buckley's mind was torn by a terrible pain. So many conflicting desires confronted each other in the realm of his loneliness. He thought how lucky he had been when suffering was just a matter of deprivation; when he had confronted the wilderness with his simple wants, first for food and shelter, then for companionship and sex, and freedom from the terrors of the night. How simple was his grief at the loss of Torraneuk, Wombalano Beeaar, and Tro wernuwil. In all his past suffering he had been the victim before forces beyond his control. Now his misery was of his own making. Yet he could not find the wisdom or the strength to resolve these impossible contradictions.

He wandered distractedly along the beach away from the Karaaf. The weather was mild but he was unmindful of it and the possibility of a harsher climate as he moved south. He lived on a few shellfish, his appetite not keen enough to urge him to hunt.

After several days and some distance south of Mangowak, he found himself slouched on the beach of a bay he remembered from long ago.* He gazed out to sea, still in great despair. Life had never seemed more worthless. After all his struggles for it, all his luck and perseverance, his strength and courage stretched to their limits, it all seemed a waste. What value was his obstinate hope now?

The sun was out and an arc of mist hung over the

* Loutit Bay, Lorne

beach around the little bay. He dozed fitfully, his face falling on to the sand. In a dream he looked at a hill sweeping around a river valley so that the top of it appeared like a pair of giant shoulders spreading out. In the middle of them a clump of trees made a head shape. It was Burmbo Merio. He looked into Burmbo Merio's face; the infinite blackness loomed at him. He asked for a sign. Just then Bunjil soared across the face of the hill. He turned and ran towards the sea. He ran on and on but seemed to go so slowly. Kooring-kooring laughed uproariously at him as he vainly tried to reach the Karaaf.

Suddenly he woke, startled by the sound of a footfall. He leapt up, whirling around with leonile and malka held ready. Before him stood a beautiful young woman, shrinking back in fright at his club. She wore a murrakul or headband of twisted Wollert-fur, a reed necklace, a waist-fringe or kyoong made of strips of Ko-im skin, and a little round nose-bone. All she carried was a fire-stick, her kurniang, and a beenak with a few roots in it.

He let his arms drop and smiled. She nodded and smiled also. He introduced himself as Murrangurk and, wary of revealing his tribal associations, added quickly that he was lost, having come from the sea. She told him her name was Yanathan-lark, meaning 'Movement-of-Clouds'. He could not believe his ears, let alone his eyes. On asking where she was from, she explained that she had fled from the lake country where her tribe was fighting another. She had feared capture by a strong and fearful enemy.

Two fugitives lost on a distant shore. Easy to find something in common; easy to find love. Buckley, even if he was going grey, was a fit and healthy man with a good appetite. Death was not looking for him yet. In his hour of greatest despair; at the moment of realising his own limitations; when time and life seemed to be running out, he was given the best. Yanathan-lark was everything he could have wished for, the one thing above all that would completely reverse his sinking fortunes.

The day waxed warm and they sat together on the beach chatting about the things they knew in common — the places around the country, the tribes, the kinds of food they liked. She was a rather short woman; slightly stocky but rounded, all trim and taut and obviously fit, and about twenty years of age. Buckley was finding it nearly impossible to mask his desire.

In the afternoon he waded into the foam in an attempt to regain control of his feelings. The sea was blue and sparkled in the sun, the surf gentle and refreshing. He sat down in the water, letting the broken waves wash over his body, and beckoned Yanathan-lark to come in. The sea was strange to her but she was keen for fun and stepped gingerly in. Buckley urged her on. Every cell in his body had anticipated contact with her from the first moment. His very excitement seemed a barrier to making an advance, but playing in the surf was a start. After a little while, when she had become accustomed to the water, he pounded it with his open hand, showering her with great sparkling drops, and dived away laughing under a wave.

Yanathan-lark needed no prompting in this game. Two butterflies flew around each other over the water. 'Look,' she pointed, ' I am Bollam-bollam,' and threw herself over a wave and down into the water.

Buckley took the implied invitation and dived after her. The merry game soon evolved to the point of pushing and ducking. Laughing at the way touch had been established, they finally stood and embraced for a long time, the sea caressing their thighs. She breathed mischievous smiles into his ear. 'Shall I call you father?' she asked impishly. Buckley grinned and shook his head. 'Shall I call you brother?' He shook his head again. 'Then I shall call you husband.'

They walked up the beach together in silence, Buckley smiling at the sensation of her skin. Their bodies entwined, they stretched out on a grassy dune. She lay over him looking down into his eyes, and he could make out the dark outline of her rounded young face surrounded by the frizzy hair that seemed to explode out of her head. He would never forget, when at last their energy was spent, that there was a big, yellow full moon behind her, risen out of a shimmering silver ocean.

In the morning raging hunger struck them both. With good humour they set out into the bush, gathering roots and berries. In the afternoon Buckley got two Wollert, so that evening they had a little feast on the side of a dune overlooking the ocean. During the days that followed they settled into this place for a long stay. He built a comfortable mia-mia and extended his hunting excursions further into the bush. With two people gathering food they ate well and lived a good life. They got some tarnuks and made themselves quantities of a delicious drink called beal to slake their hot, salt-water thirst. This was done by soaking the flowers of various plants in water or by dissolving native honey, gurring and manna in it. The result was a variety of sweet, cool drinks.

On their walks to gather the flowers and other treats Yanathan-lark would try to teach him how to tell the character of the trees. If you looked at them in a certain way, she said, you could see that some were dancers, some happy and laughing, some sad, some angry. Buckley would laugh, but he wondered all the same, remembering what Mirri Mallo had said.

Summer came, and the warm weather and his more than adequate sex life eased every tension in his being.

Yanathan-lark was an easy woman to love. She was very playful, and sang and laughed often. It was hard to imagine her being unhappy. One day Buckley asked her what was her dreaming. She told him it was Tutbring the flame robin. She tried not to take things seriously. She was a little like Barroworn. She liked to wander around her country with a few friends, sometimes alone, and just enjoy herself. Many men had fought to possess her. Sometimes she had changed hands with bewildering rapidity, and so she had never seemed to have time to have children.

One night she pointed out the constellation Buckley knew as Pleiades, or the Jewel Box. This, she said, was the Kururuk (Seven Sisters). They came in the spring bringing the warm seasons to the earth, and left in the autumn, leaving winter across the land. They had once lived on earth but had climbed to the sky and become stars in order to escape a man and his son who had relentlessly pursued them. After many adventures he had become a star in Orion's belt, and so still followed them to this day.

Buckley loved these stories and these hours. He loved to listen to her talk and tell of her life. Her warm voice vibrated with the same soothing feelings that he absorbed from her body. They would lie together and listen to the surf. It became like music from an unknowable instrument played by a spirit far across the water; the roar of the breakers lulled by the infinitely soft breathing sound of waves draining back across the sand.

Once he speared a Koorman, the seal that abounded in the straits. They roasted it on a big spit as the sun set. This was one of the most delicious feasts. Where Karbor tasted like pork, Koorman meat was more like bacon. The feast was quite unforgettable for another reason, too. When they had gorged themselves the very unpredictable Yanathan-lark proceeded to smear the fat of the animal all over her body. Buckley was apprehensive, but his qualms melted like the fat as her body heat turned it to oil and her whole sleek figure glistened in the flickering firelight. He sat smiling with delight as she began to dance before him, her hips swaying and beckoning in an openly lustful manner. She held her arms above her head and swayed them while placing her feet together and rapidly swinging her knees out and back together so that her thighs made quick slapping sounds. Sharply aroused, he stood before her. She moved closer to him, her dark eyes shining. Then suddenly she flashed a big smile and wrapped herself around him. Almost as if she were climbing a tree she drew herself up, until their faces were level, and declared her love for him. He pulled her down to his rug then, and they laughed as she rubbed him with oil.

Once again Buckley wondered how long his good fortune could last. Yanathan-lark's tribe had not come looking for her, as might have been expected. Neither did she show any desire to search them out. He raised the subject several times for his own peace of mind, as he knew retribution against him was possible if they were found together. She just made excuses and evaded the subject. Buckley was not going to press the point, and let himself relax and take things as they came, trying to resign himself to the fact she would certainly go if her tribe came for her.

The summer began to pass, and food was growing scarce in their district. He did not wish to penetrate too far into the mountains behind them because of the risk of falling in with unwelcome company, friendly or not. They decided to move further down the coast and try their luck elsewhere. They marched slowly, taking their time. Yanathan-lark was easy to travel with and they enjoyed exploring as they went.

Two days after they left their but they passed by the rock-shelf under Nooraki where Buckley had spent his first summer and first learnt to survive alone. He told Yanathan-lark about those days; the hut he had built and how he had found the stone and then gone on to meet his family.

She caressed his face and hair and told him the story of the Bullum-Boukan, two mischievous spirits in one female body. One day at the camp of the kulin the men had gone hunting and the women fishing. Having had a good catch the women returned and cooked their fish. Bullum-Boukan smelt the delicious aroma and came to ask for some. Mindful of their old tricks the women chased Bullum-Boukan away.

The next day Bullum-Boukan came to the deserted camp seeking revenge. They took the live coals from the fire in a tarnuk and dowsed the ashes with water. In the evening the kulin returned and discovered their misfortune. Bellin-bellin tried to blow the damp ash back to life but without success. He had to get Thara to fly off and search for their fire. At length Thara found the Bullum-Boukan with it on top of a mountain. He swooped and knocked the coals away, causing the country to catch fire. Tutbring managed to get some coals and fly back to the kulin with them. Her breast was scorched from holding them too close.

The Bullum-Boukan were disgusted with the kulin and left the earth. As they rose into the sky the kulin saw them separate into the sun, which retained the fire that gave the world its life-giving warmth and light, and the moon that, although it only kept a pale light, had the power to move the oceans.

They moved on. The coast was mostly inhospitable. The hills came down, big and chunky fortresses, sometimes dropping away in cliffs to the water. The shoreline was easily passable but rocky. Sometimes there were small beaches but often these were washed by the high tide, especially when the weather was rough. Whenever it was possible to climb away from the shore the scrub was almost impenetrable. A few hundred yards would prove exhausting and result in very scratched legs.

Persevering with the shore they at length reached a river known as the Danawa which flowed down out of the high mountains of the interior. They camped here for a few weeks, finding adequate food supplies. On one hunting excursion Buckley made a three-day round trip further down the coast. He reached a cape that appeared to be its southern limit.* From this point the coastline ran to the north–west. He could only see about twenty miles further to the next headland, but there were cliffs and more rugged, cloud-covered ranges in the densely forested hinterland. It looked forbidding and inhospitable. A cold and strong south-westerly blew in from the sea, buffeting the landscape. He turned back satisfied there would be no point in travelling further.

The cold weather began to close in with increasing frequency. On some days clouds and mist moved in across the water and visibility along the beach dropped to a hundred paces or so. There would be no wind, and small wavelets would lap the sand, and a light rain fall through the mist. The world was then quiet and subdued, but not gloomy. Walking on the beach assumed a dream-like quality. On other days the coldest winds howled and raged, packing the clouds against the mountains until teeming rain gradually stilled the air. This was Brinbeal's country. Rainbows would be everywhere, often springing out of the ocean and arching over the land.

At these times Buckley and Yanathan-lark suffered as the weather hampered their food-gathering. He yearned again for the safety of a stable home and dreamt of his hut by the Karaaf. Yanathan-lark was fully agreeable to trying the

* Cape Otway

comforts there, and they slowly made their way on the long journey back up the coast, sheltering when they could in caves and crevices.

After many days of hard travel they reached the Karaaf. Again Buckley experienced the build-up of anxiety over his but on their approach, and again the pleasure when they came and found it completely undisturbed. The first night there, bedded down in the warmth with Yanathan-lark by his side, was one of the most satisfying he could remember spending in the wilderness. Within days he had re-established his weir, and they settled down for a quiet winter together, living mainly on bream and mirrnyong.

Many months and much laughter passed by. Buckley felt the agonies of his tragic experiences recede in his mind. The companionship he had found with Yanathan-lark engendered in his mind a certain detachment from the world. He gained with her a greater sense of enthusiasm, and of the humour and pathos in things. One of those things was himself; himself growing old.

The inevitable day finally came. They were busy drying their fish in the usual manner when the strangers arrived. Buckley froze when he looked up and saw a party of men approach along the beach. They were Yanathan-lark's relatives from the lake country. He knew she had to go. They were amiable enough, but declined to stay. They wanted her to come back to her country straight away. He knew they would use force if necessary. He had understood long ago that she would go without question if they came. They looked a long, silent goodbye into each other's eyes. And then she was gone.

21

He watched the little group as they marched out of sight towards the distant hills in the west. Even Buckley, who had so often had his loved ones torn from him, could not accept such a sudden change. One moment they were together in harmony, the next he was alone in an empty universe again. He tried to comfort himself with the rationalisation that he had only had Yanathan-lark because he could never keep her. Tutbring never stayed. Like the most beautiful sunset awaited through the longest day, such an experience could only be had because it was ephemeral. Its quality, like a freshly-bloomed flower, was inseparable from its passing nature. Never look back, he kept telling himself. But his heart ached for her until it burst. He thrust the fish away from him, stumbled across the sand, and wept.

He would never forget her, the young woman who laughed a lot. For the rest of his life, every time he saw the Pleiades he would think of her. He would look for their return in the spring when Tutbring came, and mourn their passing in the autumn as another winter seeped into his bones.

The days passed again and the necessities of physical survival structured his world enough for him to get by. He tried to be thankful for his good memories when he struggled with his will to live, but it was hard.

He dreamt once that he had come to die at a little cabin

by a pond in a lost forest. Everything was old and covered in moss. There were strange-looking birds around the cabin, a little like chooks and a little like Tarnwil the plain turkey. But the birds were doomed because there was no male to fertilise their eggs. The blackest melancholy weighed upon him. It was becoming cold and late in the day. Dank shadows closed in. He lay down by the pond with a fowling-piece to shoot himself. He had to move it back from the water as the tide was coming in. The eggs were floating away on the water.

He awoke feeling the same terrible gloom. But he had no fowling-piece. The surf pounded outside. Suicide was always there, but he knew he would be dead and buried soon enough. He lived on; eating and sleeping, walking about, occasionally doing something with his hut.

Once on a moonlit night he walked along the Karaaf, half-heartedly fishing for Boonea by torch-light. A high wind was blowing and he looked at the sky. It must have been a trick of the moonlight. Above the hill to the north–west, numbers of small clouds seemed to appear from nowhere. They sprang out of the inky blackness in the middle of the sky and ripped across the landscape up the coast. He watched the movement of clouds and remembered Yanathan-lark with a sudden terrible vividness. A bitter loneliness blew through his soul and he started to cry again, but stopped himself. For so long he had been inspired by the new; new people, new experiences, new ideas. Now that seemed to have run its course. Life only offered that which it would snatch away. Now he would have to find his motivation in the barren wastes themselves; have nothing to live for and yet still want to go on.

A long time passed again. He lived with a growing feeling that life could not, should not, stop here. He still felt the vigour of youth in his body and life was still to be lived. But, even though he was free in many ways, there was nothing he could do, because he was alone. He had survived alone time and again, but always the loneliness came to subvert his freedom. Finding himself in the same old hind again, he felt that this time the only solution was to look inwards. The stability of his existence allowed his mind to dwell more and more upon the ideas and stories that his old friends Torraneuk and Wombalano Beeaar had imparted to him, and upon the strange turn of events that had ended in catastrophe.

For them the world was a living thing. Everything within it was somehow alive in relationships with everything else. Sky and earth, wind and rain, the animals, trees and plants, and the waters were all characters in their own right, and with some they and all their people entered into a personal relationship. All these things, and the kulin themselves, were manifestations of the ancestral spirits. They did not need to look for these spirits within because they were sure they were within them. Buckley had prayed to a god in some of his most desperate hours when death seemed imminent; a god that he had taken to stand outside the world, looking down on it. Such a being was unknown to the kulin. Bunjil and the other powerful and creative spirits had their home in the sky, the upper world, but that world was only above, not outside the world of the earth. And so the sky seeded the earth with the rain so it could give life. He remembered some of the strange preachers of his youth who taught that God was manifested in the whole world or in nature. These beliefs seemed close to what his friends had lived by. At times when his loneliness weighed heavily upon him he yearned to understand such a way of thought so that he might be comforted.

One day he wandered along the Karaaf and into the scrub and timber on the gently-sloping hillside that rolled away inland. He was lazily noting places where he would come in future for roots and berries, and was watching the stream for Boonea and fish. The day was warm and still, with fluffy white clouds rolling out from behind the hill and along the coast. Lying on the bank he gazed up watching the clouds. His mind wandered back over the years; back to his first contacts with the Wothowurong. He thought about the feelings that preoccupied him then. So young, he had yearned for society and the presence of women above all, even when he had been self-sufficient in those first months before hunger had driven him from under the mountain he now knew as Nooraki. It all seemed so long ago, and he marvelled at what he had lived through and swore he could not do it again.

Then he remembered the stone he had found in the stream that gushed from the rock-shelf above his hut; how he had kept it and made a little pet of it. He sat up and smiled and laughed at himself and his odd behaviour. At that very instant his eyes dropped to the shallow waters of the stream. Here it flowed only a few inches deep over a broad bank of clean sand. His eyes fell to the only object on that sandbank. It was a round, smooth stone about the size of his fist. The colour and texture were uncannily like the stone he had just been remembering. It wasn't the same one, of course, but there was no denying its distinct resemblance, and it was the only one there.

This strange coincidence struck Buckley's mind with great force. He took the stone and returned to his hut, where he ate some fish and wondered. To accept the view of Torraneuk was to know that this was clear proof of the living universe. There could be no doubt; something bigger than he could see had revealed itself to him; and it probably signified a birth of some kind. He was exhilarated by this profound experience. He placed the stone on a small shelf by his chimney. This one would be more than a pet perhaps a piece of a great spirit to be held in his hand, in his memory, in the times ahead as he grew old alone; when he had to accept the world as a living thing or be crushed by loneliness. He laughed to think of Torraneuk. 'I don't know . . . might be something,' he would have said with a twinkle in his eye.

Buckley was bolstered by a new confidence now. As the days rolled by he resolved to try and take a more positive attitude. After all, he had at least been given something. He could have been dead long ago, or lived as a vegetable without any society at all. Perhaps he would never have ecstasy in his life again, but there were still things to do. He felt he could place a certain part of his heart in the direction of a god, but he could not sustain himself by an obsession with such a relationship. He was not the kind of man to spend all his spare hours in prayer or meditation; he knew he was inevitably involved with others. His path would still take him among the people of his country.

He began a very constructive and rewarding period. It gradually came to him now that he was not only growing old — he knew he had been perhaps twenty years in the wilderness — but was by that very fact becoming ngurungaeta, something of an elder among his tribe, the Wothowurong. He had seen a whole generation of children born and grow into maturity, and many of the old people die. By his caution in mixing with them, especially the women, and by his gentle and peaceable manner he had acquired a certain influence. His detachment was now a valuable asset that he sought to restore after the painful separation from Yanathan-lark. If he could retain it while actively involving himself he thought he could accomplish some good.

His old urge to make himself useful had created opportunities for him in the past and he resolved to try it again. Despite the shocked revulsion he had experienced numerous times at the violence of the kulin, he now felt a great fondness for them. After all it was from and through them that he had had all the life he could have missed. This love needed action, interchange between himself and the tribes. He found he again had the desire to make contact with them, no matter what befell him. He knew now what cruelty and violence could be expected, but it occurred to him that these incidents had perhaps been few enough considering his long years in such wild company. He felt himself too old now to be upset by any foolishness. Besides, he became bored with spending all his time at the Karaaf. Huts were for shelter from the wind and rain, not for hiding in. He liked to go walkabout every now and then. Perhaps the peace and contentment that was so elusive, yet so curiously unattractive to him in his restless youth, could now be found in a free involvement in the affairs of the kulin.

So he began to make regular visits around the Wothowurong country, visiting the bands and family groups as he found them. He liked to see his favourite places like Moodewarri, Mangowak, Corangamite, Gerangamete, and the waterfalls at Boonea-yallock. He began to use various caves and hollow trees as regular stopping places, making use of them as refuges from the weather when he needed them. Everywhere he went he was always greeted with sincere welcomes and kindly-given gifts of food. They enjoyed his company as he brought them news of the district and the other groups, and told interesting stories of his past experiences. In time they became used to his wandering nature. Whereas at first he often had to overcome a certain resistance to his leaving after a visit, they eventually let him go without fuss because they knew he would return again with new things to tell them. He was able to come and go as he pleased, and greatly enjoyed the freedom to choose between having company and being alone at his but or in the bush.

He saw Mirri Mallo several times, and she was well. There could never be the same thing between them again. She was becoming a young woman, and Waraduk had taken his place and was growing her up. He also saw Weeitcho taerinyaar, Koronn, and Terragubel sometimes, but he never saw Yanathan-lark again.

Sometimes he accompanied Wothowurong groups to a mountain called Noorat, far in the west past Corangamite, where they went to trade. Other tribes brought certain spear woods, stones and food specialities from remote regions. The Wothowurong also brought food like Boonea, but their most valued items were the materials for making kallallingurks — the stone axes. They had karkeen, the dark and most valuable stone from the Woiwurong country and some other inferior stones from the north, and from their own country. Their most reliable trading item was gurring. Big lumps were traded to the Western tribes who always carried it and used it for cementing splits and joins in tarnuks, or stone and bone barbs into their spears. It was essential for sticking tarks together and for making kallallingurks. A suitable length of wood — perhaps from a moiyan tree — was split open at one end and a stone wedged in, cemented with gurring, and bound with Ko-im tail sinews. Sharpened properly with a hard stone it could readily be used to fell a large tree.

One day Buckley was visiting a group at Kooraioo when a dispute broke out between two young men over a girl. Immediately each of them had allies from among their brothers and a bloody fight was threatened. Buckley was in an extroverted and energetic mood. He chided the young men for their behaviour and walked over to them, questioning the need for such antagonism. He was aware that a hot-tempered young fighter could have attacked him for interfering, but was feeling confident enough to take the risk. He moved among them and began to take their weapons away, eventually throwing them to one side in a heap. He then demanded to hear the complaints of both young men. For some time the whole gang argued, Buckley questioning each for evidence of any wrong-doing. In the end it seemed that both of them were victims of false promises, and conditions were agreed to which would in time settle the dispute.

This dispute became the first of a number that Buckley was able to help solve in a bloodless manner. Although the kulin were still ready to fight if necessary, their respect for his age and experience remained high.

These developments further strengthened his resolve to stay among the kulin, and he enjoyed himself more and more. He was so keenly involved that he hardly grasped it when he was visiting the Bengali once and they told him some hunters of Koorman had settled on an island in the great bay on the other side of Port Phillip.* They had forcibly taken some wives from the Bunerong and killed several men. The Bunerong were angry but too afraid of the fierce men to attack them, and so had to avoid the island.

Buckley had long expected to run into some sealers. He had known of them for a long time; the Bengali still had their iron kallallingurks. It was obvious they were trouble and he was not keen to brave a journey right through the Bunerong country to try and contact them. However, his curiosity was sparked when a bihar from the Yawangis told him some other Murrangurk men had settled on the far shore opposite the sealers. It seemed they had some strange carrying devices drawn by large four-legged animals. It must have been a more substantial settlement, which had landed horses and carts. In time, he heard the Bunerong had made some contact with them but were generally avoiding their

* Phillip Island

settlement. He began to wonder if he should make some effort to get there, but at this time was so pleased with his life among the kulin that he never did. The existence of a distant but probably reachable settlement at least meant there might be somewhere to go if life became impossible again. He had hardly formed these ideas when he heard they had all gone and the Bunerong were again masters of their country. Time passed. One day Buckley was at Bangeballa, not far from Lib-lib, when he saw a group of Yawangis coming towards him. He felt a chill of excitement flash through his veins when he realised one of them was carrying a flag over his shoulders. He hurried forward to meet them. It turned out they had raided a bullito-koorong or sea-ship in the bay and it was still there, as far as they knew. They had first seen it stop offshore from Beangala, where they had watched it for several days. It had moved up the bay where a little koorong had left it with a number of men and proceeded up the Werribee. They watched for a while and, seeing no movement on board, swam out to it, boarding from both sides as a precaution. There were many interesting things they wanted, although they were afraid to go down into the cabin. They had taken the flag, some rope and sails, glass bottles to bark and sharpen their spears with, and a number of other objects. Before they could get back, the men had returned and fired on them, but without effect. Buckley presumed that the Yawangis must have been out of range, as they seemed to have no idea about the effect of guns. The last they had seen of the ship was when it moved further out into the bay. They had sought out Buckley to ask him to come and help them lure the crew ashore again, so that they could continue their happy plunder.

Buckley was trembling. After all these years, he was wary about rescue and a return to his own people. But he felt he had to see the boat, even if only to prevent a fatal clash between the kulin and the amadiate. It would take him a day or two of solid travelling to reach the shores where it had last been seen. He was adamant that he would not involve himself in his friends' scheme and warned them of the danger of being shot, describing to them the nature of the weapons. They set out together, jogging steadily when the terrain allowed it.

Unknown to Buckley, the ship he pursued was a cutter of fifty tons called the *Lively*. She was a small, single-masted vessel belonging to a mother ship and fitted for rowing or sailing. The *Lively* had become separated from her ship during a storm. After days of buffeting on rough seas the crew managed to put into Port Phillip in April 1831. Meanwhile, half of the original crew of ten had died of scurvy. The remaining five, weakened by illness, anchored and got ashore with some provisions and made camp. While they were resting it seems the ship broke anchor and went aground higher up the bay. She was recovered two weeks later in the process of being plundered. The crew claimed they drove the natives off, refloated her and sailed off to the Derwent River where their exploits were reported in the Hobart Town newspapers.

On the second day they arrived breathless, and Buckley half desperate, at the beach on the north–west side of the bay. He looked across the water. Not seeing the ship at first glance his heart began to sink; but there it was, lying at anchor some distance further along the coast. He insisted on approaching it alone and drove himself on, cursing the effort of running on the sand. Finally, he reached the point opposite the ship and proceeded to build a large fire, watching anxiously for any sign of preparation to make sail.

As the smoke began to billow up he advanced into the water. Then he realised how completely he had forgotten his English. For years now he had actually been thinking in the Wothowurong dialect, as well as fluently speaking it. His frustration was immense as he tried desperately to remember any word or hailing call that might inform the men on board of his race, but all he could do was use the universal 'cooee' of the bush. To them, especially at some distance, his huge, dark-tanned, hairy figure wrapped in skins must have looked like that of a peculiar and dangerous savage.

He could see men appearing on deck occasionally, sometimes looking in his direction. They must have been about a mile offshore, but he felt sure they must have seen him. He was almost in tears with frustration, even while still reasoning to himself that he had no real cause to become desperate to meet them. But once he had seen the ship and other white men in the flesh he felt overwhelmed with a desire for contact. He was afraid to swim so far. There could have been sharks around the boat, and he was sure he would never make it back if they turned him away.

In the middle of the following day a small boat put off and began sailing in his direction. His heart leapt and he jumped up in excitement. He waited until they were about half a mile out, and then began to signal. But, alas, it was a fatal mistake. They eventually saw him and, when only a few hundred yards away, changed direction, fearing that they were falling into a trap. If only he could have hailed them in English they would have waited; instead, they set course for a small island two or three miles up the coast.

Buckley followed them on shore, running as fast as he could. He saw them land on the island and begin working as if they were cutting wood. When he reached the island he swam the narrow channel and ran towards them. But they had finished their work and were beginning to embark as he ran along the beach to them. They laughed and pointed at him as he yelled to them and made desperate gesticulations. Exhausted, he reached the spot where they had embarked;

but they were already hundreds of yards out. Cursing miserably, he collapsed at the water's edge, utterly unable to believe their callousness.

When he recovered his strength he regained his sense of perspective, and realised that, considering the way he appeared, he was lucky not to have been shot at. He went and examined the place where they had been working, in the hope of finding an axe or something useful. Mystified, he found they had not cut wood but, for some reason, had made a mound of earth about the size of a grave. His dazed mind failed to understand, still concentrating on the idea of finding something of value. He dug down, and was shocked to find the body of a white man wrapped in a blanket. The weather was cold, but he could not bring himself to rob the dead. He had his skins, anyway, and so refilled the grave, covering it with boughs and heavy stones to protect it against Garl.

He passed another night in miserable frustration, trying to think of some way he could hail the ship. He thought of paddling a raft out, but the more he thought about it the more he grew afraid that he would be shot down. In the morning he returned to the Yawangis where they were camped on shore, and stayed with them, watching. To his amazement, another landing party did come ashore and cooee. He could see they were all armed, and so, reluctantly, he remained hidden and let them go. They sailed out of the bay a few days later.

While he was there some of the older men revealed to him something they had never told him before. Apparently, another vessel had anchored there a long time ago. A group of four or five white men had brought two others ashore, tied them to trees, and shot them dead, leaving the bodies where they were. They then sailed off and were never seen again.

* * *

After the departure of the cutter, Buckley returned to the Karaaf to restore his equilibrium. He lived there for several months, making occasional visits to the kulin. One day he was patrolling the beach near Beangala when he found a stranded boat. It was a whaler, a large rowing-boat with eight big oars lying around it and half buried in the sand, evidently beached in a storm. Three blankets were rigged as a sail; the ropes, mast and other articles were all there. He washed the blankets and, seeing some distant fires, searched out the Bengali. They danced joyfully when they saw him, as they always loved his surprises. He cut up the blankets and shared them out among the families present, and they all settled down to a feast and corroboree in honour of their old friend and ngurungaeta.

While they ate, their principal man at this time, called Pewitt (mudlark), told Buckley that they had seen the boat before. Two men had come from it and wandered into the bush. They had been very sad and bruised and cold. They had been treated well, being fed on Tu-at and Ko-im until they recovered. When they were well the Bengali had tried to tell them about him and bring them together, but the two white men had left, marching across the plains towards the Yawang mountains.

Buckley sadly surmised that they had probably started out just as he had done, seeking to climb the hills with the idea of spying out the land. They had two days' start and could have been anywhere by then. He asked the Bengali to spread the word for any news of them, and returned home. Some months later word came that they had been speared to death by the Woiwurong while crossing the Barrern river.

22

A long time passed again. Marching along the beach on a visit to Mangowak, Buckley found a hogshead cask partly buried in the sand. As it was too heavy to move he dug it out and knocked the head in. The stench was terrible and the flavour even worse. The cask had been full of ale but, perhaps because seawater had seeped into it, it had putrified. It seemed a waste, but he had to abandon the contents. He hadn't had a drink of anything like ale since his youth, and wondered what it would be like again. With his friends he had generally drunk nothing but water or occasionally beal. He broke up the cask with an axe and took the iron hoops. On his return to the Karaaf he broke these into pieces for scrapers and, on his next walkabout, gave them as gifts to his best friends.

On this walk he began to realise that he had not been involved in settling any disputes for some time. Unless they were keeping quiet when he was with them — and this was unlikely, as they had no propensity for such deception — he felt they seemed to be more peaceable. Perhaps it was the result of his long years of becoming used to their ways, but he fancied not.

Not long after this a bizarre thing happened that once again brought him to think that a terrible pattern was emerging. He had joined a large group of Wothowurong on a hunt. They circled a valley in the Boordek country, and fired it in order to make a clean sweep of the game.

But consternation and fear broke out when it was found that among their catch was a great Kaan, about nine feet long with two heads. The fire had burnt the body in two. Everyone left the area without staying for the corroborees they had intended.

Buckley had no idea what he could make of this, but his suspicions were confirmed not long after. A terrible plague swept through all the tribes, coming down along the river valleys in the north right to the coast. He was terribly afraid and saddened to see the kulin everywhere laid out with fever, then breaking out into terrible sores. Often only a rash would have time to develop, and they would be dead within a few days. Hundreds died, the strongest seeming to be the greatest victims.

Before he could grasp the severity of the plague and isolate himself, he felt the fever begin to come over him. He managed to get back to the Karaaf and, with reserves of food and water, secluded himself. Within a few days scores of large pimples appeared all over him, and were especially bad on his face and the backs of his arms. They soon oozed pus, but at least his fever left him. In time they cleared up to leave characteristic white pockmarks. He thanked his Maker once again for another reprieve.

The kulin believed the plague to be a punishment Bunjil had visited on them by the agency of Mindie, and therefore called it Monola Mindie. The terrible ulcerous sores it brought were said to be Lillipook Mindie, the scales of Mindie. It was by far the greatest disaster Buckley had seen since his days in the sand dunes of Holland. The tribes were decimated and all began to despair, unable to know how they could appease the dreadful power which had unleashed this upon them.

Not long after this trial, when all were still stunned from the universal loss of loved ones, another awful fear swept through the country. Bihars ran with urgency, passing on the story that the sky was in danger of falling. Buckley had heard of the belief before that since Barroworn had raised the sky in the Dreamtime it had been supported by great props at the farthest ends of the earth, which were looked after by a certain old man. In the current climate the story spread unquestioned that, unless the old man was given a supply of kallallingurks to cut more props, and rope to tie them with, the sky would fall and doom come upon them all. Buckley had a special interest in such a problem, due to his relation to Barroworn. He knew this to be nothing more than a robbery, not unlike those performed in countries of so-called Christendom. He scoffed, and tried to use his influence against the panic, but the tide was against him. There was talk of finding the highest mountains and fleeing to them for safety. The required articles were donated and gathered and sent on to the distant tribes. Some parties of kulin from several of their tribes went to the Bunerong country and raided the old settlements, taking rusted tools, rope and even the metal parts of old drays. These too were sent on. Buckley could only watch, and wonder what distant confidence man was getting the windfall of treasures.

At length the madness passed, and the badly shaken kulin began to rebuild their lives. It was during this period that Buckley was given another wife. His steadfastness and reputation as a ngurungaeta had steadily increased through their terrible ordeals, and it was considered a wise arrangement by all. Her name was Parrarmurnin Tallarwurnin, and she was about fifteen years old. Her family had suffered from Monola Mindie, and she joined him so that he could grow her up. She was from the Buninyong group, a distant section of the Kurung who lived mostly in the interior. He was delighted to have someone once again, especially a young and energetic girl. She had passed through those vital years Mirri Mallo had just been entering when he had felt he had to give her up. This young woman and he would form a very practical partnership; she helping him as he grew old and he teaching her what he knew. They would be lovers sometimes but, especially for Buckley, the companionship and assistance were more important. Together, they returned to his hut by the Karaaf, accompanied by an old acquaintance of Buckley's, an old man called Nullamboid who came with his wife and children.

They lived on, and when the time came for a walk again, they went to a place called Jeringot, one of a string of waterholes on the south side of the Barrabool hills supplying the Barwin. This place was known to abound in Boonea, but was also a favourite haunt of the Bunyip, so no-one stayed there long. While they were there Buckley tried spearing them several times but, as usual, without success. They did not have the same significance for him now as when he was a young man. Whatever they were he was sure they could not impress him much compared with the things he had experienced over so many years as Murrangurk.

One day Buckley and Nullamboid were out gathering roots. It was a cool winter's day. A blanket of grey cloud hung over the land and all was quiet, apart from occasional passing birds. Suddenly, they saw two young men coming through the marshes in their direction. Buckley again felt that chill of excitement flash through his body. The young men had coloured handkerchiefs attached to their spears, and they were deliberately waving them about in anticipation of attracting his attention as they knew he was in the area.

He ran to meet them, wondering what sort of trouble he could be faced with this time. One of the lads, named Bullbul, told him they had met three white men and six weird blacks they had never seen before over at Beangala. He asked if they had a koorong. 'Ye, ye,' they replied, but added it had gone, leaving the men behind with two little white houses and many provisions such as blankets and axes. They were angry, because the Bengali had been given gifts which sounded like scissors and knives, while they had been refused anything except the handkerchiefs. They said they were going to get allies so they could kill the invaders and take possession of their goods.

Their plan alarmed Buckley, but he didn't know how to circumvent it. He was wary of a direct approach to the strangers, for he neither wanted to frighten them into shooting him, nor did he want to be seen to directly betray his friends' plans. Again he was frustrated by his loss of language.

They discussed the situation until sundown, and the next morning Bullbul and his friend left in search of their brothers. Buckley reluctantly prepared for the march to Beangala. As he left, Parrarmurnin Tallawurnin, Nullamboid and his family all began to weep bitterly. He was perplexed and tried to reassure them all would be well, but they just cried that he was leaving them. His concern at the situation deepened, but he set off, determined to find out what was happening. White men at Beangala! He could not ignore such an event.

He reached his destination the next day, when the weather was cold and tempestuous. After searching about he saw the smoke of a camp fire just in from the shore, and approached with great caution until he saw a flagpole with the Union Jack hoisted upon it and some tents pitched nearby.

The sight of this outpost had an unexpected and distressing effect on Buckley. Suddenly, standing alone in the forest and looking at that flag, his mind was flooded with ancient memories. This was no simple matter of being rescued from savagery and returned to civilisation. He was reminded now that he was a free man with a place of his own in this land, a man who had once been a miserable prisoner and could find himself enslaved once again. He sat down and thought about this, reluctant now to present himself at the camp.

Shortly, he saw one of the white men. He was carrying a bucket and went to the well they had nearby. When he returned to the camp Buckley crept over to the well. He was almost shaking with distress over his situation. Taking a drink of water and splashing his face, he tried to recover his senses and decide what to do. He could see the white men sitting around a fire, talking excitedly. The strange blacks were camped with their tents near those of the whites. He could see old Pewitt, the cousin of Barroworn, and the Bengali all seated around the camp watching them. In his quaking distraction he neglected to keep himself properly secluded. Soon one of the Bengali saw him and called to him, pointing him out to the startled whites. They rose from their fire, calm but very apprehensive, their guns within reach at their feet. Buckley was fully armed with spears, leonile, malka, and kallallingurk.

He approached slowly, looking the three whites in the eye, one by one, and glanced around, nodding to the Bengali. Finally, he stood before them and let them inspect him for a time, and then seated himself with dignity, his weapons held between his legs. He heard one of them gasp an astonished query about what on earth he could be. Another of them came forward and asked him questions. They could not make him out at all. His distress quickly changed to mirth at their innocent confusion, and he had to bite his lip to stop himself from laughing. He still could not remember anything to say to them. After they had all talked at and about him for some time one of them came over to him with something in his hand. He held out a crisp, edible-looking substance and said, 'Bread. Do you want some bread?'

Buckley looked at the food. Bread; bread. Ye, ye, bread. His memory began to return. He repeated the word 'bread', and a cloud appeared to pass from over his brain.

Part Three

23

Buckley would take some time to realise it, but his benefactors were bringing with them the fate which had already spread, like a plague, across most of the South Pacific. In Van Dieman's Land, hunger for pasture had led to the systematic elimination of the local tribes, but still the pastoral economy was bursting at the seams. For some years, men had wanted to bring their sheep to Port Phillip.

Two years earlier, in 1833, John Batman and others had read avidly the full report published by Hamilton Hume who, with Hovell, had penetrated south to the shores of Jillong in 1824. Batman, and a group consisting mostly of Launceston professional men and merchants, had formed the Port Phillip Association with a view to forming a colony of free settlers. By 1835, Batman was anxious to get going, as the previous year had seen a settlement formed in South Australia and the Hentys' departure for Portland Bay. Everywhere there were signs of a new land rush.

Batman sailed in May in the *Rebecca* and, by the end of the first week of June, had completed a brisk excursion into the west and north sides of the bay, and had signed his 'deeds' on vast tracts of land in both areas with the first 'chiefs' he could find. When he departed again for Launceston he stopped on the way out of the bay at a small cove named Indented Head, and left a so-called party of occupation. It comprised three white men called Gumm, Todd, and Thompson; several of his old Sydney black friends with whom he had grown up — Pidgeon, Joe the Marine, Bullet, Bungett, and Old Bull; six dogs; and three months' provisions. The party was commanded by his servant Jim Gumm, who was given written authority to chase trespassers off Batman's 'property'.

Later that month Batman strode into the Cornwall Arms in Launceston, a tavern where he drank with old Straitsmen. He threw up his arms and announced to the crowd: 'I am the greatest landowner in the world'. The patrons, and most of all the proprietor, John Fawkner, listened intently to his adventures. They also noticed that he was soon slumped in a chair by the wall, gazing distractedly out the window. He was a sick and exhausted man. Syphilis had broken his health.

At Indented Head, Batman's men had established their camp and met the Bengali and other kulin. One of them — Murrodanuck, headman of the Yawangis — and his wife beat time on skins while sixteen men did the 'kangaroo initiation dance'. Jim Gumm gave him two dogs — Ball and Spring — and Pidgeon corroboreed for them. They all camped together without trouble, except for the rapid reduction of their provisions.

At two o'clock on Sunday, 6 July, they looked up startled when one of their guests made an exclamation, and pointed out a strange-looking giant of a man wrapped in kangaroo skins. He was heavily armed, and walked slowly out of the bush into their midst, seating himself with dignity among the blacks. They were slightly fearful of approaching him, suspecting he was a hostile chief. But Gumm made their standard gesture of peace, and offered him some bread. William Buckley heard his first English words in a lifetime.

Other words began to return to Buckley's memory, and he repeated each of them until he could begin to converse.

He soon had them realise he was a European and, to their further amazement, an Englishman. They took him to their tents and showed him the provisions they had and offered him a meal and clothing. He was presented with a shirt and trousers that felt at first strangely close and cloying to the skin and limbs. He then seated himself for a meal prepared for him by Jim Gumm, who gave him tinned meat, fried over the fire. Its salty flavour brought back strong memories of his youth — the army and prison in particular. It was otherwise rather greasy and inferior to his palate, long accustomed to fresh roasted meats and poultry straight from the fire or mirrnyong. With this he had some more of the dried bread or biscuit, and a mug of tea which he found a real treat, although it lay rather heavily in his stomach for a while.

As he ate they began to question him further. He began to understand them much better than he could express himself. They were asking his name so he pointed to the tattoos on his right forearm, which included the initials W.B. Gumm hazarded a guess and said to him, 'W for William; B for Burgess.' They repeated this and he nodded first that he was called William, but he couldn't get his surname. It was strange. He knew he still knew it; he just could not remember how to say it. After more trying from both sides it was at last understood by all that he was William Buckley. Next to the W.B. were tattooed in a row a sun, a half moon, seven stars, and a bird with a human face. On his upper right arm was a mermaid. They nodded understandingly at this and took it he was a castaway seaman.

By the time he had finished eating he had a feeling they were in the country to stay. As time progressed and his words returned he came to understand what they were saying about the land. They claimed to have exchanged a large number of provisions for certain parts of the country with certain 'chiefs'. They kept mentioning these chiefs and Buckley soon understood that a terrible mistake was afoot.

When they showed him to his bed that night his feelings were greatly confused, but he felt buoyant. He was still worried about the danger of attack when Bullbul and his friends returned. Added to this was the gnawing thought that this party represented a gigantic hoax the white man was about to perpetrate on innocent victims. He couldn't help feeling a deep and growing suspicion, for surely they understood there were no chiefs, there was no-one at all who could trade off the sacred places. Despite these feelings he was overjoyed at his 'deliverance'. He thanked God most humbly that an ageing man like himself could pass through such a world and come back. He slept long and soundly.

The next morning he was awoken by the sound of Barroworn piping sweetly and persistently in a tree over the camp. He lay in bed for a time listening and enjoying the comfort of the blankets and pallias. Barroworn made him think. This party must have strong reinforcements behind them or they could not be serious in making the claims they had. They were not going away so he would have to try and create harmony between the two races. Barroworn reminded him of Torraneuk's teaching about getting the best of both worlds. This was the way he felt. He thought he could get it himself, but could the others? At least the idea gave him hope and his joy grew again. He heard Jim Gumm call him out to the camp fire where he presented Buckley with a fresh and sizzling breakfast.

Their kindness he could not deny, whatever his suspicions of their activities. In order to make a good start he once again joined in with the situation as he found it, and determined to make himself useful in whatever way he could. He answered their questions about the surrounding country as best he could. Naturally, his answers were rather limited, so he offered to take them on a tour. They replied that it would be better to wait. Their ship would shortly arrive from Launceston, across the ocean to the south, bringing many more provisions and people, among whom were some who would come on the tour. For the time being Gumm's party was preoccupied just with maintaining their camp. They had to make continual exhausting kangaroo hunts that even knocked up their untrained dogs. Buckley, remaining at the camp at their request, tried hard to persuade the kulin to leave, knowing that Bullbul could return at any time. They were trying ruses, such as a false alarm at a ship arriving, in order to trick the whites away from the camp.

Gumm and Todd continued to query him about how he came to be there. After about ten days he was speaking fluently enough and had to tell them something to avoid arousing suspicion. He said he was a soldier, one of four survivors from a wrecked convict transport bound for Van Diemen's Land. He told Todd that the captain had gone off looking for help and the other two had died. He had then walked for forty days until the tribe had rescued him. They had no reason to doubt him, and the story satisfied their curiosity.

Towards the end of the month his worst fears were realised. Although Bullbul had soon returned unaccompanied, many more kulin had started to appear. On some days all the kulin would leave the camp, and on others just the men would go. But sometimes there were up to ninety gathered there. At length he nervously went among them and spoke with the older men. They were looking at him with suspicion. He suddenly felt very self-conscious of his new clothes and tried to make light of them, but it was obvious many of them suspected he had already deserted them. They told him bluntly that they intended to massacre the invaders and made it plain he would be killed too unless he actually helped them.

Buckley had to think quickly. To run and warn Gumm and the others would have created a panicky confrontation, with blood spilt on both sides and no telling where it would end, especially when the other whites came. He answered at once that he agreed with their plan but advised them to wait, telling them about the koorong coming soon that would bring many more provisions, and how this greater prize would be lost unless the party at the camp were left unharmed in order to receive them on shore.

This plan succeeded for a few days but eventually they became impatient and suspected that Buckley was trying to deceive them. He was now forced to make the situation known to Gumm. The achievement of his hope for harmony and mutual benefit was obviously going to require great efforts. Even now, before the establishment of a settlement, he found himself having to risk his life and take sides against his old friends in order to protect the weaker party. He armed himself with a gun, something he had once wished for so much. Now he reluctantly bore it against the very people who had promoted his survival without one.

Walking steadfastly over to the tribal camp he stood before the men and stated loudly and strongly that he personally would kill the first man to harm the strangers, repeated his promise of gifts on the arrival of the ship, and strode firmly off. There was no man strong enough to challenge him, and the aura of the ngurungaeta returned again. They muttered among themselves and agreed to wait. The tension of the previous days of growing hostility had distracted everyone from food, and they now turned their attention to some relaxed hunting and fishing. It was the season for kalkeeth again and many dispersed around the peninsula in pursuit of the annual treat.

Buckley stayed with Gumm's party, and they all took turns keeping watch day and night in case of a surprise attack. Buckley was now in a terrible position and wondered if Gumm and his friends were being honest with him. This made him question his own dishonesty with them. But more importantly he realised that if he was ever going to mingle with his own kind again he could not live a lie. The truth would be found out and he would have to face that. If there was any chance of a pardon it would have to be now with these men or their masters, who might be able to get it for him in exchange for his vital services. After much soul-searching he made his decision and told them he was an absconder. But he didn't reveal the full story, telling them he had bolted from a ship in Western Port. They were not worried by this disclosure, runaways being common enough around Bass Strait. Buckley was too important to their safety.

The problem of maintaining peace blanketed his concern about the future, as each day he waited with growing anxiety for the appearance of the ship.

Some days later, at mid-morning, Buckley spotted her as he watched despairingly over the bay. She was a schooner and stood out gamely in a stiff south-westerly until touching on a sand-bank about three miles off. He almost wept at the sight. The sails were so white and beautiful, her movement so indescribably graceful and gentle, and this time there was no worry; he would meet those on board beyond a shadow of a doubt. Things had to be looking up now. He whooped for joy and ran laughing to the camps of both parties, roaring out the news. The whole Beangala shoreline seemed to erupt into excitement as everyone poured on to the beach.

It was 7 August 1835, and they were watching the *Rebecca*, carrying a party that included Henry Batman, his wife and family, two more of the Sydney blacks — Blacksmith and Johnny Allen — and John Helder Wedge, the Port Phillip Association's surveyor, who would shortly become a friend of Buckley's.

The Wothowurong flocked around, slapping Buckley on the shoulder, expressing their delight that he had not deceived them. As they watched, a whale-boat put off and made for the shore carrying two passengers. Some of the Wothowurong asked Buckley if it was safe for them to stay on shore or whether they should wait in hiding back in the bush. He told them to stay on the beach as they had done no wrong and should expect to be treated with respect and to be presented with gifts, and further advised them to remain calm and not to do anything to frighten the strangers or they could be shot. He knew privately that they would probably all be shot or hanged at the slightest provocation, but this meeting had to be successfully concluded if there was to be any hope of harmony. He sat on the beach surrounded by his tribe, Gumm and his party waiting warily nearby.

The boat landed and was pulled up on to the beach, and the two dignified-looking passengers approached cautiously. Buckley rose as they approached, looking in their direction. Batman and Wedge were astonished to see his shaggy visage. The first words they uttered were to ask who he was and remark amazedly at his height, as he was head and shoulders above every man present. Gumm briefly told them the story he knew, quickly adding that Buckley had been preserving them from attack. The new arrivals remained calm, and greetings were commenced all around.

When things had settled down again Batman, seemingly a little suspicious, began to ask Buckley questions. Buckley elaborated on the story he had given Gumm as best he could express it. He told him he had come on a ship many years ago, he could not remember how long, having lost all recollection of time; and then he changed the subject to the question of presents for his friends, manipulating Batman's obvious need to make peace at once. Batman asked him to remain with their party, and solicited his advice on what presents to give. Buckley suggested the first need was bread, and so the boat was dispatched for two large bags of biscuits.

Soon the *Rebecca* was refloated from the sand bank and anchored closer in shore. Provisions, blacksmiths' and carpenters' tools were unloaded. Late in the afternoon, when suitable accommodation had been prepared, Mrs Batman and her four children were landed. She was the first white woman Buckley had seen since Sullivan's Bay.

That night a great corroboree was held and more biscuits were generously handed around to one and all. Buckley became slightly drunk for the first time since his days as a militia-man. Henry Batman enjoyed a drop, and freely gave out from his supplies. The Wothowurong enjoyed their gifts and the visitors enjoyed the entertainment. Buckley, the happy and so far successful mediator, sat among both races, with high hopes for future harmony between his friends old and new.

24

Buckley took a great liking to John Wedge, who was an open and good-humoured man. Early the next morning they went out walking along the beach together. Buckley showed him how he could throw his tark about eighty paces and quickly retrieve it. They laughed and joked as Buckley answered his questions about the land, its people and his experiences. He thought he would have to trust somebody, and told Wedge his true origins as a runaway from the *Calcutta*.

Wedge was astonished and asked Buckley if he knew what year it was. He hadn't thought to ask. Wedge told him it was 1835, and thus he had been thirty-two years in the wilderness. Buckley himself could hardly believe it was so long, as he had taken it to be some twenty years. With Wedge's assistance he calculated his age to be about fifty-five.

He suddenly realised just what an old man he was becoming, and stopped on the sand, holding his breath and looking inside himself down all those years. He sat down and looked at Wedge and told him that he would not go back as a prisoner.

Wedge smiled and assured him he would argue his case. The *Rebecca* sailed later that day carrying dispatches from Wedge. He made an articulate petition to Arthur, describing Buckley and the circumstances in which they had found him. He added an account of the assistance Buckley had already provided and his future potential. This was accompanied by a similar letter to the Colonial Secretary, Captain Montagu. A letter to his partner John Batman explained the situation.

Buckley waited quietly over the following weeks. He knew that if the worst came to the worst he would go bush again and live on without the white man until the end of his days. But he lived in the hope of a free pardon. Surely after thirty-two years he had absolved himself. At night he would lie in bed repeating the figure over to himself. It was virtually his whole life. He could not expect to see much after that, but he still felt fit and energetic with life left in him yet. He certainly wanted to visit the settlements in Van Diemen's Land. It was possible some old friends of his were still alive down there. What could they have made of their lives, he wondered. He reckoned there were probably some farmers among them.

He spent the days working as an interpreter, staying close to the camp in case any dispute arose; but things remained amicable. Fruit trees were planted and they started building a house with Buckley's keen advice.

When he had first presented himself, the main reason for the settlers' inability to recognise his origin immediately was the fact that he was magnificently adorned with half a lifetime's growth of hair. It came down over his shoulders and mingled with his long flowing beard, uncut since Sullivan's Bay, apart from a very occasional rough trim with a sharpened shell. He enjoyed its natural feel and protection from cold winds, but it was very hard to keep clean and free of lice. There was soap at the camp, and he finally took the plunge and submitted to a haircut and complete shave before having a wash. John Wedge laughed at his mock protestations and made 'before' and 'after' sketches of the transition. At length he was refreshed and presentable, greatly pleasing the Batmans, but feeling rather foolish in front of the Wothowurong.

After several days Wedge said he was ready to go on a tour of the countryside so he could report to the Association. They set off on 12 August in good spirits, accompanied by Alick Thompson and three of the Sydney blacks. As they travelled Wedge noted down the names of different places as Buckley described them, and added brief descriptions and sketches alluding to their magnificent pastoral and agricultural potential. They crossed the Bellarine Peninsula and camped on the shore of Lake Connewarre, where Buckley had first joined his tribe and seen bloody battle so long ago. His nostalgia and excitement made him swell with pride. He talked as much as his language would allow, relating tales to the enthusiastic Wedge.

When they returned to the camp for a day on 17 August, Gumm told them a schooner called the *Enterprise* had entered the bay on the previous day. Pidgeon and the others had rowed out and become drunk on board before it sailed up the east coast of the bay. There was no way to investigate these rivals at this stage, and Wedge decided to continue his surveying. The next day they set off east to the Iramoo. On 20 August he made a sketch of the falls at Boonea-yallock where Buckley had joined the great eel party and seen the beginning of a strange and tragic chain of events. He named them Buckley's Falls in his guide's honour. They camped at this idyllic place.

As Buckley squatted by 'his' falls and let his mind drift away into the sounds of the rushing waters, the aptly-named *Enterprise* was entering the mouth of the Barrern. Its owner was John Fawkner, the man who more than any other represented the forces that would sweep away Buckley's world forever.

Fawkner epitomised the Australian colonist. Transported

as a boy on the *Calcutta* with his convict father, he had had a hard youth in Van Diemen's Land as a poor farmer. As a young man he was flogged in front of his father's house for assisting in an escape plot involving some ticket-of-leave men and convicts commandeering a ship. He served three hard years as a convict in Sydney. The harshness of his youth had embittered him and he certainly knew injustice. A weedy little man, he overcame all this with indomitable energy and returned to Van Diemen's Land where he tried his hand at various businesses. By the 1830s he was a tavern-keeper in Launceston; his business adventures had not gone well and he was badly in debt. In 1835, at forty-three years of age and with creditors closing in daily, he bought the 55-ton *Enterprise* and waited impatiently on the docks for it to arrive from Sydney. His desire to leave and make a fresh start while he still could had been made even more urgent by Batman's activities. He had approached Batman at his estate near Launceston, seeking to join the Port Phillip Association and accompany him to Port Phillip. Batman had rejected him as undesirable.

His schooner finally arrived and he loaded up forthwith, setting sail for Western Port on 27 July. But matters were not to be so easy. When the master of the ship, Captain Lancey, found out his boss was on the run from creditors he refused to co-operate. After three days, when they were in Bass Strait, he turned back to Van Diemen's Land and dropped Fawkner at George Town on the north coast. A cover story of seasickness was provided, and Fawkner left to hire a horse to ride back to Launceston. The expedition continued without him.

Lancey sailed to Western Port where Fawkner had some intention to settle. It was no more appealing than it had been in the 1820s when the settlement Buckley had heard about had been attempted on the basis of Hovell's mistaken report on his journey with Hume, and abandoned after a year or so. He sailed into Port Phillip, making a brief stop at Indented Head. After several days spent exploring the eastern shore of the bay they entered the large river at the north end and sailed to the falls where they anchored on 29 August.* At this stage they had no real idea what the Port Phillip Association laid claim to, and so proceeded to establish themselves, unloading their provisions and livestock, which included horses and a pig.

Ignorant of these developments which were long feared by John Batman, Buckley and Wedge continued their tour. On their way they shot ducks and swans on the rivers and lakes, and Buckley was able to demonstrate his cooking methods learnt from Wombalano Beeaar and others, providing delicious roasts that showed how well one could live in this country. Several of these shoots were conducted in front of bands that Buckley had spotted as they travelled, in order that they should fully understand the power of the guns. He told them all that they would be given gifts of blankets, knives and other useful things if they went to Beangala, and many promised to visit him there. But in his new role and with new feelings he was failing to sense the mixed reactions that these events were having on his old friends.

From Buckley's Falls they travelled on to the Barrabool hills, and Buckley pointed out the vast open, grassy plains that ran from the Yawangs around the Yalloak and upper Barwin valleys, and disappeared over the horizon to the lake country in the west. They went south past Moodewarri and Paraparap. But coming down the Karaaf towards his old home Buckley received a shock that made him face the reality of what he had been doing for the preceding weeks. They met Nullamboid and his family, and Parrarmurn in Tallarwurnin was still with them.

*Opposite the Flinders and Spencer Streets intersection

They were overjoyed to see him in spite of his neglect of them. Old Nullamboid was amazed by his companions. Without the slightest self-consciousness he walked straight up to Wedge and opened his shirt to see if he really was white all over. After some time chatting with them, Buckley explained that he was showing the strangers around and they would have to go on. He urged them to come to the camp at Beangala for gifts, but it was not what they wanted to hear. They again cried bitterly when he left, and he was still disturbed when he proudly showed Wedge his hut and fishing weir and told about his life there.

When they returned to the camp at Indented Head on 25 August, Buckley immediately sensed a changed mood that alarmed him somewhat. The various Wothowurong families and bands that now arrived were becoming very suspicious of the invaders. The aloofness, suspicion and condescension in the settlers' manner only aggravated these feelings, and the gulf between the two sides was widening.

He felt unable to effect any real change of heart in either party although, on the outward formal level, relations remained polite and peaceful. Privately the Wothowurong were beginning to favour completing the task they had come to do before the return of the *Rebecca;* they began to blame Buckley for not instigating an attack, considering he was in a position to arrange a state of false security among the small party of invaders. He was very distressed. These developments added to his guilt over leaving his family, but he had other priorities. His anxious wait for news of his pardon came before all else. Beyond that he still wanted to work for harmony, and knew that in any open confrontation the guns of the whites would, even if eventually silenced, take a toll far worse than a few provisions were worth. He lived in a state of continuing tension for a couple of weeks, trying to balance these conflicts. He was forced to use the same strategy as before; promising greater wealth to one party upon the arrival of the next ship and watching for any panicky call to arms by the other.

Meanwhile Wedge had gone without him on another survey walk around Port Phillip. He told him what little he knew of the Woiwurong and Bunerong country and how one could follow the coast around. Wedge surveyed the Yawangs and the grassy plains of the Iramoo, crossed the downs of the Barraring country and came to the Barrern river valley. To the north he found open plains; in the northeast and east, moderately wooded hills. There was good grass everywhere.

At a point on the banks of the Barrern he met some Woiwurong and asked them the name of the river. They misunderstood the question, and answered 'Yarra Yarra' which meant 'ever-flowing'. And so the Barrern was renamed.

Coming back to the south on about 2 September he was surprised to see the *Enterprise* and find Lancey and his party camped on the bank of his Yarra Yarra River. Lancey received him hospitably, giving him a meal and a bed for the night. Wedge explained to him that he was on land claimed by the Port Phillip Association; John Batman's block, in fact. There seems to have been no hostility or argument between the men, Lancey taking it all calmly. But Fawkner later claimed that Wedge had made use of Lancey before becoming nasty and ordering him off. It was the first round in the great Batman–Fawkner feud. Wedge went on his way and Lancey sailed a few days later, leaving Fawkner's two servants, Charles Wise and James Gilbert, to carry on. Several days later they commenced ploughing the land at the foot of 'Batman's Hill' on the river bank.

At Indented Head, Buckley waited.

On 13 September the great day came. The Henty's cutter *Mary Ann* sailed into the bay under Captain Scott and anchored about two miles out. Buckley sat on the beach and watched intently as Henry Batman was rowed out to her in the launch the *Rebecca* had left them. Buckley had asked him to fire a gun, on boarding the cutter, if there was any good news for him. He could hardly take his eyes off the diminishing figure as it boarded and walked the deck. The next few minutes were an eternity. But then he heard it — the crack of gunfire.

At the sound of the shot Buckley leapt for joy, roaring 'Ko-ki!' as though he had just speared a big Ko-im. He hugged Wedge in gratitude, practically lifting him off the ground in his joy. Wedge was to record that Buckley was 'most deeply affected . . . Nothing could exceed the joy he evinced at once more feeling himself a free man, received again within the pale of civilised society.'

John Batman had made a personal representation to Arthur after receiving Wedge's letter. The astute Lieutenant-Governor was amenable, but for purely practical reasons. He was unsure of his jurisdiction but wrote to the Secretary of State for the Colonies in London, Lord Glenelg: 'From dear bought experience I know that such a man at the head of a tribe of savages may prove a most destructive foe, and his good offices cannot be too soon propitiated by an apparent act of good grace.'

Without waiting for a reply Arthur promptly had the usual document prepared. A free pardon was granted on 15 August, and dispatched with a letter from Montagu warning that the business did not imply any official recognition of the Port Phillip Association. In fact the following day in Sydney Governor Bourke issued a proclamation voiding their treaties and prohibiting the occupation of Port Phillip.

The launch shortly returned and Batman brought the pardon and accompanying letter to Wedge. Unaware of the machinations which had preceded it, Buckley was grateful for its prompt granting and for the flattering testimonial for service which was given with it. The happy man then reminded them of his promise to the Wothowurong, and the boat was dispatched for more biscuit, subsequently distributed the following morning.

25

Buckley again felt himself to be the equal of any other man. With these documents he felt confident that he could now wield great influence in the new settlement and see that it developed to the benefit of all.

Later that day he had the first major setback to his fledgling ambitions. The *Mary Ann* not only brought his pardon and the testimonial that gave status to his position as interpreter; it also brought instructions from the Port Phillip Association ordering the main camp to be moved to a site on the Yarra Yarra. Whatever his standing with the whites, his only standing with the Woiwurong was as a member of a tribe they had been feuding with for years. His knowledge of their customs and language could only be of limited use.

They spent two days packing and loading the *Mary Ann* before they were ready to sail. A small camp would be left, but they were compelled to move in order to counter the threat from Fawkner and others who had begun to arrive and see the grazing prospects for themselves. Wedge, Buckley, Henry Batman, and his family were to go.

Buckley explained to the Wothowurong where they were going and left it to them whether they would come. They were angry that the settlers were leaving with all their possessions, and clearly felt they were being cheated. They were also upset at Buckley's departure. He was not above feeling guilty about what was happening but he had to take the challenge and follow his own path.

How strange it was to see the shores of Beangala and the waters of Jillong recede far behind him as he once more trod the deck of a ship. His heartfelt sadness was swept away by elation as the wind filled the sails and he revelled in the sensation of speed over the water. The weather was blowing from the north and they had to beat about the bay for two days. Finally, they anchored opposite the site Batman had chosen for a village, and found Fawkner's servants farming just across the river.

They commenced unloading, and began the construction of temporary workshops and dwellings.

Shortly the Pootnaroos and Woiwurong visited. There were about two hundred of them, but they were peaceable and were given gifts of blankets and tools. Buckley was amazed to see a tall, handsome, light-skinned woman among them. It was Karrie Ael — the first time he had seen her in many years. He pointed her out to Wedge, but there was no real contact between them as her father was unknown to her.

A few days later Buckley had his second serious setback.

John Wedge left for Launceston on the *Mary Ann*. This left Buckley in an invidious position. With only Henry Batman, the four Sydney blacks, and Fawkner's men at their camp to back him up in case of trouble he was in a hopeless position. He didn't feel close to either party anyway, and began to deeply regret having left the Wothowurong. He felt trapped. But Batman's brother and Wedge had got him the pardon, and other settlers would come soon, so he had to wait and see what would happen.

Throughout October, other boats began to come and go and the settler camps began to swell to perhaps a dozen men with families. Few were associated with the Port Phillip Association. They were mostly independent or with Fawkner. Toward the end of the month Fawkner himself finally arrived, having sorted out his affairs in Launceston.

He detested Buckley from the first moment he saw him. Buckley seemed the incarnation of everything he hated. Fawkner had made a stop at Sullivan's Bay to see the place where he had first landed in New Holland when ten years old. The mere fact that Buckley was from the *Calcutta* and a direct reminder of his bitterly resented youth was bad enough. But to see that he had run away and gone native was proof that he was even more degenerate than the licentious blacks themselves. However, Buckley's real undoing was probably just the fact that he was working for Fawkner's hated rivals in the Port Phillip Association.

Fawkner began to disparage Buckley among the others straight away. He referred to him as a mindless lump of clay, derided him for preferring to live with the blacks, and accused him of having two wives, 'or more properly slaves', as he wrote. He questioned Buckley's value and ability as an interpreter, accusing him of having a bad influence over the natives and of being an altogether dangerous character. For Fawkner and his supporters it was probably true. An aggressive Buckley would be trouble.

But Fawkner also hated John Batman, regarding him as a cheating braggart, and was out to subvert his purposes from the beginning. He had come to Port Phillip with his family to build a new life free of his past. Together with his supporters, he claimed to want a free colony open to working men rather than squatterdom. However, he immediately became a squatter himself and, before long, had trouble with new arrivals camping on his selections and doing what he had done to John Batman. He led the settlers in disregarding Batman's cursory attempt to make a formal agreement with the Port Phillip tribes, although he was quite active in befriending them on a personal level.

This campaign of slander, and the ill-feelings it promoted, deeply hurt Buckley. He was already on the defensive with the Woiwurong, his language and the fire-power behind him being his only assets. This tenuous position was further undermined by the fact that Fawkner's party had not been idle during the weeks they had been in the district. They had also given gifts to the Woiwurong and befriended them more closely than anyone in the Association that employed Buckley. This friendship centred around a strong mutual liking that had developed between two young blacks, Baitbanger and Derrimut, and a young orphan lad raised by Fawkner, William Watkins. They had been teaching each other their languages.

These and other people aligned with Fawkner treated Buckley with contempt, and he could hardly miss the nasty looks directed at him from many quarters as he moved about the settlement. He felt abysmally isolated and depressed as all his ideas were obviously failing, and the personal odium was at times unbearable.

Early in November a boat was expected from Launceston bringing more settlers and provisions, and John Batman himself. Clearing had begun on the site Batman had marked the previous June, and other preparations were being made for his arrival.

Other tribes of the kulin had been drifting in to swell the ranks of the Bunerong and Woiwurong, as word spread through the country about the activities at the Barrern. By the beginning of November the bulk of the Taungurong, Jajowurong, the Kurung, and Wothowurong had also arrived.

Henry Batman instructed Buckley to assemble them all together for his brother's arrival, in order to extend the big welcome they were planning. There were some eight hundred blacks gathered in an orderly arrangement of camps at a place about three miles north–east of the settlers[*]. This was a great and unique occasion, certainly the last gathering of the Port Phillip tribes, the kulin 'nation', before their rapid decimation by the invading settlers.

Buckley's unease grew with the strain of his position. There was only a remote possibility that he could control such a large group by diplomacy if any hostility arose.

One day as he walked around their campsites he realised with sudden horror what was really happening. There were eight hundred blacks and only a handful of settlers. The temptation was too obvious. His feelings were confirmed when he noticed that the last bands to arrive from the remote areas were composed only of men. They had left their families behind. This was a sure sign that they planned an attack and that word had been spread in advance. He drew aside some of his old friends from the Wothowurong and asked them what the plan was. At first they were shy of confiding in him, but there was mutual understanding that Buckley himself would forfeit his life if he betrayed them. In venting their anger they soon revealed that a general attack was indeed planned.

The tribes had evolved a cunning strategy that was already in action. They were pretending friendship. As the settlers moved around the camp at their work two or three men were slowly attaching themselves to each one, offering assistance as they went. They had kallallingurks concealed in their skin rugs and were dragging spears, concealed in the grass, with their toes. The settlers had left their guns on the boat in the river in order to avoid provocation. At a given signal the settlers were to be killed before they could group themselves and get their weapons.

Buckley was stunned. His feelings polarised violently. He had always hated the fighting and bloodshed that had marked the lives of the tribes, especially when he had seen the strong mercilessly destroy the weak and helpless. But

* Probably on Rucker's Hill, Northcote.

now it was different. The settlers were weak and vulnerable at this particular moment, but they represented only the beginning of an invasion that could destroy these tribes and take all they had. He could not in all honesty blame the kulin for their hostility, and was impressed that for once they were united in a common cause and had devised a bold plan of action that would obviously bring success and perhaps even lead to the abandonment of Port Phillip. He dreaded the thought of seeing harm come to the women and children, but that worry was equally there for the kulin. On the other hand he was not about to forfeit his life or the trust of the Wothowurong for the likes of Fawkner and his grasping associates.

By now he was despairing that the best of both worlds was possible. He was powerless to influence so many people in such a difficult situation. It seemed to be either one side or the other. If there was to be bloodshed then so be it. He wished he could stop it but he could see no solution. He only hoped that the women and children, who were then safely aboard Fawkner's ship in the river, would be spared. In a state of vacillation and near panic he sat by the settlement on the river bank, desperately hoping an acceptable solution could fall out of the sky. Unknown to him his dilemma was being solved for him.

Whereas the Wothowurong, Jajowurong, Taungurong, Kurung, and Bunerong were solidly united for attack, the resident Woiwurong, while privy to the plan, were predominantly pro-settler. They were the favoured tribe with the people in Fawkner's group, having already received many gifts from them and being greatly influenced by the friendship of their young men with Watkins. Shortly before the planned attack, Derrimut told Watkins about it but, owing to their mutual imperfection of language, Watkins was unable to grasp the full import of what was being said. However, he could tell it was something alarming, and went to warn Fawkner.

Fawkner called Buckley to his tent and demanded to know the truth. Suddenly confronted with his enemy demanding the information from him, Buckley's mind seized. He both wanted to tell and didn't want to tell. Refusal to talk would be an admission something was going on, but he could not lie about it.

Finally, with Fawkner and others interrogating him insistently, he snapped, and roared out the truth, adding that if he had his way he would spear Derrimut for the betrayal. The little merchant recoiled in horror and dismissed him.

So it was done. The moment passed, and at least death was cheated for the time being. Fawkner spread the word, and within minutes the entire camp was strangely animated. The men slipped away to their guns as subtly as the alarm would allow.

The kulin were promptly cleared from the settlers' camp by threat of shooting. A party of settlers approached the kulin camps. A large party of men, apparently a battle council, was broken up by muskets fired over them from a distance. The settlement was saved and the danger was over for everyone except Derrimut. An attempt was made by someone of another tribe to spear him. He was very lucky to escape alive by finding refuge with the Fawkners, who fed and clothed him for the rest of his days.*

After this incident generous gifts of blankets, bread, knives, scissors and such items were promptly handed out with assurances that many more would be forthcoming when the next boat arrived in a few days. The tribes dispersed, never to show their full strength again. Their society could never successfully counter the organisation soon to emerge in their powerful enemy.

* He died in the Benevolent Asylum on 28 May 1864, in his fifties. His grave is in the Melbourne General Cemetery.

26

On 9 November 1835, the *Norval* arrived with John Batman and five hundred of his sheep, Joseph Tice Gellibrand, the Port Phillip Association's solicitor, and his sixteen-year-old son Torn, and others. At last Buckley met Batman and thanked him for his efforts in gaining his pardon. The much sobered Henry still spoke favourably of him, despite Fawkner having told everyone about their clash. That night they drank and talked about their adventures. Gellibrand and the Batmans were not about to dismiss a valuable aide on account of Fawkner's stories. John Batman now had to confront his ex-tavern-keeper on his own block. They made an agreement, and Fawkner moved south of the Yarra.

Everyone entered a relatively constructive period. One of the pioneers and chroniclers was George Evans; a servant of his named Evan Evans made Buckley his first pair of boots. The two races mingled peacefully as the settlers gave useful gifts and proceeded to establish themselves. The warmer weather settled everyone down as the first Christmas approached. During this time, the wife of Fawkner's servant, James Gilbert, gave birth to the first white child at the Yarra settlement.

The settlement was now being referred to by a variety of names. Barraring or Barrern was corrupted to Bearbrass, the most popular. There was also Bearbury, Batmania and Dutigalla, a corruption of Gnuther kalk kalk, meaning 'no trees', the kulin name for the river flats around the mouth of the Barrern.

Gellibrand officially hired Buckley as a guide and interpreter at fifty pounds per annum plus rations. Some time in January 1836 he proposed a trip to Geelong, as the western shore of Jillong was now being called. Buckley leapt at the idea, but quickly added that he did not think he could walk it. There was a growing stock of horses at the settlement now and he did not see why he should walk while the new squatters were all riding. On 1 February, Gellibrand hired a large carthorse for him from Fawkner, and summoned his guide to his tent to discuss certain matters.

They arranged the tour and Buckley was thrilled about the horse. Gellibrand informed him that he was to be made Superintendent of the natives with a fixed stipend, and then asked him if he wanted land himself. He had not thought about this; it did not occur to him that he might ever need it. The wilderness, especially in his own country, was still untapped; his beloved Karaaf was remote from the settlement. He replied no to the land question, but greatly approved of the stipend. That would secure his position in his old age and leave him enough to give a few presents to his friends. He assured Gellibrand, who had long been aware that the treaties had been voided by the government, that the tribes understood them and were looking forward to the next payment of blankets, axes and flour.

Their discussion continued, and he became nervous and irritable as Gellibrand went on with questions and conversation about the natives' moral conduct, taking it for granted that Buckley shared his assumptions about their licentious and uncivilised character. He was not articulate enough to argue the point with the well-spoken lawyer. He muttered a few things about their rights to live on an equal footing with the settlers. It was really their land, he added, rather timidly reminding his employer that it was a rental arrangement rather than a purchase. He wanted to talk about the best of both worlds. It was a good chance but he could not express himself.

Gellibrand kindly assured him that everything possible would be done to meet his views. He urged him to use his new position to further good relations through his interpreting, and most importantly to teach the blacks civilised habits and Christian principles. Buckley was so overwhelmed by the poor understanding of the man he did not know where to begin replying. He hesitated and eventually just asked if he could think about it, and nervously begged leave. Gellibrand glowered with goodwill as Buckley quickly departed.

The next day they set off on tour, accompanied by some other settlers. Gellibrand wrote that as soon as they crossed the Saltwater River* and Buckley saw his country 'his countenance was much changed and when we reached Geelong he took the lead and kept us upon a trot. He seemed delighted and proud of his horse.'

And no wonder; after four and a half disturbing months at Bearbrass he now found himself out touring his old haunts on horseback and looking forward to seeing his old friends. They rode down through the Yawangs and on to Geelong, to Buckley's Falls and the Barwin, where he showed them a cave and a hollow tree he had lived in on his wanderings. They reached the Indented Head camp on 4 February.

It was not a very pleasing visit, especially for Buckley. He learnt that the Bengali and others there had not been given food for three months and were angry about what was happening. They had stolen a sack of potatoes from the garden, then left that morning when threatened with shooting.

The next day they rode on across the Bellarine Peninsula. Gellibrand sent Buckley a quarter of a mile ahead in case

* Maribyrnong River

they encountered any hostile Wothowurong. About eight miles later he heard a 'cooee' and when they arrived at Buckley's spot they 'witnessed one of the most pleasing and affecting sights'. Three men, five women, and twelve children surrounded Buckley, who had dismounted. They clung to him, with tears of joy and delight running down their cheeks. It was Nullamboid and his family and friends. They missed their friend and ngurungaeta and wanted him back. They had never seen a horse before and Gellibrand kissed his to show there was no need to fear them. The younger men were encouraged to mount and a thirteen-year-old girl was given a ride.

Nullamboid and the others begged Buckley to stay and he tried to explain his position to them. Gellibrand gave the old man his blanket to reassure him. Nullamboid explained to Buckley that Parrartnurnin Tallarwurnin had gone away with some young men of another tribe. Buckley had hardly thought about her during the overwhelming changes of the previous months. He could hardly blame her for leaving; in fact, he said it was the best thing and told them to send her his greetings and tell her that he hoped he would see her again one day. After exchanging other news they had to depart, neither Buckley nor his friends feeling very happy.

They rode on to Lake Connewarre. Gellibrand noted the huts there — about one hundred of them along the water. Tom shot a large musk duck which Buckley ate for dinner when they camped that night. In the morning they rode to Paraparap, and up to the Barrabool Hills.

Accompanying them on this excursion was a young man named William Robertson who, with his brother John, owned a share in the Association and ran a Hobart Town merchant business. Buckley and Robertson took a great liking to each other. Robertson, like Buckley, was tall, strong, and genial. Buckley admired him when he took the flagging Gellibrand's knapsack as well as his own. He was to enter Buckley's life again after many years. They returned to Bearbrass a few days later. A ship had arrived laden with provisions, including a cargo of potatoes and bricks. It was so long since he had eaten chips that Buckley had forgotten how good they were. He had grown fond of roots, like the mirrnyong, that he had lived on in the bush, but the potato was hard to better. He distributed these and other items to the kulin, and the mood of the settlement was amicable again for some days.

He felt sad about Nullamboid and the others, but resigned about the young Parrarmurnin Tallarwurnin. At this time he was not thinking about going back to the hard life in the bush. He had a job that provided him with plenty of food and other things he had long gone without. He was now engaged in supervising the construction of the brick chimneys on Batman's house*, the first proper dwelling to be built at Bearbrass. As an old bricklayer, he fondly remembered his youthful days under his 'good old master, Mr Wyatt'. Soon after its completion the chronicler George Russell passed by, and Buckley cheerily asked him if he did not think it was pretty good work for a man who had lived thirty years with the blacks. These days were happy ones for him. There was ale and wine to mellow the summer heat, and he had his pardon. He would visit Van Diemen's Land when a chance came, but at the height of this beautiful summer his only real concern was the continued sniping from Fawkner and his associates. His hopes even resurged that a society of mutual benefit to both races would grow up about the beautiful woodlands and downs of Port Phillip. Within days he would begin to find out that the real problems were yet to come. Suddenly, things took a dramatic turn for the worse.

A number of minor conflicts had begun to take place over the women. The Sydney blacks had been causing

* On Batman's Hill, now the site of Southern Cross Station.

jealousy with their activities, but the growing number of single white men began making serious trouble.

On 13 February things flared into the open. A young Woiwurong woman, about twenty years old, came to Buckley in great distress. She had been on her way to Bearbrass to see her mother when a shepherd had accosted her by the Saltwater River on the Association's No. 10 block.* He had dragged her to his hut, raped her, and tied her hands behind her to a post and left her there all night until she had eventually escaped. One hundred and fifty kulin gathered around to accompany Buckley, who took the woman to Gellibrand and explained the situation and pointed out that justice was being demanded.

Gellibrand had just returned from a tour of the blocks north of Bearbrass. Two men were brought to him, but they were only identified as having been in the hut at the time. Eventually, the guilty shepherd arrived. Confronted with the accusation he swore his innocence, but Gellibrand was convinced the woman was telling the truth. With a show of strength he publicly reprimanded the man and dismissed him from the Association's employ. He tied a red handkerchief around the woman's neck to cheer her and saw the shepherd on to the *Caledonia* himself, as he had to leave that day on a business trip to Van Diemen's Land. Buckley was left to explain the 'punishment'. The Woiwurong, who would have preferred him speared, dispersed again, only just satisfied.

After a visit to Port Phillip the following March, when he saw the woman living there happily with her husband, and after Buckley had rather weakly assured him they were satisfied with the deportation of the shepherd, Gellibrand wrote: 'It was in fact all the punishment which we had the *power* but not all that we had the *will* to inflict.'

Other incidents continued to occur. In March, a party

* Sunshine

of wattle-bark strippers fired on a Bunerong camp near Western Port, wounding several people. They had tried to take a thirteen-year-old girl for gang rape. She lived, but was crippled in one leg by a musket ball through one thigh and into the other.

The settlement had been established for only six months, and these incidents were consequences of its rapid expansion. By this time, Batman had fifteen hundred sheep on his block, although he had yet to settle at Bearbrass himself. Wedge had just returned and was running a flock by the Werribee. Captain Swanston, Robert von Steiglitz and others were also expanding their flocks. Shepherds, wattle-bark strippers, and the like were now penetrating thirty miles and more from the Yarra Yarra with increasing frequency.

During this first summer Bearbrass had its first taste of bushfire, but it did no harm. By April the autumn rains had raised a coat of shimmering green grass on Batman's Hill, and the whole country looked very pretty. The settlement was still only a collection of three or four wattle-and-daub huts and twelve or fifteen tents — some only tarpaulins slung over a branch supported by a forked stick.

On 20 April, John Batman finally arrived to stay. He came on the barque *Caledonia* with his wife Eliza, his six daughters, and their governess. His health had continued to decline, but he set about making a home in the house Buckley had helped prepare for them.

Meanwhile, other boats continued to arrive with increasing frequency and the population began to burgeon. News of the opportunities opening up in the Port Phillip District had spread through Van Diemen's Land like wildfire. Families and speculators started touring to see the prospects and decide whether to move there.

Nevertheless, by the winter of 1836 the permanent population was still only a few dozen. The problems of the present, and especially the future, began to demand more than individual solutions, and the white citizenry of Bearbrass began to gather in the open air to discuss and vote on certain issues. Buckley recorded his vote along with the others. A meeting on 1 June voted on various matters to constitute a government. Another made a submission to Governor Bourke for a magistrate. Von Steiglitz had noted the country was so new that there was no power whatever to uphold the law. This problem was made more pressing by the violent incidents which had already occurred, as Gellibrand had indicated. In fact, according to Bourke's August 1835 Proclamation, they were all breaking the law by being there. Confident, however, that the colonial authorities were not going to come and evict them, they pressed for recognition. Officials arrived from Sydney to make reports.

But before these attempts to form ordering institutions had come to fruition, another violent incident took place that would serve to justify the need for official law and order, and provide a turning point for Buckley.

In July, a man called Charles Franks and a shepherd, James Smith, were found dead in the homestead at Mt Cottrell on the Werribee Plains. The premises were robbed but there were no witnesses. Gellibrand took a party out to retrieve the bodies. So-called justice was summary and brutal. A posse was organised, including a contingent of Woiwurong and the Sydney blacks. They went out and tracked a band, probably Kurung or Wothowurong, finding them with stolen goods. Most of them were massacred on the spot.

Everyone had known Franks as a kindly man, and this only increased their sense of outrage. However, Buckley knew that von Steiglitz had recently passed by Franks' place and been given some lead to make what Franks had jokingly referred to as 'blue pills [buckshot] for the natives'. Convinced that Franks was not entirely innocent and more than likely provoked his own destruction, Buckley had refused to go with the posse. He was living in an annexe to Batman's storehouse, where he acted as a watchman. When the revenge party returned he was struck with horror at the news of what they had done. They expected to leave the bodies of Franks and Smith in his but for the time being, and to their astonishment he savagely refused.

Up to this time the level of violence between the settlers and the kulin had not — with massacres in the first months narrowly avoided — extended to killing. It was a problem, to be sure, but relations with the settlers were no worse than or very different from what they had been among the tribes. Now Buckley was savagely confronted with the truth of colonial occupation. Any provocation, real or imagined, from the kulin would result in immediate extermination. The same behaviour by the settlers would be subject to 'justice'. The immediate difference lay in the possession of firearms; in the long-term in numbers and organisation. Now he had no regrets over his reluctance to betray the planned attack the previous October.

On 12 July he stood in front of Batman's smithy in a state of frustrated outrage. It was a grey Port Phillip winter's day and the funeral procession of Franks and Smith filed past him*. Virtually alone he saw the injustice and felt no sympathy.

The settlers walked past bearing the coffins, their faces set with righteous sorrow. In Launceston the *Cornwall Chronicle*, expressing the typical sentiments of the time, roared that the massacre had not been sufficient revenge and called for more blood. Buckley was not an articulate man, especially in English. He just looked at the farce and snapped inside. He laughed; laughed loudly and rudely in

* They were buried in the first cemetery at the Flagstaff Gardens

the faces of the mourners.

That act was the beginning of the end for Buckley in Port Phillip. From then on he was increasingly vilified and treated with contempt. Fawkner and his friends had continued to criticise him, but had remained a minority. But now the majority, ever increased by newcomers, was more and more solidly against him. His unpopularity made the job of interpreter, always complex and demanding, finally impossible. Soon after he resigned, and stayed on as a helper and boarder with the Batmans, who were among the few who at least understood his feelings.

27

John Batman was battling with a multitude of personal problems made worse by his ill-health. By the time of Franks' funeral he could hardly walk. The sheer effort of establishing a home and starting to grow food was as much as any man could cope with. But as well as that he had many time-consuming problems with the Association, the settlers, and the blacks. People were coming and going daily from Van Diemen's Land and now also from Sydney.

Once he had resigned, Buckley was able to avoid being exposed to these pressures himself and relax more, doing the simple labouring jobs with which he was happy. He got on well enough with the Batmans, often enjoying a drink and a talk with them. They were certainly kind to him, and one day he gave Eliza Batman his old Ko-im skin that he had been wearing when he walked into the Indented Head camp. She had made him a shirt that was the best present he had received since Wombalano Beeaar had once given him her rug.

Their eldest daughter made him a pair of slippers. He found the Batmans much more easy-going than most of the colonists now flocking in. So many of them were, to him, extremely stodgy people. Unlike the kulin they were deeply reserved and phlegmatic. The men would never cry, the women never show desire. In fact most of the whites seemed to deny they had sexual feelings, whilst looking resentfully at the free ways of the kulin. He became afraid to show his feelings, began to withdraw in their company.

It was a different age to the one he had left behind. The Victorian era was about to dawn and everyone now, especially the well-to-do, favoured tight formal suits and dresses and dark forbidding colours, black being universal. The victory over Napoleon and his French Empire was safely in the past. No power rivalled Britain or her navy, and no-one seemed to want to remember the situation that had festered during Buckley's youth.

After some months of quiet life, just miserably watching the inevitable growth of the settlement at the expense of the kulin, a new opportunity came for Buckley

Although the Port Phillip Association's treaties had been repudiated, it had been successful in obtaining recognition as the official coloniser of Port Phillip. In September 1836 the settlement was formally recognised by the authorities in Sydney. Batman had requested that someone be given authority from the beginning, offering assistance with money and buildings from the Association. The Government understood the advantages, fearing that convicts would run away to Port Phillip from Van Diemen's Land and lead lawless lives or, worse still, create high wages in a settlement that would tend towards a chronic labour shortage. Bourke appointed as magistrate the thirty-six-year-old Captain William Lonsdale. He chose Bearbrass as the official centre of the settlement and arrived in H.M.S. *Rattlesnake,* under Captain Hobson, with a detachment of troops. They were of the Fourth or King's Own Regiment of Foot, Buckley's old corps from his Holland days.

This put him on a good common footing with Lonsdale, who had instructions to appoint him to his staff. On 10 October he became interpreter, constable and attendant to Lonsdale, and negotiated a rise in salary, getting sixty pounds per annum plus rations. This time he was determined to at least get a decent wage for attacking the terrible problems he knew would plague him once again. He had mixed feelings about the job, but Lonsdale was telling rather than asking. He could not expect it to be any easier, even with military authority behind him; but, like everyone else 'received within the pale of civilised society', he needed the money. His standing was also helped by the fact that Lonsdale was staying with the Batmans.

At first he assisted in constructing buildings for the corps, the barracks, a storehouse, and a residence for Lonsdale. For help he employed several Woiwurong, paying them in food. They were not servile, but willing to help out of courtesy and fair exchange. They worked cheerfully, thinking it a huge joke, but the soldiers' red jackets were objects of terror to them.

With their camp functioning, Lonsdale sent Buckley out on a series of missions among the settlers to see if there was any trouble with the tribes, and to settle disputes as best he could. Things looked up for a while, and he enjoyed travelling about the countryside. But it had been a year now since the colony really began and great changes were obvious. The most distressing thing, which he should have known but had not really thought about, was the extent to which the forest was being cleared. Everywhere he went settlers were busy with axes, chopping down trees and grubbing stumps. Wimba and Ko-im were disappearing from many areas, along with many other creatures, old landmarks and familiar sights. His ideas on the scale of farming had been gained in the neat counties of his native England. It was only now that he began to grasp the vastness of the Australian pastoral system, its hunger for acres and the speed of its growth. By that summer there were about three hundred people at Port Phillip. But the number of sheep was about seventy thousand.

He could not convince himself that this was progress, even if it was necessary to the people he had welcomed as his rescuers. The settlers were often mean and aggressive people. He realised more and more that his ideas had really been a terrible illusion.

For some weeks, at least, Buckley's problems were simply those of adjusting to this awareness. Things were going well. The settlers had enough land and work to do, but there was still land enough left for the tribes to have somewhere to go. But then the trouble started again. First, two stockmen were killed about seventy miles from Bearbrass by a band avenging an attempted rape of two of their women. Then a Wothowurong man was seized and accused of robbery. He was tied to a tree, shot dead, and his body thrown into the Barwin. Buckley had to go with two other constables and apprehend the killer.

The man was sent for trial in Sydney and acquitted for lack of evidence; the witnesses, of course, were in Geelong. It did not matter, in any case, as no court in the entire colony would accept evidence given by a black.

These incidents, and the generally hostile feeling towards Buckley, disillusioned him once and for all. His work became a burden because people feared and mistrusted him. They could not understand a man like him. He had to be bad to have gone native the way he had. Stories spread. There was the massacre plot and the Franks funeral incident. Then someone had seen human flesh in a 'lubra's' basket and become indignant, only to have Buckley rebuke them and tell them not to put their heads in other people's baskets.

As the summer wore on into 1837, he made it no secret that he regretted the whites coming at all and disturbing the life he had had with the Wothowurong. Settlers like Gellibrand and Hoddle chronicled his unhappiness and its cause — he blamed the whites for what was happening. They began to think he could go back to the kulin and agitate in a way that would cause real damage. More stories went around, and Buckley was looked at more darkly than ever.

The truth was that he was now incapable of such action. He yearned for his old life but he could not go back to it. Time had overtaken him. As a young man he had bolted without thought of anything but freedom, with the mad confidence of youth that comes of not really knowing just what can happen. Only eighteen months after his 'rescue' he felt he had aged. The fit and active hunter who had guided the amazed John Wedge was now feeling too old to think of braving the hard life of the Wothowurong. Even the tough conditions of the pioneers had softened him. Worse, as he admitted to McKillop, one of the many Scots settlers in those early years, he had even become afraid of the kulin, especially the hostile Woiwurong with whom he had most contact. His position of authority did not endear him to people already resentful of his presence in their country.

In the meantime, during December, Lonsdale had appointed George Langhorne, a missionary. He was to bring civilisation and religion to the natives by gathering them into a village settlement where they were to live on charity until they learnt farming or wage work. Buckley was attached to Langhorne as interpreter. When he arrived and commenced his duties in January 1837 he found 700 kulin, mostly Woiwurong, waiting for their handouts. They were hostile to Buckley because of his Wothowurong connections, and Langhorne was soon forced to ask that Buckley be transferred to Geelong to be amongst his own people.

Buckley couldn't get on with Langhorne and was uncooperative with what he saw as a stupid scheme. Langhorne later wrote: 'He appeared to me always discontented and dissatisfied, and I believe it would have been a great relief to him had the settlement been abandoned, and he left alone with his sable friends.'

The village mission went from failure to failure, ending in 1839. Handouts were no substitute for the freedom of the bush, especially when they had to be earned by boring work and the recitation of Holy Scripture. At one stage all fourteen children in the school ran away together and were never seen again.

Between 1 March and 29 March 1837, Governor Bourke visited the colony along with a retinue including civil and military officers of the New South Wales Government and their wives. A parade was held to receive him, and Buckley was given the dubious honour of presenting 100 blacks in ranks, all saluting the Governor at his command.

Bourke renamed the Bearbrass settlement Melbourne, in honour of Lord Melbourne who was then prime minister of Great Britain, and approved a plan for the township naming the principal streets. He saw to it that clothes were distributed to about a hundred and twenty natives. It was he who suggested food should only be given for work done, so presumably the free clothes were to save the ladies of his retinue or perhaps himself, from embarrassment.

The official party was subsequently taken on a few quick tours of the countryside. Buckley went as guide on the tour of the Geelong country, showing the Governor his cave at Buckley's Falls. The Surveyor-General was with them, and he and the others were delighted with what they saw. Blacks found on the way were promised gifts at the settlement. The conquest of the Port Phillip District was now official and complete.

One night, as they were camped on their way back to Melbourne, there was a quick series of loud shocks like explosions. The sentry gave the alarm, thinking that natives had got into the powder wagon.

It was an earthquake; the only one in Buckley's lifetime in that country.

On his return to Melbourne, Buckley found the settlement aflurry with disconcerting news. Gellibrand had returned from one of his trips to Hobart Town with a barrister friend of his, George Hesse. On 22 February they had left from Point Henry in Corio Bay to travel to Melbourne on horseback. Some three weeks later they still had not arrived and everyone wanted a search begun.

George Russell had met them when they anchored at Point Henry and spent a night on board with them. Gellibrand had asked him about the Leigh River valley and said it was his intention to follow the Barwon to the Leigh. From there he would proceed up the Leigh some distance before cutting across through the Anakie Hills to Melbourne. It was just over a year since Buckley had taken Gellibrand on his guided tour of this country. He must have retained the impression that it was more extensive than it was, for he was adamant that the Anakie Hills could not be seen from the ship at Point Henry. Russell knew that they could be.

Despite his fatigue after the long journey guiding Bourke's party, Buckley was ordered out immediately to search for them. He rode fifty miles to the but of a grazier, Mr Reibey. Here he hired two Wothowurong trackers. One of them was Beruke, who later changed his name to Gellibrand and became well known around Melbourne. Buckley awaited the arrival of Torn Gellibrand, who soon came with a number of other white men. They rode to the station of Captain Joseph Pollock, an ex-merchant seaman running stock on the Barwon at Pollock's Ford. He had sent one of his stockmen along with Gellibrand and Hesse as they passed through, in order to show them the junction of the Barwon and Leigh Rivers. They had passed it by a few miles when the stockman realised his mistake and urged them to go back. Gellibrand had insisted it was further on and dismissed the stockman, who then returned to the station.

The search party included Cowie and Stead from their station at Bell Post Hill, Geelong, where Gellibrand had first stopped, von Steiglitz and others. After refreshments Pollock joined the party, and they rode out to the place where the stockman had left them, tracing their hoofprints to the west until the trail was lost in a recently-burnt plain near Birregurra. The trail was headed in the direction of the unexplored Otway Ranges in the south–west.

They travelled on until they spotted a camp in the distance. Buckley suspected correctly that this Koligon band would be hostile to whites, and insisted on approaching alone. What was more he knew some among them from the Burnarlook days. The Koligon and Wothowurong were still feuding over some of those old killings so he couldn't be sure how they would receive him either. Relying on his old status as a non-combatant he called out to them. They had never seen a horse before and did not recognise him at first. They ran off, but he gave chase, calling again. Soon they realised who it was and they all came around with friendly greetings, marvelling at the horse and his new clothes and hairstyle. They were co-operative, and Buckley sat down with them and began to explain his problem.

Before he could get any information Pollock and the others rode up, one of them barking out in a jargon that he evidently thought was a dialect but which no-one else could understand. This foolhardy action frightened off the Koligon just as Buckley was feeling sure they could be enlisted to search out the missing men. They refused any further discussion, but told Buckley he could come alone to their camp, and withdrew. The rest of the party were too afraid without him, however, and would not let him go.

This panicky behaviour may well have set the tragic seal on the fate of Gellibrand and Hesse. If they were still alive, or their killers — if they had been killed — still about, that band would have provided some answers. As it was, they were never found: no bodies; no horses; no trace of any kind to give a clue to their disappearance. No blacks were ever seen with any of their clothes. The two hills on the plain between Lake Murdeduke and the Colac lake country, Wallan-wallan and Mookatook, were called Mt Gellibrand and Mt Hesse as silent reminders of the mysterious swallowing up of the head of the Port Phillip Association and his friend by the Wothowurong country. The search party returned to Melbourne, 'discovering' Lake Colac on the way, and riding north to Mt Buninyong before turning east to the Yarra.

Bourke had returned to Sydney and the settlement resumed its business. Three friends of Gellibrand led by C. O. Parsons came from Hobart Town in order to mount another search. They wanted Buckley to come with them. He gave them all the information he could but refused to go. They were angry, and Lonsdale was forced to call Buckley for an explanation. On hearing about the interference, and how it could have caused them all to be speared, he was forced to agree that Buckley could achieve far more by travelling alone. Gellibrand's friends were fired by all the indignant anxiety befitting concerned colleagues, and they determined to take the situation into their own hands. They engaged several Woiwurong, gave them all fire-arms, and set off.

A strange thing now happened. Three days after this party had left, Lonsdale cleared Buckley to go on his own search. His horse, the one Gellibrand had acquired for him, had a sore back. He decided to wait a couple of days to rest it, leaving it tethered in the rear of his quarters at

John Batman's. One day a black ran up to Buckley as he was talking to Batman and said that the horse was nearly dead from bleeding. They hurried to it and found someone had hamstrung it — all the hind sinews of its legs were cut through. They were sure a white had done it; it was a white man's thing to do. The horse died.

Buckley took a boat to Geelong, intending to get another horse there and ride on; although by this time he was sure it was futile to continue. When he got to Mr Reibey's station he learnt that the search party ahead had shot dead a Wothowurong man and his daughter. The shock of this act of terror and bloody revenge made him stop immediately. There was absolutely no reason to believe these Wothowurong had anything to do with Gellibrand and Hesse, or even that they had ever seen or heard of them. It still was not even certain they were dead. The murderers had frightened themselves with their terrible act and returned to Melbourne. Buckley lost all interest in the search and returned, desperately wanting to get away from these horrors. It was not the only one he had to confront.

Not long after this incident an immigrant ship arrived in Geelong from Van Diemen's Land. Among the passengers was a carpenter who employed a black to help him carry his tool chest and baggage up from the beach. This was a common practice then as no wharves or even houses had yet been built there. In payment the black was given an old suit, and the two men parted company. Several days later another ship came from Van Diemen's Land and the same man went down to look for a little job. The master of the ship, a personality not unusual in that sort of position of authority, regarded himself as something above mortal men. When he saw the black in the suit he thought it could not be his by honest means, and promptly accused him of having murdered Hesse and stolen his clothes, and further claimed that red spots on the coat were Hesse's blood. The black was promptly handcuffed and sent to Melbourne, charged with murder.

One of Fawkner's employees questioned him, but his language was hopelessly inadequate. Buckley was disgusted that anyone so ignorant should give evidence, and took it upon himself to defend his Wothowurong brother, who explained his innocence and how he had got his suit. Unfortunately, the carpenter had left Geelong and his whereabouts were unknown. The captain persisted in his charges and the poor man was locked in the guardhouse pending trial. Even the Chief Constable was sympathetic to him.

Fate intervened. One day Buckley was walking along the bank of the Yarra Yarra discussing the case with a friend. A man and his wife within hearing stopped him and asked to see the suit. The man had once given one away in circumstances similar to those Buckley had been relating. He subsequently identified the coat, the black, and the red spots as paint splashes from a job in Launceston. The black was released and cried bitterly at his ill-treatment. The ship's captain left, with nothing against him. Fortunately, Captain Lonsdale went by due process of law. He ordered Buckley to take the freed man to his own house, where the Lonsdales treated him with great kindness. He was given all the food he could eat, and blankets, tomahawks, bread and meat and other gifts as some compensation for the wrong done him. Buckley escorted him part of the way back to his people, leaving him in high spirits. His extraordinary luck was an exception in these repeated cases of injustice.

Buckley himself was not so fortunate. As 1837 wore on the prejudice and hatred against him continued to mount. The maiming of his horse was only one sign of it.

Fawkner and others had been spreading stories that he

had eaten George Pye and other runaways when he was living in the bush, and these rumours began to surface in the Van Diemen's Land press. Fawkner also charged him with conniving with the blacks to steal sheep and kill shepherds. Two of Captain Swanston's men and a runaway had been speared while bringing provisions to Indented Head. Later, one of the suspected Wothowurong had been shot in the back, and Buckley accused Baitbanger of the murder. Articles and letters that expressed a widespread desire to have him removed from the colony had been appearing over several months. Apart from the hatred and insinuations of cannibalism, the predominant reason was a fear — fed by Buckley's own expressions of unhappiness — that the ageing bushman was going to go back to his 'sable friends' and instigate rebellion. The word 'insurrection' was being muttered around Port Phillip again.

These feelings were well known to Lonsdale, who was now under increasing pressure to dismiss Buckley. A fair man who adhered to the rules, Lonsdale did not readily give in. Buckley himself was keen to get away for a while. His estrangement from most of the other colonists was now extreme. Money could not buy what he wanted, and without the drive to make money there seemed to be no place for him. The colonists, all rivals, seemed to take little joy in each other.

28

At length the chance came for both Buckley and Lonsdale to calm the situation. An absconder had been captured at Port Phillip and was to be taken back to Van Diemen's Land. Buckley was not enthusiastic at the reversal of roles, but the man was going anyway; and so he readily agreed to take him.

The trip provided an exciting breath of fresh air in his troubled life. He gloried in the voyage across Bass Strait and marvelled at the extent and development of the settlement in Launceston.

Having delivered his prisoner to the gaoler, he made enquiries with some contacts he had been given by John Batman and others, and found out that one of his old shipmates from the *Calcutta* was living on a farm of his own some miles out in the country, and rode out to visit. The countryside was well settled and the scars of clearing the bush had begun to heal. There were no blacks anywhere. No-one seemed to give them a thought, unless prompted by direct question. The issue was either avoided or brought surprisingly venomous and contemptuous comments from people who obviously knew nothing about it.

Buckley's friend almost collapsed with astonishment when the ageing man stood before him and identified himself. Recognition came only slowly and after a long look, despite Buckley's height. He was welcomed like a long-lost brother and they spent many long hours in the comfortable little but over jugs of home-brewed ale, swapping yarns and laughing about the old days. The other man just kept shaking his head in disbelief.

After a few happy days Buckley had to leave, according to his instructions. He had no desire to simply desert his kulin friends, but he was strongly leaning towards the idea of coming back to this happier isle. Mr Samms, a member of the Port Phillip Association and the Launceston Under-Sheriff, treated him hospitably and gave him flour and other provisions to pass on to his friends at Port Phillip.

His ship was a paddle-wheel steam vessel, the first he had seen. They were still new, having only sailed the Pacific since 1835. This one was carrying convicts in the charge of Captain Foster Fyans, who had been appointed the first Police Magistrate at Geelong. Buckley still remembered the *Calcutta* and felt uneasy, but a lot better, about travelling such a ship as a free man. How his luck had changed.

How Port Phillip had changed in so brief a time. It was only two years since those joyous days when Wedge and the others had come and seemed to change his life for the better. Since then all his dreams of the best of both worlds had vanished. One illiterate man, who could hardly speak English, could not hope to have any significant influence on a settlement expanding like a fire fanned by wealthy and influential winds; by men whose driving concern was to seize the rich lands of Australia Felix in order to make more wealth and win More power.

Even men like Lonsdale — public servants who took seriously the idea that all people were equal subjects of the crown — were helpless in controlling these forces. A man like Buckley had no hope alone. As an old man in white society, a remnant of the past in the great era of progress, he was suspect if not despised. His only hope would have been to have had allies, but he had none. The three men closest to him were never able to see what he saw, and could not help anyway. Gellibrand was gone, and his death signalled the early end of the Port Phillip Association. Wedge was hardly to be seen, and in fact went to England for five years in 1838. His station was sold to Chirnside and called Werribee Park. John Batman was a sick man battling for his own survival, and Henry had returned to Van Diemen's Land. Others in the Port Philip Association, like Simpson, were kind to Buckley, but their own pioneering labours were inevitably their predominant concern.

After they had landed in Melbourne, Buckley was instructed to accompany Fyans and his party across country to Geelong. As they rode, Peret-peret the spur-winged plover warned of bad weather and, sure enough, as they were crossing the plains near the Yawangs a rainstorm began. It poured down, soaking the struggling horsemen. Suddenly, life caught up with the gentle giant. His old frame sagged and he began to collapse. Half falling from his horse he turned pale and stumbled under a tree, unable to continue, his mind racing with a jumble of events from the past two years. Fyans and the others were alarmed, not knowing what to do, but Buckley insisted they go on without him, making it plain where to go.

He remained under shelter, resting his exhausted body and trying to still his mind. He suddenly realised that he might be going to die. He was fifty-seven and knew he could not last forever, especially after his strenuous life. He had survived by courage, the help of others, youthfulness and sheer luck so often before when death had stalked him. But he could not defeat time. Now the inevitability of his end was becoming undeniable. The rain poured down and the blackness of the coming night closed over him.

He had thought he would still have a few quiet years to himself, perhaps in the refuge of Van Diemen's Land;

and he swore he would have them if he saw out the night. Loneliness and misery over the conflict and destruction of the past two years pressed on his heart. He dreamt of the old times as he never had before. He had spent his life never looking back; always casting the past away behind him. Now he was struck by an irresistible urge to go back; back to the bush, the wild, free country; back to his country. He wanted to go back to his old house by the Karaaf and see and feel it all there — the hush, the sea — one more time before he died, to find that spirit once more, before it was lost forever.

It was not far to the Karaaf from where he was, and this would probably be his last chance. He felt better, and grew anxious for the night to pass so he could set out. He dozed a little in the bushes, but the wet made sleep impossible. By first light the rain had eased to a series of isolated showers that drifted like stately grey curtains across the plains of Iramoo. He rode off, determined to avoid Geelong and any other white men's camps on the way. He moved slowly, conserving his strength, savouring the countryside one last time. Crossing the Yalloak and Barwon Rivers some miles inland he passed along the eastern flank of the Barrabool Hills and down through Jeringot, where he had left his now lost old friend arid young wife to run like a fool to Beangala. He could see now that he could not have gone bush again, because his old country was rapidly disappearing. By now probably only the more remote corners like Mangowak and Gerangamete were untouched, and that would not he for long. Sheep-runs were pushed in along all the streams; huts and clearings were appearing everywhere.

He reached the headwaters of the Karaaf near Paraparap by nightfall and made camp. He could almost see the ocean. In the morning he rode triumphantly along his stream towards its mouth in the east. It was over two years since he had last walked that way to show John Wedge where he had lived. The little valley had sheep well ensconced, but he saw no-one.

At mid-morning he at last approached his campsite; a little of the old nervousness as to what he would find returned. He tethered his horse and stepped over the dune and down on to the beach. It was gone. The ruins were still there but it was completely wrecked. It had to be expected, he told himself, shuffling around, reconstructing from the bits and pieces he could still recognise, the place he had once loved more than any other. The stone was not to be found.

He realised the hut had not been destroyed by the elements. It had been wrecked. He saw hoof-prints, bits of paper; it was obvious whites had wrecked it, no doubt assuming it was just a strange native mia-mia.

His weir had long since washed away. Two stakes still protruded from the sand where they had once held their bundles of sticks. He stared down at them and let his mind wander back. The world had seemed so fresh then. He could hear Burmbo Merio and Mirri Mallo splashing with Yeraobo in the water nearby, and Yanathan-lark singing one of her songs by the campfire. An old man could at last look back.

He slowly forced his mind back to the present. He mounted his horse and said some goodbyes. It seemed the only path left was to leave the colony. He wondered if the settlers would ever know what it was like to lose the sacred places, the true homes of their hearts. Perhaps they had lost theirs so long ago that even the memory of them had been forgotten, swept away in the tornadoed oceans of the globe as generations of people had washed away on the tides of time.

For some reason he forded the Karaaf, and rode across the plain toward Maamart by the lagoon at the mouth of the Barwon. Shortly he came to the big old tree where he had first been found by the Wothowurong aeons ago. It was still the same. He had seen lifetimes come and go but it looked as if time had stood still. He dismounted and went up to it, looking fondly over its mighty form. Just then Barroworn alighted on a branch and made a sad little cry. Buckley was ecstatic. The spirit was still there and he was with it. No matter how much the world had confused his heart, the friend was still within it. Now he could go.

So long Barroworn, he thought, and turned and walked away. As he approached the horse, for a minute that was unique in his life, he felt his whole body fill with an overwhelming self-love. It was all right. He knew that he had done right, no matter what mistakes or what was said now or ever by the Fawkners and their ilk. A great sense of release swept through him. Half-weeping, half-smiling with relief and gratitude to something he could never name, he mounted and set his horse at a walk. As he rode away the sun came out, and Barroworn began to sing as if the world were a mere shadow of its light. He turned and waved a distant goodbye, roaring out a great cheer and kicking his mount into a canter.

At Geelong, Buckley was recovered in strength and determined to wait out the last of his duties before resigning.

He returned to Melbourne by sea and spent several weeks searching for sheep said to have been driven off by natives. Things were not becoming any better, that was certain. He now feared for his life as he travelled around on his work. There were too many lonely tracks where it would he possible to waylay someone and have him disappear without trace. Influential men were keen to be rid of him. There were few people of either race he could trust now.

As the end came near and it became obvious he was going to have to resign very soon he began to have mixed feelings about leaving. He realised something he felt he should have seen long ago. If he had his own land he might be independent enough to hold out against the pressure to get rid of him. He might have been able to find his friends — even find Parrarmurnin Tallarwurnin and Karrie Ael and do something for them. He had never thought to join the land grab, even when Gellibrand had raised the matter nearly two years previously. Now it was obvious there soon would be nothing left in the entire kulin country.

In a final bid to save the situation, in November 1837, he sent a petition to Bourke for 'a grant of land, or such other assistance as your Excellency may seem fitting, in order that your petitioner may not in his old age be reduced to distress.' Ever the optimist, he added that a pension of £100 per annum would be satisfactory as a substitute.

Bourke sent the petition to Gipps, who forwarded it to London recommending the pension but not the land. Glenelg rejected it in a reply of 4 June 1838, stating that he would not have given land anyway and refusing the pension on account of Buckley's 'former history'. Buckley probably never knew the fate of his petition. According to the correspondence of Superintendent Latrobe in 1841, the authorities in Sydney were only then made aware he had left Port Phillip. It was in connection with a scheme proposed by Wedge, then in England, to give aid to the blacks, using Buckley as intermediary. Latrobe rejected the idea.

But things at the settlement were moving too quickly. Lonsdale finally had to submit to the pressure on him. By mutual agreement Buckley resigned in December. How worthless his pardon seemed then, but at least it gave him a way out. He had saved some money and was given a reasonable severance payment. With Lonsdale's advice he booked a passage for Van Diemen's Land. Instead of his longed-for best of both worlds, he had been caught in a crushing grip between them.

He sailed out of Port Phillip Bay for the last time on 28 December 1837, on the *Yarra Yarra,* less than two and a half years after his 'deliverance', and just thirty-four years and two days after his brave dash for freedom. With him were two Kurung brothers Fawkner was sending over to Hobart Town, to impress on them the power of the settlers.

He stood on deck and watched the mouth of the Yarra Yarra River recede. He saw the Iramoo, Jillong, Beangala, and Sullivan's Bay one last time. He was still telling himself he would go back to the bush one day. There was no question he would at least visit his old friends, bring them presents and tell them of life in Van Diemen's Land.

Way out through the Heads that he had watched from the Karaaf for so many years he looked back and could see the Yawangs. Slowly they and the coast of his country sank below the horizon of Bass Strait.

29

Buckley arrived in Hobart Town on 10 January 1838. The bustling port and extensive settlement were something of a wonder, considering it was all started by his old shipmates. The master of the *Yarra Yarra* was Captain Lancey, onetime master of Fawkner's *Enterprise*. He treated Buckley with great hospitality on all occasions. On their arrival he went to the bank with Buckley to help him get his final cheque cashed, and then took him to his lodgings at the Duchess of Kent Inn in Murray Street. There he entertained Buckley with food and ale, and saw him comfortably settled.

Later Buckley was visited at the Inn by another old Cheshireman, Mr Cutts, word having spread that the 'wild white man' was in town. Cutts was the landlord of the Black Swan Inn in Argyle Street, and insisted on having Buckley as his personal guest. Good old Kunnawarra, thought Buckley, gladly accepting the offer for several weeks.

For the first time in his life Buckley had a home, money in his pocket, nothing to do and no obligations. During the day he wandered the streets of the town, marvelling at the complex web of activity. He was especially fascinated by the new machines, the tools and skills that people now had. People talked excitedly about the growth and proliferation of industry back home. Britain had become the workshop of the world. There were iron roads that had started in the coalfields and were now being built all over the world. Some of the moving steam engines on them were doing speeds of up to sixty miles per hour, and there was no telling where it would stop.

But the city life was not for him. It never had been really, except for a few fast-living years in London. He knew he didn't want to spend the rest of his days in the noise and dust of Hobart Town. If he had to stay away from Port Phillip for the present, then his visit to his friend outside Launceston had left him with a clear idea of how he would love to spend his days. What he wanted was land; just a small block where he could run a few sheep and while away the rest of his time along the streams and in the mysterious hush of the bush. The money he had was far too little to consider buying anything at the prices he found in this advanced and prosperous colony. The only hope was a grant, but he was pessimistic of ever attracting such a favour from the government.

The desire was never out of his mind as the months of inactivity in Hobart Town began to roll by. Nearly every day on his walks people would accost him for advice and information regarding Port Phillip. The whole of Van Diemen's Land was inflamed with stories about the future opening up there. Every second word was land, and boatloads of emigrants and sheep and all the paraphernalia of the colonists were leaving almost daily. Many knew who Buckley was, and his information was keenly sought. He answered questions politely and honestly, but never told tall tales to inflame the desire to go. He privately wondered where they were all going to go and how the tribes could withstand such a floodtide, and how Batman and Lonsdale could be coping.

One day a man stopped him on the street and gave him a ticket to the theatre. After a chat he was invited to come along to the show, which was about to start. This Buckley did, and greatly enjoyed himself. After the show one of the actors invited him to come again the next day and join them on the stage. Buckley was flattered and not averse to letting his reputation gain him such favours and save him a little money. He came the next day, expecting a seat for the performance. To his shock he found he was to join the act as an exhibit, billed as the 'Anglo-Australian Giant'. Far too shy and retiring, he vigorously rejected any idea that the wild white man should be so humiliated, much to the chagrin of the stage manager who had advertised his appearance. Such were the traps of city life.

After several months in Hobart Town a chance came to leave. Another old shipmate from the *Calcutta* learnt he was in town and looked him up while on a business trip from his farm. He had built a prosperous property near Green Ponds, about thirty miles out, and was now a wealthy and respectable settler. A few days later when he had settled his business, he invited Buckley to his home. Once again Buckley enjoyed the pleasures of reunion in the quiet and refreshing rural world; this time staying nearly a month. There were many walks to go on and there was time to learn what birds and animals lived in that country.

At length he tired of his indolence. Never one to be inactive as long as there was life in him, he yearned for something to do. Besides, his money from Lonsdale was not going to last forever. His friend was on good terms with the Lieutenant-Governor, Sir John Franklin, and Buckley asked him if he could make a request to Franklin to help him find work. He returned to Hobart Town and, to his delight, soon received an invitation from Government House, asking him to come first thing the following morning.

Franklin had replaced Arthur as Lieutenant-Governor at the beginning of 1837. A man of liberal views, he had been welcomed by the free colonists who, while benefiting from convict labour and the removal of the blacks, resented the cruel and arbitrary dictatorship that had made Van Diemen's Land the most dreaded penal colony. But the sensitive Franklin was no match for the political machine Arthur had left behind and which was run by the Colonial Secretary, John Montagu.

By the time Buckley came to see him, Franklin had resigned himself to letting Montagu run the colony while he pursued his interests in exploration and science.

Buckley was up well before dawn that morning and nervously prepared himself for the meeting. This would be his big chance. If he could ever hope to get that land this was the day.

In his best clothes he presented himself at the gate before eight o'clock. He was shown into a large dining-room where the Lieutenant-Governor and Lady Franklin were breakfasting with a group of their gentlemen friends. Franklin greeted him cordially and invited him to join them. A maid gave him tea and buttered rolls, and conserves were passed to him.

Franklin had a keen interest in his story, and they all asked him many questions about his life and the state of things at Port Phillip. Buckley's mind raced; he drank tea but was too nervous to do more than nibble the food as he tried to talk. The session must have lasted an hour. Finally the big question came when Franklin asked what he would like for himself. Buckley sipped from his cup and said at once that he wanted a small allotment of land.

Stifled smiles went around the table. Flanked by some smug faces, the not unsympathetic Franklin apologised and patiently explained that he could not grant land, but he would find him work. Buckley did not smile, but thanked him with a sinking heart. The breakfast concluded and he went back to his lodgings, his hopes dashed.

Over the following days he revived them a little with the thought that at least with a job he might be able to accumulate the necessary capital.

Several days later he was appointed Assistant Storekeeper at the Immigrant's Home, a temporary establishment the government had provided as a hostel for new arrivals from Great Britain. The work was simple and easy for him; some lifting and carting, but time for sitting and minding the store, and swapping stories with the new chums and his fellow workers. The job only lasted three months, after which the Home was disbanded, as all its occupants were settled. While he was there he met the Eagers family who had recently landed from the old country: a pleasant and friendly labouring man, his cheerful and diminutive wife, and their charming daughter. He became good friends with the whole family and visited them frequently at the house they were able to rent in the town.

After the hostel had closed the government kept him on, transferring him to a job as gatekeeper at the Female Factory, as they called the establishment employing convict women at the Cascades, South Hobart. It was an easy but boring job. The shifts were inclined to drag as he stood around the little gatehouse nodding to the regulars as they came and went, or as he had repetitive chats with people who approached him with questions about Port Phillip and his past life. But it was a living.

Time passed, and he was into his second year in Van Diemen's Land. His dreams of a future on the land were still there but not so immediate. His mind began to return more and more to his past, especially to the last two years at Port Phillip. He wondered if he had done enough to try and help the people who had done so much for him, and whether he could ever go back.

Then, in 1839, he received the stunning news that Batman had died on 6 May. Buckley wept bitterly for his friend; for all his friends whose dreams he knew were lost at the hands of his old enemies.

30

Not long after the death of Batman another fatality was to change Buckley's life. His friend Eagers had gone to Sydney to look for work, as he was making little progress in Hobart Town. Having no luck, he decided to look around Port Phillip. He set out to make the journey overland, no doubt under the misapprehension that the military posts Gipps had established along the way only several months previously had made the route secure. He was killed by blacks near the Murray River, leaving his family unprovided for.

Buckley had hardly been able to think about women for four years. His advancing age, the tendency of women coming to Port Phillip to be guarded like the crown jewels, and the prejudice against him, created a problem. Nevertheless, he had grown extremely fond of Julia Eagers and her daughter during his frequent visits to their house. Their friendship had developed into a close relationship after Eagers' departure. Julia's natural cheerfulness and sense of humour suited Buckley's easygoing nature, and they always laughed together when he went to her home for a meal. She would mock him, passing his dinner saying, 'Eat, wild man!' and digging him in the ribs.

He waited several weeks after the news of her husband's death came and the mourning was over. Then, for the first time in his life, he proposed. Julia Eagers accepted; she liked the gentle older man, and she and her daughter had need of a breadwinner in the house. They were married by the Reverend Mr Ewing of the Episcopalian Church at New Town on 27 January 1840. The difference in their height was so great that, when they went out walking together, Julia could not reach his arm. He would tie two corners of a handkerchief together and attach it to his elbow. Julia then slipped her arm through the loop that hung down.

Buckley was very happy with his new family, and things went well for a short time. But soon after they had settled in together he was struck down by a sudden onset of headache, chills, pains, and fever. When sores and blood-poisoning developed after a few days he thought he was finally about to fall victim to his old enemy Monola Mindie. But this affliction was diagnosed as typhus, and he would live yet. He spent many days in great suffering. Fortunately, he was now a family man, and Julia and her daughter nursed him with great affection, always raising his spirits. After several weeks he was restored enough to return to his post as gate-keeper, but his health would never be quite as good again. His iron constitution began to fade.

While he was sick he thought a great deal about his old friends at Port Phillip and about the increasingly remote possibility that he could ever visit them again. He wondered about Parrarmurnin Tallarwurnin and Karrie Ael. Eventually he had a letter written out and sent to them. Parrarmurning Tallarwurnin's people received it and, on learning of his marriage, despaired of his ever returning. It was Buckley's last contact with his beloved kulin.

He lived on to 70, working at the Female Factory and helping Julia raise her daughter. Once he heard that his brother was still living in Middlewitch, Cheshire, but he couldn't find out about Karrie Ael. He would never know that the first overlander to Port Phillip, who had been on the tour with Buckley and Gellibrand, John Gardiner, saw Karrie Ael near Kilmore — his stockkeeper fell so desperately in love with the 'tall, noble-looking' woman that he wanted to kill her husband. Buckley slowly despaired of ever going to Port Phillip again. He couldn't afford to leave his job, or even to buy a ticket for the boat. He was trapped.

As time passed he found his reputation and fame began to fade. Very few people ever came to see him about Port Phillip. Up-to-date news of that settlement became more easily obtainable elsewhere. Rarely did anyone express interest in his life in the wild. Except during the depression years of the early 1840s, everyone seemed to be too busy rushing around in the one true pursuit of life in the Australian colonies — making money. His income was meagre, and he began to toy with the possibility of selling his story somehow to the public. After all, Daniel Defoe's *Robinson Crusoe* had been a bestseller, read by every literate boy since its publication in 1719.

Buckley felt that his story should be of equal interest, and could perhaps make a few pounds or, even better, help him gain the publicity that might persuade the government to grant him a decent pension. Even Bourke had written to Arthur in September 1835 saying: 'I wish that someone of Mr Batman's party would obtain from Buckley the history of his adventures and give it to the public. If Buckley is of the least observation or talent it could not fail to he interesting.' Unfortunately, no-one had done it while his memory was fresh, and Buckley himself could not make notes. Langhorne had taken a statement from him in early 1837, but Buckley could not explain to the missionary what his life was like. Besides, he didn't like Langhorne, and avoided his questioning. When he had arrived in Hobart Town, a Daniel Bunce, later the curator of the Geelong Botanical Gardens, approached him. It seemed a blatant attempt to use him, and he answered Bunce in monosyllabic grunts until he left in disgust.

This was not the only attempt to use him made by

people who really had no sympathy for him and were more than likely antagonistic to any ex-convict and any other race besides the English. James Bonwick, a prominent contemporary writer who later published a book hostile to Buckley, observed:

We lived for seven years in the same Town with Buckley, almost daily seeing his gigantic figure slowly pacing along the middle of the road, with his eyes vacantly fixed upon some object before him, never turning his head to either side or saluting a passerby. He seemed as one not belonging to our world. Not being divested of curiosity, we often endeavoured to gain from some one of his acquaintances a little narrative of that savage life, but utterly failed in doing so. Several newspaper folks tried repeatedly to worm a little out of him, through the agency of the steamy vapour of the punchbowl: but though his eye might glisten a trifle, his tongue was sealed.

After rejecting these earlier approaches time passed, and the story inevitably began to get confused in the old man's memory.

Sometime in the late 1840s Buckley met John Morgan, an ex-Royal Marine then in his fifties. Morgan had had a grant of land at Swan River resumed by the British Treasury, in order to make good some debts he had incurred in running a store there. He had come to Van Diemen's Land as a police magistrate, had tried farming, and then had worked in Hobart Town as, amongst other things, a journalist and as a secretary to various organisations. Morgan was a liberal and open-minded man who, as a journalist and publisher, fought for various social, political and religious reforms. About this time he aroused some attention by writing to the Governor of California, protesting at the racist exclusion of Indians, Africans, Mexicans and their descendants from the guarantees of freedom in the new Californian Constitution, which was then being touted as a model of progressive statecraft.

Buckley liked Morgan, they shared similar attitudes on such issues. He put to him the idea of writing his story, suggesting that they share any returns. Morgan was busy with an editing job at the time, and Buckley was still on the gate; but Morgan kept the idea in mind. In 1849, he was refused a marine corps pension because of his old debts, and the following year an alteration in the establishment at the Female Factory saw Buckley out of his job with a miserable pension of twelve pounds per annum from the Convict Department. Now both men had time to collaborate.

There remained one problem with their project — money — and here Buckley's past came to his aid. Assistance came from William Robertson, the tall, genial merchant Buckley had befriended, along with Gellibrand, nearly fifteen years previously at Port Phillip. Buckley had seen him occasionally before he had gone to Colac, and Morgan knew a relative of his, George Robertson, who had also been a journalist and editor in Hobart Town before leaving to join William and work for him. Morgan was easily able to persuade the prosperous Robertson, then living on his farm, to sponsor their book. So they got down to work.

In 1852, Morgan finished the laborious task of gathering a consistent story from the old man and editing it into book. A lithographic portrait of Buckley was included, probably taken from a daguerrotype, as craftsmen of this technique had toured Australia in the 1840s. At about seventy years of age, Buckley still looked strong but gentle, calm but wary. With Robertson's money, Morgan commissioned an edition from Archibald MacDougall, a fellow journalist turned printer. Morgan may have planned another, but time passed. It is not recorded how many copies were sold or whether Robertson, Morgan, or Buckley made any money from the book.

Buckley, although a legend in his lifetime, was by then a forgotten man in person. However, the book, or Morgan's eloquent plea for a pension on its last page, must have aroused some attention, for later that year the fat and prospering colony of Victoria added forty pounds a year to Buckley's pension. He and his family scraped along a little more easily, but he took odd jobs when possible. He was still a big man, but he had to be careful. He had by then given up his dream of land. It was said that Bourke had once ordered him to be granted 200 acres at Port Phillip; perhaps the Victorian Executive gave him the pension as a substitute.

In December 1854, Morgan brought Buckley news that there had been an uprising on the Victorian goldfields that would have repercussions throughout the colonies. The miners had been waging a campaign against the way Latrobe's military administration had been harassing them. Their immediate grievances, were the unjust licensing system on the diggings, and the need for other reforms in the administration of the goldfields and a revision of the laws relating to crown lands. But they also raised the demands for parliamentary reform originally made by the English Chartists, who had led the last great uprising in England in 1841 during the terrible depression of the early 1840s.

Buckley nodded to himself. The struggles of his youth were still not dead, then. The ideas had been carried halfway round the world, and the nation growing in Australia would yet be shaped by them. The merchants and graziers would not have it all their own way. The flag of Yukope and Dantun had been raised. But still, he was an old man now, and it was not for him to worry about the outcome. He thought that maybe he was lucky. The poor people fighting for their future on the goldfields were entering a hard world. The good things in life: freedom, adventure, women, children, and even love; he'd had them all in his own way and lived to tell about them. He tried not to think too much about Port Phillip, for he only felt the bitterness rise in him. He wanted to die knowing that he had lived, with no regrets.

On 30 January 1856, Buckley was out helping a neighbour on his cart. It was a beautiful, hot Australian day, and the dust swirled along the road. As the cart trundled up the street he let his mind slip away through the warm air. He would have loved to be by a cool stream in the bush with a couple of jugs of ale in the water. He kept thinking of Barroworn; his old friend was on his mind.

As they turned a corner he lost his footing and fell forward. His giant old frame went down, his head striking the road, and the wheel of the cart bounced over his body. The man who had wanted the best of both worlds was dead.

Epilogue

William Buckley was buried near the corner of the Davey and Harrington Streets entrance to St. David's Park, Hobart (then a cemetery), on 2 February 1856.

Later in the nineteenth century, visiting Buckley's Cave and Buckley's Falls and other of his localities for picnics became something of a vogue. Children passed the folklore of his exploits from generation to generation. To this day, anywhere in Australia, people can be heard mentioning his name. When they want to say that someone has one chance in a million of achieving something, they say, 'You've got Buckley's hope' (or 'Buckley's chance'). There is said to have been another Buckley, in the eighteenth century, who had the rope break when he was hanged. Like him, our Buckley survived against all odds. He was the courageous and adaptable old Barroworn.

From the time he left Port Phillip the story of the tribes became the story of their destruction; black died as white prospered. The House of Commons tried to help the blacks by establishing a body called the Port Phillip Protectorate under the authority of G.A. Robinson, of Van Diemen's Land fame. However, by not granting land rights, the Protectorate was doomed to fail; and so it did, at the hands of aggressive graziers and the blood thirsty press that supported them. The many massacres in the area testified to the frontier's isolation from effective authority.

In July 1838, Governor Gipps in Sydney wrote to the Secretary to the Colonies, Glenelg, in London, depicting a state of sporadic guerilla war.

'A statement of the principle outrages committed by or on the Aborigines ... of which reports have been received since April 25th last.

Your Lordship will observe that a great proportion of these acts of violence have occurred in the neighbourhood of Port Phillip . . . the reason of which is, that large herds of cattle and flocks of sheep have been recently driven through these extensive tracks of country . . . often not more than in the proportion of one man to several hundred sheep . . . migrating in search of pasturage, advancing often so miles in a single season, and in the case of Port Phillip, having stretched to a distance beyond our former limits of between 300 and 400 miles in the last three years.

If proprietors, for the sake of obtaining better pasturage for their increasing flocks, will venture with them to such a distance from protection, they must be considered to run the same risk as men would do who were to drive their sheep into a country infested with wolves: with this difference, however, that if they were really wolves, the Government would encourage the shepherds to combine and destroy them, whilst all — we can now do is, to raise, in the name of justice and humanity, a voice in favour of our poor savage fellow-creatures, too feeble to be heard at such a distance ...

There followed a list detailing numerous incidents of sheep and cattle stealing, several involving armed attacks on stations and overland convoys. It ended with the note:

N.B. A great number of less important outrages have come indirectly to the knowledge of the Government, or been reported in the newspapers. And it is said that a white woman, the wife of a soldier, has been murdered between Melbourne and Geelong, though no official account has been received of it'.

It is said that a white woman was murdered. Or was it defiled by black hands? Important rumours like these served to justify a lot of violence as self-defence.

Gipps, in demonstrating the impossibility of effective military pacification of the situation, had covered only a three-month period. Many other incidents were recorded. One black, caught in a raid on a Moorabool River Station, about two miles from Fyansford on 19 October 1839, called himself Picaninny Buckley.

This resistance continued spasmodically into the next decade, but it inevitably crumbled as everything went against the kulin. As Buckley had witnessed, their numbers had already been greatly reduced by plague — the dreaded Monola Mindie was smallpox. Starting in 1789, it swept through the tribes of south-eastern Australia in several waves. The death toll could have been as high as half the population. The tribes often testified as to how numerous they had been within living memory, before the settlers came.

But the black population was hit both ways. As the death rate went up, so the birth rate went down. Whites took the women. The chances of raising children were lowered by alcoholism, prostitution, tuberculosis, venereal disease, and other health problems associated with the new sedentary existence, a shortage of marriageable partners of the right 'skin', malnutrition, and the general breakdown of the social fabric. William Thomas, assistant Protector for the Western Port and Gippsland District, was convinced infanticide, the traditional form of birth control, had increased. 'No good pick aninnys now no country', they told him. The sacred places and the ceremonies of initiation were gone. The blacks saw the whites break all their laws and customs and yet still flourish. They lost their dreaming, and began to believe themselves that their end was coming. They stopped building permanent huts. The earliest reports noted many domes or beehive-shaped mia-mias, roomy and sturdily built for use on regular visits as they wandered about. Like Buckley's hut, they were destroyed too easily to be worth rebuilding.

One of the worst features of settlement was the effect that white expansion had on intertribal relations. Neighbouring tribes were territorially pushed in on one another, invoking and aggravating intertribal conflict. Revenge killings began tragically to augment the accelerating death rate. Francis Tuckfield, the Wesleyan Missionary from Geelong, in his 1843 report made testimony to this; some of the killings were taking place at his mission.

The Protectorate was abolished at the end of the 1840s and its depot given to squatters. Later there was a station established at Framlingham near Warrnambool. Parrarmurwin Tallarwurnin would end her days there.

Where the 1840s had seen a steady, relentless decline in the situation of the tribes, 1851 saw the floodgates burst open. With the goldrush the population quadrupled in three years to about three hundred thousand. In 1851 there were already six million sheep, arid that number continued to increase.

Adventurers, fortune hunters, the poor and hopeful of many lands came in search of a fortune. Many of them were Irish. This flood became the foundation of a future working class in the new colony. The embattled remnants of the tribes were swept aside. Only pockets like the Kurnai in Gippsland were to survive.

The settler estimate of the number of Wothowurong around 1836–7 was 173, but they were already being killed. In 1853, there were thirty-four, with one under ten years old; in 1858 nine males and five females. In 1863 the combined Geelong and Colac figure was twenty-eight. The last Wothowurong died in 1885. He was 'King Billy Gore', the son of Billy Wa-Wa, the last headman, who had named him Worm Bunyip after returning to their camp by a lagoon in Jacob Street, Geelong from Jerringot, where he had seen a bunyip. The last Yawangi — 'Billy Leigh' — died in 1911. The Wothowurong died mostly of pulmonary diseases, liquor and unknown killings.

By this time white society was long accustomed to using the ideas of Charles Darwin to sanctify the 'passing of the aboriginals' as a law of nature. Curiously, there was little interest in using these ideas to justify the fate of the animals and birds. Here, at least, the white man seems to understand that guns, poison, and the rapid artificial destruction of native habitats break the rules of natural selection.

Karbor and Koorman were massacred to the point of extinction, to be saved in the end by the concern of a few dedicated people. Like the blacks, their numbers have grown again but not yet their distribution. The fate of Gandu still hangs in the balance. Mighty Ko-im is fed to Garl, save a few tails kept for soup for the well-to-do. Kaan still awaits the unwary Garl, as Djurt-djurt and Thara still hover in wait for the foolish. Tuan-tuan and Turnung and their friends Wollert, Bemin and Yundool still lurk in the night to cast fear into the uninitiated. The silent Kokurn still watches all; Yukope and Dantun and their friends still flash their colours as they screech and chatter joyfully through the bush and farmlands. Bunjil, hunted and shot in thousands by the angry white man, is still the lord of the air when the city is left behind.

The wise old Waang still gets by all right and can even be seen in the cities, sadly commenting on what he sees. Kooring-kooring survived to announce the dawn and to laugh at the white man. Balayang and Ngaribarmgoruk still fly out of their hollow trees in the dusk when the soft light calls lovers forth. Norngnor still lives in the bush gullies when cover is left. Kunnawarra and Kururuk still thrive in the more remote waters. The defenceless Karwer has been pushed back to more and more remote areas, as foxes, cats and humans destroy her young.

Yern and Bo, once common, have become rare; those not shot or trapped were decimated when disease swept through Australia's marsupial population in the years 1900 to 1903. Whether Yern will ever return to challenge the dogs only time will tell. Narrut still calls up the life-giving rains. Tutbring still comes in the spring when the Pleiades drive off the winter, and still goes high into the mountains for the summer. Wimba still lives a rather lonely life in the bush, close to where Ka-warren can be found digging with his strong claws to get those bastard Collenbitchik. Everyone wants the Kumbada now. Murrin mooroo, shy and vulnerable, has had to retreat to the most remote mountain streams until that millenial day when it will be safe to once again swim in the white man's waters.

And Barroworn? He has of course survived the best of all. More than any other creature Barroworn has survived and adapted to the coming of the white man. At home on the edge of bush and paddock, or in parks and gardens, Barroworn can still be heard piping with incomparable beauty. He can be heard early in the mornings greeting the sunrise, and sometimes he can be heard on moonlight nights piping a lonely call to the moon, which always comes to life again.

Glossary

Wherever possible the vocabulary of the Port Phillip tribes has been used. In some cases use has had to be made of Western District and Gippsland words. Most have been drawn from Bride (1898); Dawson (1881); Howitt (1904); Massola (1968 edns); Morgan (1852.); Morrison (1965); Tindale (1940); and Smyth (1878), which has a chapter on pronunciation. See bibliography for details.

amadiate (animadiate, amadeat, amygeet, amerjig) refers to one who has gone to the land of the dead and been made white or, as in Buckley's case, has been and returned.

Balayang the bat; male sex-totem, brother to all men. *Bangeballa* possibly Lake Beeac or Martin, or one near Ballarat.

Ballark an inland locality.

Banor a hill somewhere above Airey's Inlet.

Barbarka the dolphin.

barngeet war boomerang.

Barrabool the hills near Geelong. The Wothowurong were sometimes called the Barrabool tribe.

Barramunga a town and locality in the Otways on the upper Barwon River.

Barraring the country between the Yarra and Maribyrnong Rivers.

Barrern (Berrern) Yarra Yarra River.

Barroworn (Perreworn) the magpie; Buckley's totem.

Barwal Swan Island.

Barwin (Barwon) principal river through the Wothowurong country: also means magpie.

beal a drink made from water in which native honey or wild flowers, for example, native honeysuckle *(Banksia ornata)* or grass-tree flowers *(Xanthorrhoea),* have been soaked.

Bearhrass (Bearbury, Batmania, Dutigalla) corruption of Barrern. First names for Melbourne.

Bearrock waterholes near Dean Marsh.

beenak women's rush basket.

Bellarine like Ballarat, Ballan, derives from *bal* meaning elbow. Thus a camping or resting place where one reclines on the elbow.

Bellin-bellin the musk crow or black-faced cuckoo-shrike.

Bemin the ring-tailed possum.

Beangala Indented Head.

Bengali band or group at Indented Head; part of Wothowurong.

berbera barbarian, referring specifically to the Kurnai.

Beruke kangaroo-rat, the name of Wothowurong tracker on Gellibrand and Hesse search party.

bihar messenger.

Bo (Boe-ung, Boo) the bandicoot.

Bollam-bollam the butterfly.

booboop infant child.

Boonea eels.

Boonea-yallock river of eels; the section of the Barwon at Buckley's Falls.

Boorang Mist-in-the-valley; Buckley's first wife.

Boordek locality in the hills west of Colac, near Boonah, Bambra.

Brinbeal the rainbow; Bunjil's son.

Bukra-ban yule home of Mindie; near Charlton.

Bullbul a Wothowurong man.

bullito-koorong a sea-going boat.

Bullum-Boukan legendary michievous two spirits in one female body.

Bunerong a kulin tribe; from Werribee River around north and east shores of Port Phillip Bay and across the Mornington Peninsula and around Western Port.

Buninyong group from near Ballarat, Mt Buninyong.

Bunjil (Bundjil, Pundjel) the wedge-tailed eagle; the higher power, virtually a sky-god (belief in such was generally confined to South-Eastern Australia); a moiety.

bunyip monster lurking in various waterholes and lakes.

Burmbo Merio younger son of Torraneuk and Wombalano Beeaar, later adopted by Buckley; means New Moon Now.

Burnarlook blackwood tree; band of Koligon.

Colac sandy place by that lake.

Collenbitchik the bull-ant; a band.

Connewarre black swan; lake in Wothowurong country. *Corangamite* from *korine* (bitter), *gnubet* (water); a lake. *corroboree* tribal dance.

Danawa remote river, probably the Barham at Apollo Bay. *Dantun* the crimson rosella or mountain lowry; one of Bunjil's six young wizards.

Djurt-djurt the nankeen kestrel; one of. Bu'njil's six young wizards.

Doorangwar (Dooangawn) Spring Creek, Torquay, where Buckley found the spear in the grave.

Dreamtime or *Dreaming* Refers to a past mythic time, a time of creation or genesis, but also to the eternal in the sense of the 'everpresent and immutable reality which underlies, and is expressed in, time' (Elkin). It is a dream, a collective dream into which one is initiated by joining a totem cult, that is, a specific 'dreaming'.

Dutigalla corruption of *Gnuther kalk kalk* meaning no trees. The flats around the mouth of the Yarra Yarra. *Eurok* the goanna; a band.

Galgal-bulluk the dog-people; a band of the Jajowurong.

Gandu the whale.

Gang-gang a species of cockatoo.

Garl the native dog or dingo; Wuruum kuurwhin's totem.

Geen-geen the currawong.

Geewar wells at the present site of Geelong.

Geiwoorn the grey shrike-thrush; songster.

Gerangamete a lake but now a locality.

Gherang a small lake.

Gnurnan the black cockatoo.

Gnurnile the white cockatoo.

Godocut Point Addis.

guram (gee-am, ker-ram) spear and boomerang shield.

gurring sap from various species of wattle tree: edible and adhesive.

Iramoo the downs and plains around Corio Bay and up to the Maribyrnong River (according to Hume).

Jajowurong (Jajowrong, Jaa˙re) a kulin tribe of the Loddon valley and Daylesford area.

jeringot a large pond; Waurn Ponds.

Jillong Corio Bay.

Kaan the tiger snake; snakes generally.

kalk wood, stick; message stick.

kalkeeth wood-ant larvae taken in August.

kallallingurk (morang) stone axe.

Karaaf Bream Creek; Buckley's favourite abode.

karalk the bright streaming rays of the setting sun on which departed souls ascend.

Karbor (Koobor, Kurberu, Koola) the koala bear; Torraneuk's totem.

karkeen Mt William greenstone (diabase); the most valued axe-stone in Victoria.

Karrie Ael Buckley's daughter; means Summer Rain.

Karwer (Ka-we) the emu.

Ka-warren (Kowurn) the spiny anteater; Tro wernuwil's totem.

Kirkedullim a place near Airey's Inlet.

kneerekeyan to dance.

Ko-im the kangaroo; a band.

Kokurn the powerful owl.

Koligon Colac tribe or group from Lake Burrumbeet down through the lake country from Colac to Camperdown and over to Cape Otway. Kolakngat was their language.

kooderoo mutton fish or abalone.

Koodgingmurrah an unidentified lake.

Kooraioo sand or sandy place on the shore of Jillong.

Kooring-kooring the kookaurra.

Koorman the seal.

koorong boat or ship.

Korok-guru the red-browed firetail.

Koronn Tro wernuwil's and Weeitcho taerinyaar's daughter; means Feather.

Krokitch and *Kaputch* the white and black cockatoo moieties of various Western District tribes, equivalent to Bunjil and Waang respectively

Kuarka Darla Anglesea River; sandy stream.

kudgerim heavy fighting club or waddy.

kulin means man,or men as in mankind and was the common term for such in the Port Phillip language group, referred to by some as the kulin 'nation', that is, the Jajowurong, Taungurong, Woiwurong, Wothowurong, Kurung, and Bunerong.

Kumbada tree-fern; Buckley's band.

Kunnawarra (Gunnawarra, Connewarre) the black swan.

Kurnai the Gippsland tribes.

kurniang women's digging stick.

Kurung (Kuring-jang-baluk) a vague group, between Geelong and Werribee and up to Ballarat; separate to the extent of having exchanged women. Seems to have embraced the Yawangis, Leigh River, and Buninyong groups. At Man.

Kururuk the brolga or native companion.

kyoong young girls waist fringe of leather strips or thong.

Lark the cloud.

leonile (leangwell, liangwil) battle club with hooked end.

Lib-lib a locality on the shore of Bangeballa.

Lillipook Mindie the scales of Mindie; the ulcerous sores symptomatic of smallpox.

Lo-an fabled ruler of Marin-e-bek.

Maamart swampy area on the west side of the lagoon at the mouth of the Barwon.

malka (malga) heavy club-fighting shield.

Mangowak (Monwak, Mangowhaz) Airey's Inlet.

Mara language grouping of tribes, west of kulin; including Koligon.

Marin-e-bek the Splendid Country; Wilson's Promontory.

marmbula kidney fat; the seat of the soul.

Marpean-kurrk ancestress who discovered kalkeeth and became the star Arcturus.

marriwan spear-thrower.

merrijig 'well done'.

mia-mia simple but or wind-break.

Millewa Murray River; means 'one big water'.

milork fat white grubs from around tree roots and rotting logs (not witchetty grub).

Mindie legendary serpent from Bukra-banyule subdued by Bunjil and unleashed by him as punishment to the kulin.

Mirro Mallo Torraneuk and Wombalano Beeaar's only daughter, later adopted by Buckley; means Sunshine Soon.

mirrnyong a tasty root — yam daisy or native dandelion *(Microseris scapagera);* also a stone-pit oven or midden.

moiyan the silver wattle tree.

mongile deadly long spear with double jagged edging.

Monola Mindie smallpox.

Moodewarri (Modewarre) the musk duck; lake in Wothowurong country.

Mookatook Mt Hesse.

Moonalelly Yawangi woman, friend of Buckley's.

moorabool monster lurking in Yalloak, or river of that name.

Moorrinno the Lightning Man.

moorup soul of the dead; shade.

mooyum karr bull-roarer.

Moriac volcanic cone north of Moodewarri.

mung black or evil magic.

Murdeduke lake in Wothowurong country.

murrakul woman's headband.

Murrangurk Buckley's tribal name; means Soul (returned from the dead).

Murrin-mooroo the platypus, Wombalano Beeaar's totem.

Myerre the swift.

nandum (karnwell, dirk, derg) long spear, jagged on one edge.

Narrut the frog.

Nellemengobeet waterholes at Bannockburn.

neram wild raspberry.

net-nets legendary hairy little people in the Stony Rises.

Ngamat the place where the sun goes down.

ngarangs man-eating, semi-human monsters living in hollows down in the roots of trees.

Ngaribarmgoruk the owlet-nightjar; female sex-totem, sister to all women.

ngurungaeta an elder.

Nooraki Mt Defiance.

Noorat mountain near Terang, important trading place.

Norngnor the wombat, a band.

Nullamboid an old Wothowurong man; a friend of Buckley's.

Pallidurgbarrans a tribe of the Otways who fell into cannibalism.

Paraparap (Palac Palac) a sandy place; a locality near Moodewarri.

Parrarmurnin Tallarwurnin Buckley's second wife, from the Buninyong group.

Peret-peret the spur-winged plover.

Pewitt the mudlark; headman of Bengali c. 1835.

Pomborneit probably equivalent to Purrumbeet — large water. A locality by Lake Corangamite.

poolyte native cherry tree.

Poorool the sugar glider.

Pootnaroos (Putnaroos) part of the Buncrong tribe.

tark (daar, tare, tirrer) reed spear.

tarluk-purn freshwater crayfish.

tarnuk wooden bowls.

Tarnwil plain turkey or Australian bustard, once common in Victoria.

Taungurong Goulburn Valley kulin tribe.

Terragubel Wothowurong friend of Buckley's; means Standing Up.

Thara the black shouldered kite; one of Bunjil's six young wizards.

Tharangalk-bek the manna gum tree country; Bunjil's country; the place of heavenly sojourn of the departed.

thundal (yarkuk) magic quartz crystals.

tooiyung crayfish.

Torraneuk Buckley's Wothowurong brother; means Heart.

Tro wernuwil Buckley's Wothowurong nephew; means Foam-of-the-Waterfall.

Tuan-tuan the tree rat or brush-tailed phascogale; one of Bunjil's six young wizards.

Tu-at fish.

Turnung the pigmy glider or flying mouse; one of Bunjil's six young wizards.

Tutbring the flame robin; Yanathan-lark's totem.

Waang (Waa, Wakee) the crow or raven, the lower power; a

moiety.

Warengbadawa hostile band of the Taungurong.

Wallan-wallan Mt Gellibrand.

Waraduk Mirri Mallo's betrothed; means Stormy Wind.

Weeitcho taerinyaar Tro wernuwil's wife; means Playful Leaves.

weenth-kalk-kalk fire-stick.

weing fire.

Werribee river on west side of Port Phillip Bay.

Wimba the wallaby.

wirrarap medicine man and/or sorcerer (the two do not seem to have been clearly distinguished with the kulin); shaman.

Woiwurong (Waverong, Wurunjerri, Wainworra) Melbourne tribe; Yarra and Maribyrnong Valleys up to the Divide; Mt Macedon and east to Mt Baw Baw. Language of the Wurunjerri.

Wollert (Willart) the silver-grey or brushtail possum.

Wombalano Beeaar Torraneuk's wife and Buckley's sister-in-law; means Beautiful Stream.

wonguim returning or play boomerang.

Woonduble the Thunder Man.

Woorer-woorer sky or blue sky; a band.

worra-worra common club or fighting stick, long with knob on the end.

Wothowurong (Wotowurong, Wudthaurong, Witowurong, Wattiwarro, Woddouro) Geelong or Barrabool tribe; Buckley's tribe.

Wotjobaluk important tribe in Western District. *Woymber Myrrnie* Buckley's first lover, mother of Karrie Ael; means Warm Wind.

Wurunjerri equivalent to Woiwurong but specific to a particular group of that tribe.

Wuruum kuurwhin member of the Kumbada; means Long Grass Burning.

Yaar-rar the galah.

Ya-itmathang Omeo tribe; source of thundal.

Yalloak (Yallock) means stream but specific to Moorabool River.

Yanathan-lark Buckley's lover; means movement of clouds.

Yan-Yan wells near the mouth of the Barwon.

varra yarra means ever-flowing, or hair. Wedge mistook it for the name of the river.

Yawangs means hills, but specifically the You Yang mountains.

Yawangis the You Yangs group.

yelum-keturuk strength-giving armband of Tuan-Tuan fur.

Yerao-bo Burmbo Merio and Mirri Mallo's dog; means Joyful Bandicoot.

Yern the quoll or eastern native cat.

Ye ye 'yes'.

ye-ye-dyileen dreams.

Yukope the king parrot; one of Bunjil's six young wizards.

Yundool the dusky glider or greater flying phalanger.

Bibliography

Age. Melbourne, 19 July 1911. (Langhorne's narrative.)

Anderson, H. *Out of the Shadow: the career of John Pascoe Fawkner.* Cheshire, Melbourne, 1962.

Argus. Melbourne, 4 and 11 March 1905. (William Todd's diary.)

Australian Dictionary of Biography. Vols 1-2: 1788-1850. Melbourne University Press, Melbourne, 1967.

Australian Encyclopaedia. Grolier Society of Australia, Sydney, 1963.

Barrett, C.L. *An Australian Animal Book.* Oxford University Press, Melbourne, 1955

— *White Black fellows: the strange adventures of Europeans who lived among savages.* Hallcraft, Melbourne, 1948.

— *Wild Life in Australia Illustrated.* Sun News Pictorial. Melbourne, 1950.

Berndt, C. 'Women and the Secret Life' in R.M. and C.H. Berndt (eds), *Aboriginal Man in Australia: essays in honour of Emeritus Professor A.P. Elkin.* Angus & Robertson, Sydney, 1965.

Berndt, R. (ed.). *Australian Aboriginal Anthropology: modern studies in the social anthropology of the Australian Aborigines.* The University of Western Australia Press for the Australian Institute of Aboriginal Studies, Nedlands, W.A., 1970.

Blainey, G. *The Tyranny of Distance: how distance shaped Australia's history.* MacMillan, Melbourne, 1968.

Bonwick, J. *John Batman, the Founder of Victoria.* Edited with an introduction and notes by C.E. Sayers. Wren, Melbourne, 1973.

— *William Buckley, the Wild White Man and his Port Phillip Black Friends.* George Nichols, Melbourne, 1856.

— *Port Phillip Settlement.* Low, Marston, Searle & Rivington, London, 1883.

Bozic, S., in conjunction with Marshall, A. *Aboriginal Myths.* Gold Star Publications, Melbourne, 1972.

Bride, T.F. (ed.). *Letters from Victorian Pioneers.* Government Printer for the Trustees of the Public library, Melbourne, 1898. (Gellibrand's memoranda.)

Brown, P.L. (ed.). *The Narrative of George Russell of Golf Hill.* Oxford University Press, London, 1935.

Brownhill, W.R. *The History of Geelong and Corio Bay.* Printed by Wilke and Co., Melbourne, 1955.

Bunce, D. *Australasiatic Reminiscences of 23 Years Wanderings.* Hendy, Melbourne, 1857.

Burton, M. *Animals of Australia.* Abelard-Schumann, London, 1969.

Calder, J.E. *Some Account of the Wars, Extirpation, Habits, etc. of the Native Tribes of Tasmania.* Henn, Hobart, 1875.

Canteri, C. *The Origins of Australian Social Banditry: bushranging in Van Diemen's Land 1805-1818.* B. Litt. thesis, University of Oxford, 1973.

Christie, M.F. *Aborigines in Colonial Victoria 1835-86.* Sydney University Press, Sydney, 1979.

Clarke, M. *Old Tales of a Young Country.* Mason, Firth McCutcheon, Melbourne, 1871.

Cohn, N. *The Pursuit of the Millenium: revolutionary millenarians and mystical anarchists of the Middle Ages.* Paladin, London, 1970.

Cribb, A.B. and J.W. *Wild Food in Australia.* Collins, Sydney, 1975.

Cumpston, J.S. *First Visitors to Bass Strait.* Roebuck Society,

Canberra, 1973.

Dawson, J. *Australian Aborigines: the languages and customs of several tribes of Aborigines in the Western District of Victoria, Australia.* George Robertson, Melbourne, 1881.

Eliade, M. *Australian Religions: an introduction.* Cornell University Press, Ithaca, N.Y., 1973.

— *Shamanism: archaic techniques of ecstasy.* Princeton University Press, Princeton, N. J., 1964.

Elkin, A.P. *Aboriginal Men of High Degree.* Australasian Publishing, Sydney, 1945.

— *The Australian Aborigines: how to understand them.* Angus & Robertson, Sydney, 1966.

The Encyclopaedia Britannica. 15th edn. London, 1974.

Farb, P. *Man's Rise to Civilisation.* Paladin, London, 1971 Fawkner, J.P. 'The Reminiscences of John Pascoe Fawkner'.

Latrobe Library Journal, Vol. I, No. 3, April 1969. Fleay, D. *Nightwatchmen of Bush and Plain: Australian owls and owl-like birds.* Jacaranda Press, Brisbane, .1968.

— *Gliders of the Gum Trees: the most beautiful and enchanting Australian marsupials.* Bread & Cheese Club, Melbourne, 1947.

Fortescue, Sir J.W. *History of the British Army.* 13 vols. MacMillan, London, 1899–1927.

Gould League of Victoria. *Birds of Victoria.* Series. Prahran, Vic., 1969–.

Grimble, A. *A Pattern of Islands.* John Murray, London, 1964.

Grzimek, B. *Four-legged Australians: adventures with animals and men in Australia.* Collins, London, 1967.

Hayden, K. *Wild White Man: a condensed account of William Buckley, who lived in exile for 32 years (1803–35) amongst the black people of the unexplored regions of Port Phillip.* Marine History Publications, Geelong, 1976.

Hiatt, L.R. (ed.). *Australian Aboriginal Mythology — Essays in Honour of W.E.H. Stanner.* Australian Institute of Aboriginal Studies, Canberra, 1975.

Hill, R. *Australian Birds.* Thomas Nelson, Melbourne, 1967.

Hobsbawm, E. J. *The Age of Revolution7- R 9-1848.* Mentor Books, New York, 1962.

Howitt, A.W. *The Native Tribes of South-East Australia.* MacMillan, London, 1904.

Journal and Papers of the Parliament of Tasmania. Vol. 5, No. 44, 1885. (Wedge's papers.)

Labilliere, F.P. *Early History of the Colony of Victoria: from its discovery to its establishment as a self-governing province of the British Empire.* Sampson Low, Marston, Searle & Rivington, London, 1878.

Lacour-Gayet, R. *A Concise History of Australia.* Penguin, Melbourne, 1977.

Leach, J.A. *An Australian Birdbook.* Revised and edited by C. Barrett. Whitcombe & Tombs, Melbourne, 1953.

Leggett, G.R. 'History of Bass Strait'. *Victorian Historical Magazine.* Vol. 25, No. 2., June 1953.

Lockwood, D. *I, the Aboriginal.* Rigby, Adelaide, 1962.

McPhee, A. *The First Chapter in the History of Victoria.* Cole, Melbourne, 1911.

Massola, A. *The Aboriginal People.* Cypress Books, Melbourne, 1969.

— *Aboriginal Place Names of South-East Australia and Their Meanings.* Lansdowne, Melbourne, 1968.

— *The Aborigines of South-Eastern Australia as They Were.* Heinemann, Melbourne, 1971.

— *Bunjil's Cave: myths, legends and superstitions of the Aborigines of south-east Australia.* Lansdowne, Melbourne, 1968.

— *Journey to Aboriginal Victoria.* Rigby, Adelaide, 1969.

Moorhead, A. *The Fatal Impact: an account of the invasion of the South Pacific 1767-1840.* Penguin, Harmondsworth, 1968.

Morgan, J. *The Life and Adventures of William Buckley.* 1st edn, Archibald MacDougal, Hobart, 1852; 2nd edn, edited with an introduction and notes by C.E. Sayers, Heinemann, Melbourne, 1967.

Morrison, E. *Early Days in the Loddon Valley: memoirs of Edward Stone Parker 1802–1865.* Daylesford, Vic., 1965.

Mountford, C.P. *The Dawn of Time.* Rigby, Adelaide, 1969.

Nepean Historical Society. *The Peninsula Story, Vol. I: Sorrento and Portsea — Yesterday.* Sorrento, Vic., 1966.

Norman, L. *Sea Wolves and Bandits; sealing, whaling, smuggling and piracy, wild men of Van Diemen's Land, bushrangers and bandits, wrecks and wreckers.* J. Walch & Sons, Hobart, 1966.

Pyke, W. *Thirty Years Among the Blacks of Australia: the life and adventures of William Buckley, the runaway convict.* G. Routledge, London, 1904.

Reed, A.W. *Aboriginal Fables and Legendary Tales.* A.H. & A.W. Reed, Sydney, 1965.

—*Myths and Legends of Australia.* A.H. & A.W. Reed, Sydney, 1965.

Ride, W.D.L. A *Guide to the Native Mammals of Australia.* Oxford University Press, Melbourne, 1970.

Ross, A. *Everyday Life of the Pagan Celts.* Batsford, London, 1970.

Rowley, C.D. *The Destruction of Aboriginal Society: Aboriginal policy and practice.* Vol. 1. Australian National University Press, Canberra, 1970.

Scott, E. 'Captain Lonsdale and the Foundation of Melbourne'. *Victorian Historical Magazine,* Vol. IV, No. 3, March 1915.

—'The Administration of William Lonsdale'. *Victorian Historical Magazine,* Vol. VI, No. 4, September 1918.

Shillinglaw, J. J. (ed.) *Historical Records of Port Phillip.* Government Printer, Melbourne, 1879. (Knopwood's journal.)

Slater, P. *A Field Guide to Australian Birds*. Rigby, Adelaide, 1970; companion volume, 1974.

Smyth, R.B. *The Aborigines of Victoria, with Notes Relating to the Natives of Other Parts of Australia and Tasmania. Vols I and II*. Government Printer, Melbourne, 1878.

Spencer, B. and Gillen, F.J. *The Native Tribes of Central Australia*. Dover Publications, New York, 1968.

Stars of the Southern Hemisphere. Rigby, Adelaide, 1968.

Stone, S. *Aborigines in White Australia: a documentary history of the attitudes affecting official policy and the Australian Aborigine 1697–1973*. Heinemann, Melbourne, 1974.

Tate, W.E. *The English Village Community and the Enclosure Movements*. Victor Gollancz, London, 1967.

Thompson, E.P. *The Making of the English Working Class*. Penguin, Harmondsworth, 1968.

Tindale, N. 'Distribution of Australian Aboriginal Tribes: a field survey'. *Transactions of the Royal Society of South Australia,* Vol. 64, 1940.

Tindale, N. and George, B. *The Australian Aborigines*. Golden Press, Potts Point, N.S.W., 1971.

Tuckey, J.H. *An Account of a Voyage to Establish a Colony at Port Philip* [sic] *in Bass's Strait on the South Coast of New South Wales, in His Majesty's Ship Calcutta, in the Years 1802-3-4*. Longman, Hurst, Rees & Orme, London, 1805.

Tudehope, C.M. 'William Buckley'. *Victorian Historical Magazine,* Vol. XXX II, No. 4, May 1962.

Turner, H.G. *A History of the Colony of Victoria*. Vol. E: 1797–1854. Longmans, Green & Co., London, 1904.

Wedlick, L.V. *The Fighting Bream and Other Estuary Fish*. Wedneil Publications, Newport, Vic., 1974.

Whitlock, D. *The Beginnings of English Society*. Penguin, Harmondsworth, 1952.

Williams, L. *Challenge to Survival: a philosophy of evolution*. Andre Deutsch, London, 1971.